Anthony Gilbert and The Murder Room

>>> This title is part of The Murder Room, our series dedicated to making available out-of-print or hard-to-find titles by classic crime writers.

Crime fiction has always held up a mirror to society. The Victorians were fascinated by sensational murder and the emerging science of detection; now we are obsessed with the forensic detail of violent death. And no other genre has so captivated and enthralled readers.

Vast troves of classic crime writing have for a long time been unavailable to all but the most dedicated frequenters of second-hand bookshops. The advent of digital publishing means that we are now able to bring you the backlists of a huge range of titles by classic and contemporary crime writers, some of which have been out of print for decades.

From the genteel amateur private eyes of the Golden Age and the femmes fatales of pulp fiction, to the morally ambiguous hard-boiled detectives of mid twentieth-century America and their descendants who walk our twenty-first century streets, The Murder Room has it all. >>>

The Murder Room
Where Criminal Minds Meet

themurderroom.com

T0352076

Anthony Gilbert (1899–1973)

Anthony Gilbert was the pen name of Lucy Beatrice Malleson. Born in London, she spent all her life there, and her affection for the city is clear from the strong sense of character and place in evidence in her work. She published 69 crime novels, 51 of which featured her best known character, Arthur Crook, a vulgar London lawyer totally (and deliberately) unlike the aristocratic detectives, such as Lord Peter Wimsey, who dominated the mystery field at the time. She also wrote more than 25 radio plays, which were broadcast in Great Britain and overseas. Her thriller *The Woman in Red* (1941) was broadcast in the United States by CBS and made into a film in 1945 under the title *My Name is Julia Ross*. She was an early member of the British Detection Club, which, along with Dorothy L. Sayers, she prevented from disintegrating during World War II. Malleson published her autobiography, *Three-a-Penny*, in 1940, and wrote numerous short stories, which were published in several anthologies and in such periodicals as *Ellery Queen's Mystery Magazine* and *The Saint*. The short story 'You Can't Hang Twice' received a Queens award in 1946. She never married, and evidence of her feminism is elegantly expressed in much of her work.

By Anthony Gilbert

Don't Open the Door (1945)
  aka *Death Lifts the Latch*
Lift Up the Lid (1945)
  aka *The Innocent Bottle*
The Spinster's Secret (1946)
  aka *By Hook or by Crook*
Death in the Wrong Room
  (1947)
Die in the Dark (1947)
  aka *The Missing Widow*
Death Knocks Three Times
  (1949)
Murder Comes Home (1950)
A Nice Cup of Tea (1950)
  aka *The Wrong Body*
Lady-Killer (1951)
Miss Pinnegar Disappears
  (1952)
  aka *A Case for Mr Crook*
Footsteps Behind Me (1953)
  aka *Black Death*
Snake in the Grass (1954)
  aka *Death Won't Wait*
Is She Dead Too? (1955)
  aka *A Question of Murder*
And Death Came Too (1956)
Riddle of a Lady (1956)
Give Death a Name (1957)

Death Against the Clock
  (1958)
Death Takes a Wife (1959)
  aka *Death Casts a Long
  Shadow*
Third Crime Lucky (1959)
  aka *Prelude to Murder*
Out for the Kill (1960)
She Shall Die (1961)
  aka *After the Verdict*
Uncertain Death (1961)
No Dust in the Attic (1962)
Ring for a Noose (1963)
The Fingerprint (1964)
Knock, Knock! Who's
  There? (1964)
  aka *The Voice*
Passenger to Nowhere (1965)
The Looking Glass Murder
  (1966)
The Visitor (1967)
Night Encounter (1968)
  aka *Murder Anonymous*
Missing from Her Home
  (1969)
Death Wears a Mask (1970)
  aka *Mr Crook Lifts the
  Mask*

Don't Open the Door

Anthony Gilbert

An Orion book

Copyright © Lucy Beatrice Malleson 1945

The right of Lucy Beatrice Malleson to be identified as the author of this work has been asserted in accordance with the Copyright, Designs and Patents Act 1988.

This edition published by
The Orion Publishing Group Ltd
Orion House
5 Upper St Martin's Lane
London WC2H 9EA

An Hachette UK company
A CIP catalogue record for this book is available from the British Library

ISBN 978 1 4719 0982 5

www.orionbooks.co.uk

CHAPTER ONE

THE FOG, that had begun as a grey mist about three o'clock, thickened as the afternoon drew on until by night it hung, a thick grey blanket, obscuring London and the outlying suburbs. It was almost eleven o'clock when Mr. Arthur Crook, aware that for once nature had superseded the blackout regulations, drew back the curtains of his office in 123 Bloomsbury Street and stared at the impenetrable fog. When he thrust out his hand he could see nothing, and might have supposed himself poised over chaos but for the distant sound of an occasional footstep muffled by the fog or a whisper checked by the atmosphere, that came floating through the dark. He was quite unperturbed by the realisation that he had to return to Earl's Court and had some way to go to the nearest tube station. He said he was like a cat, he could see in the dark, and it would be ungracious in him to decry fogs since they brought him so much business.

" Fogs are like everything else," he used to tell Bill Parsons. " One man's meat—you know the rest of it. A. walks into the road and is run down by a jeep and says, if he's capable of saying anything, This damned fog. But B.'s hanging about in an empty doorway, waiting, and the selfsame fog is a godsend to him."

As he stood at the window to-night he thought of that anonymous brotherhood of whom it might be said, Theirs is the kingdom of darkness. On such a night as this they would be lurking unsuspected in corners awaiting their victims, following them on silent feet down black roads, noiseless and insubstantial as shadows, creeping out to do their grievous work, and vanishing again like ghosts. Far off he heard the mournful strident note of a siren on the river and he thought that there, too, death was lurking. The respectable, the simple, the faint-hearted would at this hour be sitting round their firesides or hunched in their comfortable beds. " How quiet it is," they would say, " nothing moving. It's like being in a world of the dead."

1

And some of them would turn on the wireless to reassure themselves that life and colour and movement still persisted. And all the while life, arrogant, irresistible, resolved, stalked round them.

With a jerk, Crook closed the curtains and turned back to the room.

" As bad a fog as ever I recall," he decided. He knew that when he was on the pavement he wouldn't be able to see the kerb, while even the railings close at hand would be felt rather than seen. Work for the doctor, he thought, work for the wrong 'un, for the desperate, for the police and the mortician, and work for lawyers like Arthur Crook, who cater specially for the reckless and the lawless and who was known as the Criminals' Hope and the Judges' Despair.

Picking up a pencil in his big freckled fist he scrawled FOG in capital letters on his desk diary. There'd never been a fog yet that hadn't brought him work and he didn't imagine this one would be any exception. He pulled on his rough brown overcoat over his bright brown suit, jammed his brown derby hat over his red-brown eyebrows, turned up his coat collar, shoved the gloves he never wore into the pocket of his coat— a man walking alone in a fog is wise to keep his hands free— and walked out into the dark. As he closed the big street door the telephone in his office on the top floor began to ring. It rang and rang with the forlorn ferocity of neglected phones, but no one came to answer it, and after a time it stopped.

He got home without mishap. There were letters lying on the mat—there always were. There was beer in the cupboard, too, and he drew on that. And rather unusually, for he believed in riding your imagination on the curb, he found himself wondering about all those people for whom this would be the last night on earth. . . .

The young girl, Nora Deane, emerged from the south of the station of the prosperous suburb of Charlbury and stopped, appalled at the darkness. How on earth could she hope to find her way in unfamiliar surroundings on such a night ? Yet it was urgent that she should lose no more time. She began to recall the instructions she had been given by telephone earlier that day, when she was disturbed from her brief holiday to come to nurse Mrs. Newstead of 12 Askew Avenue, Charlbury.

" There is a small common opposite the station," matron

had said. " You cross that and you will then find yourself in a broad residential street. Askew Avenue is a turning on the right. It's not more than ten minutes from the station, Mr. Newstead says, and as you'll only be carrying a small case, you can easily walk."

But when matron said that she had not visualised the fog, the eerie sounds not significant in daylight, the complete absence of landmarks, her own ignorance of the locality ; and she certainly had not supposed that Nora would be arriving at eleven o'clock at night, her train having been delayed three hours by the weather and an accident on the line due to the same cause. It might, thought the girl, even be unsafe to venture into the roadway, lest some benighted vehicle purring softly through the dark, ran her down.

She advanced uncertainly as far as the kerb, and hesitated again. Perhaps it would be wisest to ring up the house and announce her late arrival. Probably they had given her up for the night. Still, that would only involve further delay and she knew, for matron had told her, that there was no one who could come and meet her.

" Mr. Newstead says his wife is quite alone except for himself," she had said. " Of course, a nurse is under no obligation to do more than the duties for which she's engaged, but I'm sure you'll do your best to help while things are so difficult. Mr. Newstead seemed so distressed about his wife. . . ." That was matron all over. A man only had to step on the soft pedal and she would start promising all kinds of things. No doubt she had said the nurse she was sending was young and obliging and would be glad to help until they got someone else. When it came to what was actually wrong with Mrs. Newstead she had been more vague. A sort of breakdown, she thought. Probably as mad as a wild horse and will throw things at me, reflected Nora, feeling the gloom of the night enter her soul.

" Lost anything ? "

She swung round so violently that she cannoned against the speaker. In the darkness it was impossible to see him properly, but he seemed to be tall and his voice was young and amused.

" I—oh, you did startle me. I didn't know there was any one there."

" I've just come up from the station. You were so still I thought you might be copying Lot's wife."

Nora laughed a little nervously. " I was just summoning

3

courage to plunge into the fog. I hate the dark. It always
seems full of invisible people."

" Which way are you going ? "

" Over the Common to a place called Askew Avenue."

" Far ? "

" Matron says it's only ten minutes, but I should think it
might be an hour in weather like this. The trouble is I don't
know the way. I've never been here before. I'd thought there
might be a cab. . . ."

" On this sort of night ? " The drawling voice sounded
amused—or was it merely supercilious? " Still, half a mile's
not a very long journey. I'll go with you and find the way.
This case all your baggage ? "

" Yes. I daresay I'll only be here a few days. . . ."

" Planning to kill or cure your patient at short notice ?
You do know your own mind, don't you, even if you are afraid
of the dark. Well, give it to me."

She felt the case twisted out of her hands by an expert
movement and made her protest an instant too late.

" It's quite all right. Really. I . . ."

" If I hadn't turned up I believe you'd have been found
standing on the kerb to-morrow morning."

" But it's quite light. . . ."

" I'm glad something's light. My mother brought me up to
be a little gentleman, and a gentleman always acts as a beast
of burden. Still, it was considerate of you not to bring a larger
case. Ready ? "

She did not know what to make of this new development. At
first she had been glad to hear another voice, but now he
seemed merely an extension of the strangeness that surrounded
her.

Before she could speak again, however, he had grasped
her arm and, saying, " Coast's clear," was leading her across
the road.

" Staying with friends ? " he asked casually. " Oh, no, you
told me you were on a case. I suppose you won't find the house
locked for the night ? "

" That would be too dreadful. I should have to knock them
up. But no doubt they'll be expecting me."

" You're what's known as an optimist, aren't you ? I didn't
know there were any left."

She explained, a little breathless from the speed they were
making, " It's urgent. There's no one else in the house but my

patient and her husband. Otherwise I could have waited till morning."

" But you didn't know about this fog when you started, did you ? "

" No. It came up so suddenly. Oh, dear." For she had stumbled and almost missed her footing.

" I can't carry you as well as the case," said the young man. " Where did you come from ? "

" A place called Roper's End. It's a little place on the river. I was spending the week-end there."

" With friends ? "

" No. Just a rest. I'd had rather a hard case before this and of course there's still a great shortage of nurses."

" So you were all alone ? Haven't you any friends ? "

" I—not many, not in London."

" That's a mistake. But perhaps you can't help it."

She was silent for a minute, but the feeling that he was waiting for a reply made her add, " I'm an orphan, you see. I had an aunt, in Scotland, but she died."

" And you came south to make your fortune."

" To work."

" That's what I said. What's the matter ? "

" You—you pinched my arm."

" We have to cross here."

" Oh, I see. It's very kind of you to come with me," she added with something of an effort.

" And at the present moment you wish nothing but that I'd give you back your case and vanish into the fog ? No, don't blame yourself. It's nothing you said. Besides, it shows you were nicely brought-up. All the same, this is no night for a young lady to be out alone. And for all you know I'm your guardian angel—for this occasion only."

She didn't know what to make of him. She even wondered if he were coming back from a party not quite so sober as he might be.

" It's very kind of you," she said again, in a confused voice. " I don't think I'd ever have found my way alone."

" That's what I thought. What's your name ? "

" Nora Deane."

" I wish I could see you, Nora Deane. I'll tell you what I think you look like. Small and dark—what colour are your eyes ? "

" A—a sort of violet."

" And you've got a small mouth—right ? And plenty of courage, and you're very independent. . . ." He was laughing now and she knew it. " How old are you ? "

" Twenty-three. You haven't told me anything about yourself, though."

" What do you want to know ? "

" What's your name, to begin with ? "

He paused, as though he hadn't heard what she said. Then, as fear began to prick through her, he replied lightly, " You can call me Sammy, if you like."

" Why ? " The word shot out of her before she could stop it.

" Well, don't you think it's rather a nice name ? What are your friends generally called ? Oh, but I forgot. You haven't got any. You know, that's very unwise. You should remedy it. Friends are often the only barrier between oneself and disaster."

" And what do you do ? " she pursued steadily, praying in desperation, Please let us get there soon. Please let the next turning be Askew Avenue.

" Do you need to ask that ? " demanded Sammy. " Isn't my profession obvious ? I'm a squire of dames—in the dark. What you would probably call an adventurer."

" I don't think I understand."

" Much better not. How many turnings did you say this street was ? "

" I'm not sure. I thought you knew."

" I ? I've never been here before."

She stopped dead with dismay, but instead of pausing with her she heard his feet going steadily on.

" Oh, please. Don't. I mean, you've got my case."

" Well, you're not going to spend the night on that particular paving-stone, are you ? You'll catch your death of cold."

" But—I must get to Askew Avenue. They're expecting me. And I'm so terribly late." She had an appalling fear that she was going to cry. " Wait a moment. I've got a torch here."

She could hear him laughing. " I don't know how much good you expect a torch to be in weather like this."

" I thought at least we could look at the names of the turnings as we reach them."

" I don't know how many we've passed already. It may be behind us."

She said desperately, " If you don't know your way about, what are you doing here ? "

" I've told you—dispensation of Providence. I'm your guardian angel, though whether you really need one or not remains to be seen. What's the name of these people you're going to ? "

" Newstead. I don't know what you meant about being a guardian angel. I'm not in any danger."

" You can never be certain. Isn't it odd," he went on conversationally, " how fog creates a world of its own ? Even if you knew this place well, it would be as strange as a foreign land on a night like this."

She said fiercely, " I hate fogs—they're cruel. They mean death."

" Why do you say that ? Are you psychic ? " He was striding forward again and it was as much as she could do to keep pace with him.

" I was thinking of ships being run down on the river—people being run down on roads. . . ."

He said, " If I wanted to commit a murder I'd choose a night like this. I don't see how they'd ever identify you. For one thing, no one's about. We haven't heard much less seen a soul since we left the station. We haven't even seen a lighted window. I doubt whether any one in the neighbourhood so much as realises that any one else is abroad."

Fighting down the terror that threatened to master her she answered him. " There was the man at the station—the ticket-collector."

" Who can prove that a traveller from—where was it you said you came from ?—Ropers End, gave up a ticket. And someone else coming in the opposite direction. Do you think that would get you very far ? No one saw us leave together."

" Oh, but they must."

" No. Don't you remember you turned to the right to come up some steps after you'd given up your ticket ? No one could have seen us. You could no more be identified than the invisible man."

At that instant, when fear threatened to overwhelm her, she found herself at a kerb-edge and, flashing her torch, made out the name of the street.

" This is Askew Avenue," she exclaimed thankfully. " I shall be able to find my way all right now. Thank you so much for coming with me and carrying my case."

" The pleasure is mine. By the way, when's your day off ? "

" I—I don't know."

" Don't tell me you don't have one. I thought nurses had a trades union or something."

" I shan't know about that till I've been at the house a few days."

" Still, you get some time off during the day, don't you? "

" I'm supposed to get two hours, generally from two to four, but some of them prefer you to take four to six. Then if they have friends coming in they can have them to tea. But Mrs. Newstead sounds quite ill ; probably she has no one coming in. I don't really know, you see. . . ."

" I shall come for you at two o'clock to-morrow," said Sammy, calmly.

" Oh, no, please. Not the first day."

" Begin as you meant to go on. I can see you're the kind to be put upon. Two o'clock. What number did you say this house was ? "

" Twelve."

" Yours is the next one then. Don't forget. Two o'clock to-morrow."

He pushed open the gate and thrust her case into her hand. " Thank you," she murmured. " It was very kind. . . ." She wanted to get out of the dark night where strange invisible men spoke to you and walked with you, wanted to get into the light and warmth of a house, see familiar surroundings, hear voices saying homely things. She hurried up the path and cannoned against a monkey-puzzler tree growing in front of the door. Extricating herself, feeling pricked and dishevelled, she found the step and felt for the bell. Now that she was here she began to shiver. That was the cold, of course. Fog always made you cold. She remembered that she hadn't heard Sammy's footsteps move away ; it might be that he was still at the gate, might even be watching to see if she got into the house. She pressed the bell and heard a trill from the darkness. Nothing whispered to her of the peril in which she stood ; no inward voice said Get away while you can, while you're still safe. Never mind the fog, never mind the strangeness of unfamiliar streets. Keep away from this house, keep away, keep away. Desperately she rang the bell a second time. Now nothing seemed to matter but that she should get inside, out of the dangers of the dark. And, unheard by her, her guardian angel of the past thirty minutes had gone ; now she was

8

defenceless indeed, like some small creature battering feverishly on the door leading to destruction. But she didn't know. She only thought of lights and warmth and the security of a job.

CHAPTER TWO

Oh, no one. No one in particular. A woman of no importance.
—Oscar Wilde.

THE SECOND TRILL had died away and she was nerving herself to ring a third time when she heard the sound of feet slowly approaching from the other side of the door. She waited, her breath coming unevenly, the apologetic words on her lips even before the door opened.

It only opened a crack. " Who's there ? " said a suspicious voice.

Her spirits chilled her again. " It's I—the nurse you sent for. I couldn't get here earlier. . . ."

" You're very late." There was no suggestion of welcome in the voice that answered her.

" It was the fog—and an accident on the line. Matron said you wanted me urgently. I'm sorry. . . ." Her voice died away. For a horrified moment she thought he was going to refuse to let her in. The door seemed to close against her, then she heard a chain withdrawn and the gap widened.

" Come in, nurse," said the grudging voice. " Quiet now. I've put your patient to bed, and if she wakes up again we may be up all night with her. That's it. Put your bag down while I chain up the door." He seemed to take a long time, and the sense of security that had lapped her for a moment as she stepped under the shelter of a roof vanished again. A sense of desolation overwhelmed her. There was no light in the hall except from a candle the man had been carrying, which threw shadows on the scanty furniture and went streaming up in a wavering pillar of gold and black towards the invisible ceiling. On the table beside it were some letters addressed to Alfred Newstead, Esq., and as though he suspected her of prying into his affairs the man turned and snatched them up and thrust them into his pocket.

" I've been so busy doing your work, nurse," he said, with an attempt at jocularity, " I haven't had time to attend to my own business. Now, as I say, your patient's asleep and there's nothing to be done for her to-night. I hadn't expected you to arrive so late, so I made do myself. I'll show you your room if you'll bring your case along. I expect you're tired."

" I'm quite ready to go on duty," she said quickly, barely able to avoid expressing her dismay at this marked lack of hospitality. It was bitterly cold, it was hours since she had had food and the general lack of cosiness in the atmosphere lay heavily on her spirits. The house itself struck chill as a tomb, as though no fires were ever lighted in the rooms and no warmth ever kindled the hearts of those who lived here. In the morning, no doubt, everything would look different, but now only the strangeness and the lack of that natural warmth that comes from a house that is truly inhabited impressed her.

" You're very young," said Newstead, breaking into her thoughts.

She turned quickly. " You didn't ask for a middle-aged nurse. Anyway, I'm the only one available."

" Now, now, don't take offence. It's only that I'm afraid it's rather a depressing case for a young lady like yourself."

He came nearer, picked up the candle ; the shadows eddied wildly. She saw him more clearly now, a middle-aged man, about fifty, with a large white clean-shaved face and a small full mouth the colour of plum. He was going bald and had a thin line of sandy eyebrow above very light eyes. His hands were very large and freckled and the backs were covered with fine pale hairs, and were of an ugly shape, very strong with long curving fingers. She repressed a further shudder.

" Cold ? " asked Newstead with some show of kindliness.

" I—do you think I could have a cup of tea ? If you could show me where things are I could look after myself, but it wasn't possible to get any food on the train."

He hesitated for a moment, then said, " Why, of course. I'd have suggested it myself, but naturally I supposed, arriving at this hour, you'd have had dinner. First of all, though, I'll show you your room. You'll have to have tea in the kitchen, but you won't mind that. I can't risk waking Adela."

He moved in front of her, going up the stairs with a peculiar soft step as though he had rubber on the soles of his feet. As they reached the first floor he moved with exaggerated care. Rather to Nora's surprise she found that she herself had been given a room higher up. As though he read her mind he hissed, " Want you to get a proper rest when you're off duty, and if you're on the same floor my wife will be after you like a dragon. It's not her fault, mind," he added, his voice becoming more normal as they went higher, " she's a nerve case. I daresay matron told you."

" She said something about a breakdown."

" That's why I was rather surprised they'd sent any one so young. You need rather specialised experience for a case like my wife's." They reached the next landing and once more he turned to mount a flight of stairs. " Perhaps I should explain. The doctor finds it difficult to account for her illness. He says that organically she's sound, except for her heart. Of course, heart trouble is apt to cause depression, but in my wife's case it's abnormal. I mean, there's no particular reason for it. She didn't suffer in the bombing as many people did, and we never had any children, so she hasn't had any anxiety on their account. We have enough money, though, mark you," he added quickly, " we have to be careful, we can't afford to throw it away. And this illness of hers has been a great expense to me. As a matter of fact, to be perfectly candid, she suffers from delusions. But don't get the idea that she's dangerous. If she's dangerous to any one it's only to herself. It all comes of her habit of sitting alone and thinking. Nature never intended women to think. It's all right for men, who have the work of the world on their shoulders, but in women it only too easily becomes brooding. Then they start living in the past, recalling this incident and that, until they've built up quite a history for themselves that doesn't touch reality at any point. I'm afraid that's what my poor wife has done."

At last they had reached the door of her room and he stopped and opened it. It had been built for a servant when the house was put up sixty years ago, and the ceiling sloped so that there was a little tunnel to the window. The outlook was drab, she discovered next morning, and the furniture poor and ill-matched.

" I think you'll be quite comfortable here," said Mr. Newstead, putting the candle down and looking at the pale saffron walls blotched with bunches of orange wallflower tied with blue ribbon. " Of course, we don't live in luxury, but then who does in a war ? No, as I was saying, my wife can't face facts. She's like most women—you're a romantic sex. She feels somehow she's been cheated—don't ask me of what

11

because I couldn't tell you. You mustn't pay too much attention to what she says. I suppose if you've expected a great deal more from life than the ordinary life can be expected to yield, sooner or later you're going to feel you've been badly treated, and if you feel that, of course you've got to blame someone. I daresay you understand."

" I'm not sure if I do," said Nora slowly. " Do you mean your wife is out of her mind ? "

" No, no, nothing like that. Please don't suggest such a thing. It's just that she suffers from acute depression. Last year she even attempted to take her life. No reason, you understand, but she was miserable and she hadn't any work to take her mind off things. And so she makes a drama out of the most insignificant happening. For instance, if a neighbour doesn't happen to see her in the street, she will come home convinced that a determined attempt is being made to boycott her. If she wants something quite unreasonable and unnecessary, something it's quite beyond my power to buy for her, then I'm trying to starve her. She has decided, without any warning, that she doesn't like this house. She says it's unlucky. You can see for yourself there's nothing wrong with the house, and it's almost impossible to get anything these days, certainly nothing as good as this. You see what I mean. She's lost her sense of proportion. If you could see the letters she writes, often to people who don't exist, or hear the conversations she holds with imaginary friends, you'd appreciate my anxiety."

" But is there no one who could come in and sit with her ? She must be terribly lonely."

" My dear, she's frightened off all her erstwhile friends. You see, sooner or later she makes up her mind that they're plotting against her in some way, and then she tells them so, and naturally they don't come again. It's the same with servants. She lives in a sort of day-dream in which she's waited on hand and foot and everything is done perfectly. Then she comes back to reality and finds dust in the drawing-room or sees that the silver hasn't been polished, and she talks to the maid of the moment as if she were a machine, and naturally the girls won't stand it. If you knew what a slave I am—and I have my own work, too. I can't tell you how thankful I am to see you. Perhaps being young will be an advantage. Perhaps it will cheer her up. I tried to get a neighbour to come and be with her, take her out of herself, but it was no good. She said such outrageous things to her that naturally Mrs. Forbes wouldn't come again."

" Perhaps she won't like me either."

" You're a nurse, aren't you ? Then you'll know it's your duty to make your patient like you. Besides, I don't suppose it will be difficult. Only—if she should take some wild fancy into her head—she's like a lot of middle-aged women, she's apt to resent young people—you mustn't take her very seriously. If you can persuade her she isn't really as ill as she imagines and get her out of bed and out of doors, you'll be doing more for her than any doctor can do."

" Has she no relatives ? " Nora wanted to know.

The man's voice sharpened. " None who're any good to her. The fact is she's becoming cunning. She's out to win sympathy, at any one's expense. That's why I'm warning you. Every one can't be rich. Now you, who have to earn your own living, don't, I'm sure, go about being sorry for yourself. That's the kind of idea I want to get into my wife's head. It's not every woman who has a husband to earn a living for her, and if you can make her understand that she's a great deal better off than many women of her age, that might be the first step towards a cure."

Nora had been nervous of the fog, had shrunk from the mysterious Sammy, had been grateful to find herself under a roof, but now she experienced a creeping dread that made her former apprehensions seem childish. The whole house frightened her ; she was afraid of the man at her side, and already all her sympathy was with the patient she was not yet to see. Privately she thought Mrs. Newstead was probably as mad as a hatter and might well set the house afire, but if so she was quite prepared to believe her husband had driven her to it. Her thought fluttered for a moment towards Sammy and she felt grateful to remember that he would be coming to-morrow. He was a stranger, but he was at least a link with a normal world. Here the shadows of insanity crept round like bats' wings. She shivered again.

" You're cold, aren't you ? " said Mr. Newstead, avoiding looking at the empty grate. " But a cup of tea will soon put that right. By the way, you've brought your rations, I hope. That's right. Oh, no, I didn't mean I wanted you to find them now. We're quite ready to share our tea with you this evening. In fact, now you come to mention it, I believe I could do with a cup myself." He moved towards the door.

" Don't forget to turn out your light (he had switched on a poor little bulb, about 25 candle power, as they entered the room.) With my poor wife in this lamentable state and no responsible woman on the premises, I have to do the house-keeping, though I must say some of the neighbours are very kind. Now, you'll be down in a minute or two, won't you ? There's a bathroom at the end of the passage on the next floor, and you better come right down to the basement. And whatever you do, don't wake my wife. Perhaps you'd better come down in your slippers. Yes, I really think that would be best."

He smiled in a way that made them seem conspirators, and shuffled off in a furtive manner that was somehow less straight-forward than the natural concern of a man for a sick wife. Nora remained motionless, staring at the unappetising walls, and thence back to her case which she supposed she should unpack. So uneasy did she feel, however, at this extraordinary reception, that she went no further than the removal of a brush and comb and a sponge-bag for immediate necessities. There was a large marble-topped washstand against one wall, but when she went up to it she found the plain white china ewer empty and grimed with dust, and a fresh foreboding troubled her.

" He was expecting me. Yet he made no real preparation. This room hasn't been dusted for days. . . . Still, I suppose if he has no servants and his wife's as ill as he makes out, it's not so odd." She took off her hat, straightened the uniform in which she had travelled and found her way to the bathroom. Remembering his warning, she came very quietly down the next flight of stairs. As she turned the corner on to the first landing, however, she was arrested by a long moaning sound as of some creature in terrible distress. Involuntarily she paused. Mr. Newstead had said that his wife was asleep, was not in any circumstances to be disturbed. It was possible of course that she was making this distressing noise in her sleep, but unable to stop herself, the young nurse moved softly to the door of the sick-room and opened it a few inches. The room was large and heavily furnished and lighted by a dim blue bulb hanging from the ceiling. There were thick curtains drawn tightly over the windows, a great writing-desk facing them, and a small glass-topped table loaded with bottles and phials beside the large old-fashioned bed in which Adela Newstead lay. A single glance was enough even in that light

14

to assure Nora that this woman's illness was more than an imaginary condition ; there was the faulty respiration, the dark, unnatural colour of the skin, the irregular pulse, for automatically she touched the sick woman's wrist, the restlessness that betokened a serious condition. It seemed to her that the woman was trying to speak but that her tongue was too big for her mouth and was choking her. Most likely she had had some sleeping-draught, and when she looked at the table she saw a bottle marked Sleeping-mixture. She took it up and glanced at it. It consisted of a number of tablets of which one was to be taken each night. She put the bottle down and leant over her patient.

Mrs. Newstead opened her eyes. " Who are you ? " she demanded in a queer sleepy voice. " You're new. I haven't seen you before."

" I've just arrived. I got held up by the fog. Is there something you want ? "

Comprehension was growing stronger in the dark eyes staring into hers.

" Where's the other one ? " she demanded. " You know who I mean."

Nora knew nothing, but she said with a nurse's instinct to soothe : " She isn't here any more."

The woman laid her head back restlessly on the pillows. " She'll come again. As soon as I've gone she'll come again."

" No one's coming but me," said the girl. " Is there anything I can do for you ? "

Something like intelligence brightened the dull eyes. " Yes. Yes." A hand came out and held her wrist. " I want Herbert," she whispered. " Quickly. I want Herbert." The breath panted between her lips.

" I'll call him," Nora was beginning, when she remembered the superscription on the envelopes in the hall. Mr. Alfred Newstead. Herbert, then, was someone else. Mrs. Newstead took her hand off the girl's arm and indicated the desk by the window. " In there," she whispered.

Nora crossed to the desk and opened it. " You want me to get something out of this ? " She half-turned. Mrs. Newstead's hand was wavering in mid-air.

" That's it. My husband. . . ."

" I understand." It was something Alfred Newstead was not to know about, and her conviction that something was desperately wrong here increased.

" The address book—the top shelf." The voice was hoarse and urgent. " Don't—tell—him. . . ." Nora found it at once a small notebook bound in dark red morocco. She came back to the bed without closing the desk.

" Herbert," whispered the sick woman again. " Get him—you understand."

" I understand." She dropped the notebook into the pocket of her apron. Suddenly the woman's face changed again.

" Water," she said in a choked voice, as though she could hardly speak. She seemed sinking back into a coma. Nora took up a glass and a carafe of water from the bedside table. The condition of both repelled her, for they were smeared, and she could not even be sure that the water was fresh. She was used to cleanliness in a sick room even when the rest of the house was imperfectly cared for. She would have paused to wash the glass and refill the carafe but for the urgency in her patient's face.

As she leaned over the bed, guiding the glass to the sick woman's lips, the door behind her was pushed open and a soft rather guttural voice said, " Come, come, what's all this ? " Alfred Newstead came into the room. " Nurse, I told you particularly not to disturb your patient. Now she'll be up all night and we shall be up with her."

" She called out," said Nora shortly, refusing to be alarmed. " She woke and wanted some water."

" I daresay she has been rambling on as usual." His eyes roamed over the room, saw the opened desk. " What's that ? " he demanded.

" Mrs. Newstead wanted me to get her something out of the desk."

" What was that ? " The big face seemed menacing. Nora glanced at the woman on the bed, saw the imploring expression and returned, " I can't be sure. I was coming over to make certain." She looked at Mrs. Newstead. " Could you tell me what it was you wanted ? "

Newstead crossed the room and closed the desk with a slam. Turning the key, he dropped it into his pocket.

" My dear young lady, my wife wants something every minute of the day. I thought I had warned you. You can't treat any one in her condition as you'd treat a normal person." He spoke as though she were not there. " She'll ask for ridiculous things, things that don't exist, things she gave away years and years ago."

Nora put her hand into the pocket of her apron, nodded slightly at her patient and said, " I'm sorry, Mr. Newstead. But perhaps I'd better stay on duty now, in case I'm wanted."

" If you're here my wife will certainly want something. The only time she gets any rest is when she is alone. Then, with no one to talk to or give orders to, she may settle. As a matter of fact, I shall stay with her for a little, and when she's asleep—and she's drifting off now—I may hope for a little rest myself." He put his hand on the arm of the shocked girl and went on in a lighter voice, " Really, nurse, you'll have to curb your tender-heartedness if you're to be of any use to me here. And you're worrying yourself about nothing. My wife's almost asleep again already. She's like that all the time, doesn't know what she wants, invents something and by the time she's got it can't imagine why it's there. No, no, you come down and have your tea, and then get some rest. I'll sit up for a bit and if I think it's necessary I'll call you later on. Now, don't argue. You can't work twenty-four hours on end, you know, and you'll have your turn to-morrow. When you've been here a short time you'll be glad of a chance to sleep."

He ushered her out of the room, came back to look at his wife who had drifted off into semi-consciousness, leaned his ear to hear what she was saying. But it was quite incoherent and after a moment he joined the girl at the head of the stairs.

" You mustn't let it worry you if you don't know what my wife's talking about," he warned her. " She says a lot of things that don't mean anything at all. I daresay it was just a babble of nonsense just then. Or do you really know what she wanted ? "

" Something out of the desk, she said."

" Did you give it her ? "

" No."

" Much better keep that desk locked up. It'll probably be something under the carpet next time. Now, here we are, one more flight, and then you can have your tea. I'm sure you must be longing for it."

The tea was made and was standing on the kitchen table. " I really think I will have one myself," said Mr. Newstead, " just give me one of those cups out of the pantry and we can be quite cosy."

Nora, however, was full of misgiving. She fetched the cup, receiving in return one he had just filled, but though she was

17

grateful for the hot tea she was uneasy at the recollection of the sick woman left alone two floors away. Mr. Newstead could say what he pleased about a nervous breakdown, but there was much behind this no doctor or nurse would be told. And who was the other one—presumably a nurse, too—who had gone away but who would, Mrs. Newstead feared, come back?

" Another cup, nurse," said Mr. Newstead, but she shook her head. " Sure ? Well, you go along upstairs and have a good sleep. Don't go into my wife's room again, mind. I don't want her roused and she'd gone off nicely."

Nora washed her cup and saucer, said Thank You for the tea and made her way up the stairs. Her feet dragged ; she didn't know when she had felt so tired. She couldn't believe it was only a few hours ago that she had received matron's summons to go to a case at Charlbury, Middlesex. On impulse she peered over the banisters from the first floor and there, sure enough, was Alfred Newstead, his round white face, like a full moon seen through water, staring up from the dark hall. Her flesh crept. If she was to be followed, spied on, entrapped if possible, she thought she would ask matron to send someone else on to the case. One week she must stay, but surely at the week's end if any one else were available she could ask for a change.

There was nothing to be heard as she passed Mrs. Newstead's door, and she climbed as quickly as her leaden legs would carry her up to her own room. She resolved not to go to bed, but to remain awake, listening for sounds in the dark silent house. There was something wrong here. Even during a war you could get people to come in and work from time to time, but the condition of the rooms showed that they had been neglected for a long time. She sat down on the edge of the bed—there was no comfortable chair in the room—and felt so tired that she lay back with her head on the pillow for a five minute rest before preparing for the night's vigil. She was, however, more exhausted than she knew. She felt sleep coming upon her like a tide against which she struggled in vain. Although the light was on the room seemed to be darkening ; the darkness approached her from all sides. For a grim moment she recalled the horrible tale of the Pit and the Pendulum, and put out her hands to push the blackness away. But it rolled over her, quelling her puny struggles. Her case stood on the table waiting to be unpacked, her apron waited to be donned, and her clean cuffs beside it ; her uniform frock was crumpled from travel and she knew she must rise, brush her hair and her teeth, be ready for an emergency. But she was no match for the darkness and the exhaustion. When Mr. Newstead came softly to her door a little later, knocked and, receiving no reply, peered in, she was sleeping " like the dead " he told himself. He waited there a moment, then crept away. But after he had gone the door opened again an inch or two and one big powerful hand came through the crack and switched off the light.

CHAPTER THREE

'Twas a strange riddle of a lady.—SAMUEL BUTLER.

WHEN she woke with the sound of battering in her ears, Nora was at first at a loss to understand where all the noise came from, and her mind fled back to the days when she was accustomed to be wakened from uneasy sleep by air-raid sirens and the falling of bombs. Then she opened her eyes, recollected her surroundings and knew that someone was hammering urgently on her door.

" Nurse ! Nurse ! " said a voice she recognised as belonging to Mr. Newstead.

She got off the bed in some confusion, realising that she had lain thus all night through, that she was stiff, tired, crumpled and in no shape to start a day's work.

" I'm coming," she said, picking up the apron she had put out the night before, but not pausing for clean cuffs or a cap. She supposed she looked a fright and wondered what time it was. It was still quite dark.

Mr. Newstead, looking almost as dishevelled as herself, stood outside.

" Please come quickly, nurse," he said. " I thought I should never wake you."

" Is Mrs. Newstead worse ? " she asked, smothering a yawn. She believed she had never felt so tired, drugged with sleep.

" I don't like the look of her at all. I'm going down to ring Dr. Langton, but I don't like to leave her."

She came out of the room after him, still fastening the strings of her apron.

" When did it happen ? " she inquired nervously.

19

" How do I know ? She was all right at a quarter to two when I left her."

" You left her ? "

" Certainly. She was sleeping peacefully. I'd no reason to suppose there was any harm. I went to my own room. . . ."

" You should have called me."

" As a matter of fact, I did try to rouse you but I couldn't get you to wake."

She looked startled. " I never heard you."

" Isn't that what I'm saying ? I couldn't make you hear. Well, didn't you notice the light was out when you got up this morning? It was blazing full on when I came to your door."

" I fell asleep," said Nora confusedly. " I suppose it was the journey."

" It didn't seem to me to make sense to wake you to come down to my wife who was sleeping quite naturally—or so I thought—when the odds were you'd go to sleep again at once. I thought it best to let you have a good night and come on duty this morning. Now then, here we are. If you can do anything for her—but you'll know about that. I'm going to get the doctor."

Newstead had left the pallid light burning and by its faint inhospitable ray Nora could see her patient lying heavily against her pillows. She was full of apprehension as she approached the bed. If anything went wrong the doctor would certainly blame her for not going on duty on arrival. He would say she knew that was her job and shouldn't have allowed herself to be over-persuaded by Newstead. She crossed to the bedside and tried to switch on the small standing lamp to see better the position was, but either the bulb had failed or the lamp had somehow become disconnected. She crossed the room and pulled back the heavy curtain. Outside the day was sharp and chill, and she was glad to open a window and let some of the clean grey air come into the stifling room. She saw that there was now a shabby fire in the grate, though she could not remember having seen it the night before. She did not need to make much of an examination to realise there was nothing she could do. She had seen death too often not to recognise it now. Heavy, flaccid, the skin grey, the jaw sagging, Adela Newstead, who must have been a pretty woman once, lay unlovely as any poor creature picked up from a tenement in her last hour. She had put on flesh of recent years and her face had none of the fabled peace of death.

Nora pulled open the door and ran downstairs. " Mr. Newstead ! " she called. " Mr. Newstead ! "

No one answered. She opened a door and found herself in a sitting-room. Dust lay everywhere, the curtains were drawn across the windows, the light only revealed emptiness. She crossed the hall and found a second room with a telephone on a table near the window, but there was no one using it.

" He can't have gone out," she thought in sudden panic. " Oh, what sort of a house is this ? It feels wrong and it is wrong. That woman upstairs is dead and I believe he knew it. I don't think he ever meant to ring the doctor. But surely he wouldn't leave me alone."

She went upstairs again to the dead woman's room, but everything was as she had left it. With the confused idea of making herself presentable she went on to the third floor, her mind dark with its own thoughts. When she opened the door silently it was as much of a shock to her as to the man within to find Mr. Newstead standing by her suitcase rummaging among the contents. His head was bent showing the fleshy back of his neck. He looked, she thought, like some gross human mole.

As she entered he turned sharply. " Why have you left your patient, nurse ? I told you. . . ."

" I left her because there's nothing I can do for her. When's the doctor coming ? "

" Do you mean she's . . . ? Oh, but that's ridiculous. I mean, she was perfectly all right last night, she was all right at a quarter to two this morning."

" The doctor will confirm that."

" Yes. Perhaps I better warn him what to expect. I suppose you are sure ? "

" Perfectly sure." She looked at him with cold indignation. " Were you looking for something in my room ? "

He gave her a peculiar glance. Then, dropping the lid of the suitcase, he came closer.

" Nurse, there's something I've got to ask you, and you'll be well-advised to tell me the truth. You may have to swear to it on oath."

" I don't know what you mean, but I certainly shouldn't tell you anything that wasn't true."

" Then—what did you give my wife out of the desk last night ? "

" I didn't give her anything. I've told you that already."

21

" I know you have. But I'm asking you again."

" And I give you the same answer. I gave her nothing. Oh ! " Her glance travelled beyond him to her rifled luggage. " Is that why you were going through my possessions ? "

He looked discomfited. " It's all so unnatural," he muttered. " I'd have sworn there was nothing seriously wrong. Nerves— yes. Delusions even—yes. But—people don't die of delusions."

There was no softening of the pale young face staring into his, no tenderness in the dark violet eyes. He hadn't known that eyes that colour could be as hard as pebbles. He looked away again.

"Anyway, the doctor is certain to ask you, and naturally I shall have to tell him that you were with her and that she asked for something out of the writing-desk."

" I don't know what you're suggesting, Mr. Newstead," said Nora, " and I certainly didn't see anything in the writing-desk that could have a thing to do with Mrs. Newstead's death. You sound as if—as if . . ."

" The truth is," burst out Mr. Newstead, " I'm worried. I suppose it's the suddenness of it. I know her heart wasn't too good, but the doctor never seemed to think of this develop- ment. However, if you didn't give her anything there's nothing more to be said. Only I felt bound to warn you he is certain to ask."

" What is it you're thinking ? " demanded Nora.

He hesitated before replying. Then he said slowly, " When I came into the room last night you were giving her a glass of water."

" She asked for it."

" Yes. Are you sure that's all she asked for ? " Nora stared. " Why, you don't think a glass of water could kill any one, do you ? "

" Not a glass of water, no. Well, if you've nothing to tell me—you're young with all your life before you and I only wanted to help you—I'll go down and tell Dr. Langton what's happened. You'd better come down, too. And don't be afraid," he added, as they came out of the room, " he won't blame you."

" He can't," said Nora flatly.

" I mean, for being so sleepy last night."

He hurried on down the stairs and she came slowly to the door of the dead woman's room, the last words ringing in her ears.

" But why should I mind ? " she asked herself in bewilderment. " I was sleepy last night. After I had that tea I felt : .."
She stopped dead, then tried to laugh at her own suspicions.
" I'm getting melodramatic. It's the atmosphere of this house, I suppose. It was just an ordinary cup of tea. This isn't a film, this is real life. People don't do that sort of thing to you when you come to nurse their sick wives. Besides, there wouldn't be any sense."

Unless, of course, whispered her brain, he wanted to be sure you were out of the way. If you'd been on duty you might have noticed some change, you might have been able to do something, you might have talked—or she might. The thoughts whirled through her head like the snowflakes in the old paperweight at home when it was taken up and shaken. She was bewildered and dismayed. Then she remembered the dead woman's words. Herbert—get Herbert—and her frantic indication of the whereabouts of the address-book. This little book, almost forgotten until now, was still in Nora's pocket. It was for this that Mr. Newstead had been searching. But did he know what it was he was looking for ? If so, then he must realise his danger. And who was Herbert ? A lover ? a relative ? a friend ? She didn't even know his other name. And anyway it was too late. All the same, she'd keep the notebook. Mr. Newstead might go through her case again, but he couldn't exactly ask her to turn out her pockets.

She came out on to the landing. The dining-room door was ajar, and she could hear Mr. Newstead's rather thick voice speaking eagerly.

" Yes, I know it's sudden. That is, you never gave me any warning. . . . Well, I suppose it was heart. . . . In her sleep. Yes, she arrived last night, but too late to do anything. Yes, she's still here, of course. Yes, naturally. Though I'm afraid she won't be able to help us much. All right. Yes, I see." He hung up the receiver. Nora retreated into the dead woman's room. It was as she had thought ; he hadn't rung up the doctor the first time. He had made the excuse and gone straight up to her room. He was suspicious of her and she was pretty certain she had not allayed those suspicions. Though she couldn't possibly be any danger to him—unless, she thought, I can trace Herbert and Herbert's a danger. Oh, dear, it's like last night's fog, only I can't be sure I shall ever get out of this one. If he'd rung up before the doctor wouldn't be asking about the nurse now. On the whole, I'd have been luckier if I'd never found the house and spent the night at the station. I don't like all this mystery. Mystery about Mrs. Newstead's illness, mystery about her death, mystery about Herbert. . . . Looking round for something to do to stop this train of thought she began to tidy the room. She found a rag in the bottom of the wardrobe that she used as a duster ; she cleared the bottles and phials from the glass-topped table to the medicine cupboard nailed against the wall. She was closing the door of this when Mr. Newstead returned.

" I was just putting things straight," she said.

His gaze was direct and angry. " What were you taking out of that cupboard ? "

" Nothing. I was putting the various bottles away."

" Indeed. That was very officious of you."

She stared at him, amazed by his manner. " But it's part of a nurse's duty to keep the sick-room tidy. And—well, I know there hasn't been any one lately. . . ."

He marched over to the cupboard and opened the door, examining the bottles as though he suspected her of having concealed one of them. Nora watched him, her mistrust and dislike increasing to match his. Before he could speak, however, the front door bell pealed and he said shortly, " That'll be the doctor," and went down to let him in. He had to draw the bolt and chain, and the doctor seemed gruff and exasperated at being kept on the doorstep. He came straight up to the sickroom, a tall man, stooping a little, with his hair growing in great·tufts over his ears. Nora was standing by the window, and turned meekly as he entered. He went at once to the bed, stooped above Adela Newstead and then straightened himself again.

" When did this happen, nurse ? " he demanded.

It was Alfred Newstead who answered. " I'm afraid nurse can't help you, doctor. She wasn't here."

" I thought you said she came last night."

" Yes. But it was eleven o'clock. We'd given up all hope of her. I'd given my wife her sleeping-draught and she seemed to have settled down."

" H'm Then you never saw her alive, nurse ? "

" Oh, yes," said Nora quickly, before Mr. Newstead could answer for her. " I went in for a few minutes last night. She seemed to want something."

" And you gave it to her ? "

" She asked for water and I gave her that, and then she

drifted off and I went down and had a cup of tea and Mr. Newstead told me I shouldn't be wanted before morning."

" So you don't know what time this happened ? "

" She was all right at a quarter to two," said Newstead swiftly. " I thought it would be safe to get a bit of sleep myself. Nurse was tired out—she had a bad journey in the fog and was delayed finding the house—and there seemed nothing she could do."

" What time did any one find Mrs. Newstead ? "

" I came in about six o'clock, didn't like the look of her, called nurse and came down to telephone to you."

" It was nearer half-past when you rang me," said the doctor, ungraciously.

" I couldn't get the connection at first. I wondered if the line was out of order. I tried again a bit later, after I'd heard from nurse that my wife was dead, and then I was more fortunate."

" Nothing wrong with my line that I know. What time did Mrs. Newstead have her sleeping tablet ? "

" About ten o'clock. She generally liked to settle down about ten."

" How many did you give her ? "

" Just one, according to your instructions. You told me. . . "

" I know I told you it would be dangerous to give her more. Where are the tablets ? "

" I think nurse tidied them away into the cupboard. She wanted everything to be shipshape for your arrival."

Nora went to the cupboard and looked at the bottles inside. She picked out the phial she had handled the night before.

" Are these them ? "

The doctor took them without thanks. " Something wrong here," he snapped. " When did I give you this bottle ? "

" Let me see. I think it was Friday."

" And to-day's Tuesday. You started them that night."

" Yes. She had none left."

" So she should have used four tablets, and I gave you fourteen, a fortnight's ration. I hoped she wouldn't need them after that. Well, that leaves ten."

He lifted his hard grey eyes and stared at Mr. Newstead accusingly.

Mr. Newstead looked troubled and perplexed.

" Yes. Isn't that right ? "

" If you mean are there still ten here, no, there aren't.

25

There are only seven. That means three are missing—missing since Friday. What happened to them ? "

" I—why, I haven't any idea. I could have sworn there were more than that in the bottle when I gave my wife hers last night."

" You may have to. We may all be glad of your help."

" But, doctor, I don't see how I . . . "

" You had the handling of them. No one else did. That is, I take it there's been no one else attending to your wife since Friday."

" Not until nurse came last night."

" You're not suggesting nurse gave her an extra dose." He flashed round to Nora. " Did you ? "

" No, sir. Just the water. But I picked up the tablets while I was standing by the bed, and I think the bottle was about as full as it is now."

" You didn't count the tablets ? "

" No, sir."

Mr. Newstead jumped in again, like a man poaching his partner's balls at tennis.

" If you've any ideas in your mind, doctor, I wish you'd tell me."

" I didn't say anything about ideas. I just point out that there are three tablets missing. Three of these tablets are a considerable dose, a dangerous dose even for someone whose heart wasn't affected in the first place. I'm bound to ask you if you can account for the missing tablets."

" No," said Newstead thoughtfully. " No, I can't. I can only assure you that I gave my wife her usual dose, and that if the tablets are missing, as unquestionably they are, they were not removed by me."

" You know best who else had a chance of removing them," snapped the doctor, " and the coroner will ask just as many inconvenient questions as I do."

" The coroner ? " Newstead sounded startled.

" I can't give you a death certificate as matters stand at present. Now then," he turned to Nora, " you didn't give Mrs. Newstead a sleeping-draught last night ? "

" No, sir. Only the water. In any case, I wouldn't have given a sleeping-draught without finding out first what she had had."

" H'm. Well, then, that only leaves Mrs. Newstead herself, assuming that the right number of tablets was in the phial last night. Is there any possibility that she took them, either because she didn't realise the effect they would have, or—because she did ? Think before you answer—it's a serious question."

" I appreciate that," returned Newstead soberly.

" In the first place, were the tablets available ? The nurse has just taken them out of the cupboard. Is that where they were normally kept ? "

" They were on the table by her bed last night," the widower confessed. " I was sitting with her, meaning to wait till she had dropped off to sleep, and in fact I thought she had settled down for the night. Then came this ring at the bell, and I came down to see who it was. As I told you, we had quite given up hope of nurse arriving at that hour and in such a fog. I was out of the room quite a while—nurse can corroborate that. I showed her her room and explained the case briefly, and then I went down to make some tea. When I came up to call nurse I found her in this room and my wife, if not precisely wakeful, certainly roused to some extent."

" So that during the time she was quite alone she could, if she had wished to, have helped herself to a further dose ? "

" I suppose she could," agreed Mr. Newstead slowly, " though I must admit it never entered my head she would do such a thing."

" I think you told me she made an attempt on her own life once before."

" Yes. About a year ago. With gas that time. Luckily I came back early and put an end to that before any real harm was done."

" So that you'd expect to be particularly careful now ? "

" Yes," said Newstead with an uneasy smile. " Yes, I see your point. You blame me for leaving the sleeping-tablets within her reach. I can only repeat that I thought she had settled down for the night, and in any case I was disturbed by the bell. Otherwise, I should, of course, have put the tablets in a safe place before leaving her alone, as I did each evening."

" I see." The doctor cove ed his long bony chin with his hand. " It's an awkward situation. I've no evidence that your wife was a potential suicide, beyond the fact that she did once try to gas herself."

" She was liable to fits of extreme depression. I was saying to nurse that it was a pity they hadn't sent someone a little older, with more experience. It's not a very cheerful case for a young lady."

" If every patient of mine who has said she'd be happier dead was to be regarded as a potential suicide I could fill a cemetery in the course of a year," observed the doctor in his grim way. " Now, Mr. Newstead, you've got to face the fact that a coroner may not accept your evidence."

" I appreciate that. He may not accept nurse's evidence either. It's a very unpleasant position for us all. Still, if you feel this matter must go to that authority there's nothing for me to say. I admit I can't quite see what they hope to prove. . . . ."

" That your wife died of an overdraught of sleeping-mixture. That's the actual cause of death. I must be satisfied how that draught was administered and frankly I'm not." He turned back to Nora. " Now, when you first came into the room, what was your impression of your patient ? "

" She seemed very restless, rather distraught. She asked if I was new, what had happened to the other one and whether she was coming back. . . . She gave me the impression of someone who was pretty ill. She pointed to the desk and I opened it, then she said give me some water in a choked sort of voice, and I came across and poured it out and I was giving it to her when Mr. Newstead came back."

The doctor frowned and seemed to stay silent a long time. Then he said, " I don't know about you, nurse, but personally I could do with a cup of tea. Is there anyone . . . ? "

Newstead took the hint. " I'll put a kettle on," he said, looking meaningly at Nora. When the door had closed behind him the doctor still maintained his sphinx-like attitude. After a minute, however, he walked over to the door, opened it and peered over the well of the staircase.

" It's all right. He's in the kitchen," he said. " Now then, nurse, there's something I want to ask you. Are you keeping anything back ? Frankly, I don't like this case. There's no doubt someone gave that unfortunate woman too much sleeping-mixture. You say it wasn't you and I believe you. If she had asked for it and you'd given it to her, you'd only have given her one, as it says on the phial. That leaves Mr. Newstead or the unhappy lady herself. Now, can you tell me any single thing that you haven't hitherto mentioned that has an active bearing on this affair, something perhaps you preferred not to mention with the husband standing by ? Mind you,

I'm asking for facts, not impressions. I don't care what you think of Mr. Newstead. You may think he looks like Charlie Peace, that's beside the point. Did Mrs. Newstead, for instance, say anything that would throw any light on the matter ? "

Nora thought for a moment.

" She said one rather strange thing. She asked where the other one was."

" Which other one ? "

" I suppose she meant a nurse."

" There hasn't been any other nurse."

" Then I don't know who she meant. I told her she wasn't here now, in the hope of calming her, but she just said in a voice not exactly resigned but as if there wasn't anything she could do about it, ' She'll come back when I've gone.' "

" She didn't explain what she meant by that ? "

" I didn't ask her. Anyway, she was, I thought, partly drugged by some sleeping-draught she'd taken. But I did get the impression that she was definitely going away—I didn't think she had any doubt about that."

The doctor frowned. " Was it after that that she asked for the water ? "

" Yes. She seemed half-choked."

" I don't like it," said the doctor, abruptly. " I don't like it at all. She didn't say anything else that would throw any light on the position ? "

" She was very uneasy."

" Anything special ? These generalisations don't help, you know, nurse."

" She wanted to get in touch with some friend, I think, or perhaps it was a relation. I assumed that Mr. Newstead wasn't anxious to help and . . ."

The doctor made an impatient gesture. " Just what I warned you against," he said. " Assumptions are no good. Now you don't need me to tell you this is a very awkward and unpleasant case. I haven't the smallest doubt that my patient died of an overdose of sleeping-mixture, and I haven't the smallest proof as to who administered it. If I send this to a jury they'll be in exactly the same position as I am. There's no definite evidence either way. Mrs. Newstead was a hypochondriac and I'd say she wasn't happy. But there are plenty of unhappy wives who don't commit suicide. I don't know anything about Mr. Newstead's private affairs—the coroner's officers can nose those out if they think they're relevant—but once this becomes a public matter the fellow's a murderer in all but actual proof. I'm being blunt with you because I can see you've got sense. Once a hint of murder is dropped against a man, particularly a husband, he's ruined. He may as well string himself up to a hook behind his own door. I don't speak without the book. I had a similar case in my practice about two years ago. I wasn't satisfied, the case went to the coroner the man was found *Not Guilty*—that is to say, the wife had been done away with but there was no evidence to affix responsibility—but the whole neighbourhood knew that the man had done it. He could be as innocent as the Archangel Gabriel—I daresay he was—but the poor wretch was finished. And when he did finally put an end to things the whole place smirked with satisfaction and said that was proof positive. And they don't call that murder." The fire that had inflamed his voice died down. " And if they say she may have taken the stuff herself, as she very well may, then you're blackening the name of a dead woman. Either way you're bound to lose." He looked at Nora again. " Was there time while you were looking in the desk for her to take the tablets out of the phial ? "

" She would have had to get the bottle, to unscrew it, screw it up again and put the tablets into her mouth—and swallow them."

" She couldn't swallow tablets without water. Some people can, but not Mrs. Newstead."

" Water ? Then you think . . . doctor, she asked me for water when I turned back."

" I hadn't forgotten. But that's not proof either. The plain fact is there's no proof. I'm no more wooden-headed than a coroner's jury and I don't want to let a crime go through . . ." (it seemed to Nora that he was talking more to himself than to her) " but I don't want to be responsible for breaking up a man's life. If any of Mrs. Newstead's relations have got anything to say, they can say it to the police. They can ask for an enquiry if they think things aren't right. And that's what they'll do if they're not satisfied. But I doubt if they will. A woman who's once tried suicide often tries again."

Nora wondered is she should say anything about her unusually heavy sleep, her suspicion that her tea had been doctored, but an instant's reflection assured her that this was only one more of those impressions that were a mile removed from proof. Why, she herself had washed her own cup, and any coroner's jury would assume that the journey, the long delay, the feeling of her way in the fog, would account for her exhaustion. So she held her peace and heard the doctor say he'd send along the certificate. Though she disliked and mistrusted Mr. Newstead she appreciated that Langton was right. There wasn't a jot of proof, there could only be suspicion, that would touch them all, Newstead himself, the dead woman, the nurse—even the doctors might suffer. Doctors don't like being involved in murder or suspected murder. It's bad for their practice and a man who had already had one such experience would strain several points to avoid a second.

" I'll send along the certificate," repeated Langton absently, " and I suppose Mr. Newstead will see the undertakers. You'd better get things in order here, unless there's someone who can help."

But Nora shook her head. She had laid out dead bodies before. They had no dreads for her. Dead people ceased to be personalities the moment the breath left the body. You could be afraid of the living, but never of the departed.

" And you'd better leave an address in case of emergencies," the doctor added. " We'll hope this is the end, but if it shouldn't be you might be wanted. But I daresay Mr. Newstead knows where you can be found. Well," he turned towards the door and almost ran against the widower who brought the news that there was tea in the dining-room, " it's been a sorry business. I hope your next case is more promising."

CHAPTER FOUR

You k'n hide de fier but wat you gwine do wid de smoke ?
—UNCLE REMUS.

MR. NEWSTEAD was very curious to know what Langton had said during his absence and as soon as the doctor had drunk his tea and left the house he began to make his enquiries.

" He simply took me through my story again," answered Nora wearily. " I think he wanted to be sure I hadn't given your wife the extra dose of sleeping-draught."

" I'd be glad to be sure of that, too," agreed Newstead,

" though the alternative isn't a very pretty one. No man likes to admit his wife has taken her own life."

" Do you mean you don't believe me ? " demanded Nora indignantly.

" Well, do you believe me ? The fact is, a case like this is bound to stay up in the air and that's unsatisfactory for everyone. I may know I'm not responsible, but that's only enough for me. It doesn't, I daresay, satisfy you. Perhaps it doesn't satisfy the doctor. I can't pretend I'm not troubled about it. I am. The truth is it's thoroughly disagreeable for all parties, and the less we talk about it the better. All we need to remember is what Langton will put on the death certificate— heart failure—and let it go at that."

He looked at her meaningly. She knew he still suspected that his wife had said something she had refused to divulge, and he was warning her to let the matter drop. She felt in her bones that he was right. No good could come out of pursuing enquiries. Yet the dying woman's face haunted her. She couldn't remember if she had promised to try and find Herbert —and even if she could trace him by means of the address-book would that improve the position ? Yet, in spite of all reason, she knew that she would do it if she could. She could only hope that she would be unable to track him down.

Remembering what the doctor had said she reluctantly gave an address in Cunningham Road, Maida Vale, where she intended to go on leaving the house. It was a Nurses' Hostel where she always stayed between jobs. Probably by tomorrow she would be out on something else, but letters sent there would reach her, and she could not be certain that she had heard the end of the Newstead affair. She went back to the sick-room to do what was necessary for the dead woman, and Mr. Newstead hung about, clearly not intending to give her the run of the house. It would be soon enough to call on the undertaker later in the day.

She left as soon as she could. At ten o'clock she was seated in a cafe near Victoria Station, having deposited her case in the luggage office, and was eagerly awaiting a large pot of coffee and some sandwiches. Mr. Newstead's hospitality had stopped short at the tea and some rather soft biscuits, and she felt she could face whatever lay ahead better with food inside her. While she drank the coffee she examined the little address-book, hoping beyond hope that she would be unable to identify the mysterious Herbert. The more she thought about the case the less she liked it, and when she had reached the letter T without success her spirits began to rise. A moment later, however, they were deflated. Under W she found an entry : Herbert Webster and an address and telephone number in Epsom. Paying for her food she made her way to a telephone booth and rang the number. A woman's voice answered and said that Mr. Webster had left for his office some time ago.

" Could you give me that number ? " she enquii

The voice said sharply, " Who is it wants him ? ' and she replied: " I'm speaking on behalf of Mrs. Newstead of Askew Avenue, Charlbury."

The voice changed. " Oh ! I hope it's not bad news about his sister. Who are you ? "

" I'm the nurse. She asked me to ring him."

" It's Berkeley 4708," said the woman, and rang off.

Nora pushed another twopence into the slot and waited. Once again the mention of Mrs. Newstead got her connected.

" Is that you, nurse ? " said a deep voice. " Mr. Webster speaking. Have you a message from my sister ? "

" Not—not exactly. That is, she was asking for you last night, and I said I'd try and get in touch, but . . ."

" Is she worse ? "

" I'm afraid so. In fact . . ." She hesitated and the man said, " Are you trying to tell me she's dead ? "

" Yes. In her sleep. It was very unexpected."

There was a long silence at the other end of the line. Then the voice said, " Are you speaking from the house ? "

" No. I'm at Victoria Station. I—there wasn't any more for me to do."

" What does the doctor say ? "

" Well—it's rather difficult . . ."

" I can't hear," said Webster impatiently. " Look here, can't you come up to my office? There's something here I don't understand. I should have expected my brother-in-law to ring me."

" I think it would be better if I came," Nora agreed. " It's not easy on the telephone. Not that I can be very helpful," she added quickly, remembering that nurses shouldn't discuss their cases even with the family, " but . . ."

" I'll be the judge of that. I'm at Berkhampstead House, Berkeley Square. Webster & Smythe, solicitors. Fourth floor. Take a taxi. I'll expect you in ten minutes."

His manner of ringing off was as abrupt as his voice. Nora hung up the receiver, wondered about rescuing her luggage, decided to leave it where it was, caught a crawling taxi and was driven to Berkhampstead House. Mr. Webster was waiting for her. He was a tall man in the late forties, with thinning hair and a big jutting nose that gave character to a face that was far from sympathetic.

" You're very young," he said as Nora came in, just as his brother-in-law had done. " What made them put you on to a case like this ? "

" Hobson's Choice," said Nora impatiently. " You can't pick and choose nurses just now."

" Well, what happened ? Tell me from the beginning."

She began with the story of her late arrival and Mr. Newstead's odd behaviour after she reached the house.

" I know this isn't what the doctor would call evidence, but I got the distinct impression that he was startled—put out, rather—by my coming so late."

" You didn't make the fog."

" No. But I think he thought I wouldn't come till next day and it upset his plans. He was very anxious I shouldn't see your sister, and angry when he found me in her room."

She went on to explain about the tea. " There's no proof there either. I know that. But I can't help remembering that he sent me into the pantry to fetch another cup while he poured my tea out."

" I don't like it," said Webster in his short voice. " I never did like the marriage and I did everything I could to prevent it. I suppose they told you my sister made an attempt on her own life last year ? Oh yes, it was genuine enough. Well, a woman doesn't do that unless there's something wrong. I wanted her to leave her husband, but I got the impression she was afraid. Goodness knows why; the money was all hers. Look here, you look sensible though you are so young—you know we're playing with fire, if that doctor really means to give a certificate. But I'd like to be certain it's all right. I want a lot more enquiries made before I'll agree to keep quiet about this. Oh, I know the fellow's arguments, but if they think Adela did away with herself—well, that can't hurt her now, and I'm not giving a brass farthing for Newstead's feelings. It won't hurt me to be mixed up in an enquiry. I've only myself to think of. I'm a bachelor without dependants, and my work takes me about the country a good deal. That explains why I haven't seen more of my sister during the past year. Most of my time I'm on Government jobs. I got three months off to attend to my own business affairs when Smythe, my partner, was killed in a raid, but I have to go out of town to-morrow for some days. It's a good thing you called me right away. By the way, what time did you say the death was discovered ? "

" About six."

" And now it's going on for eleven. If everything was all right why didn't my brother-in-law ring me up ? It's the obvious thing to do. I'm Adela's only living relative. Of course, the answer is he doesn't want any questions asked till it's too late. I bet you'll find he's hurrying on the funeral, and my being out of London would be just luck for him. It takes a lot to ask for an exhumation and most likely the Home Office wouldn't grant it. No, I fancy Alfred was backing his luck and, but for you, it would have stood him in."

" I promised his wife," whispered Nora, not much liking that hard face, the resolute mouth and dominant chin. More than ever she wished she had never found her way to 12 Askew Avenue but had spent the night at the station.

" It was lucky you did get there." But he added a minute later, " Perhaps unlucky would be a better word. Now, where can I contact you ? "

" I'll be staying at Cunningham Road—the Nurses' Hostel." She gave him the telephone number.

" You'll be there—how long ? "

" That depends. I shall have to report to Matron when I arrive."

" Will she be on the premises ? "

" No. I'm one of the outside staff. She uses us when all the inside nurses are engaged. In between jobs I stay at the hostel."

" So you'll have to ring her ? "

" Yes."

He looked thoughtful. " Look here," he said after a minute, " there's no burning hurry to get in touch, is there ? I mean, would it make any difference if you didn't ring her till this afternoon ? "

" I'm supposed to let her know directly I leave a job."

" And if she's got another one waiting she can send you on at once ? "

" If it's a rush job—yes."

" And you might go anywhere ? "

" Well, not anywhere, but . . ."

" Where I couldn't get at you easily anyway." He sounded impatient, sitting there drumming his fingers on his handsome desk. " Look here, wait till I've seen my brother-in-law. I'm going over at once. I'll ring you back by—say, not later than two o'clock, earlier if I can. I'll know by then whether I'm likely to want your help. Will you wait till then ? "

She hesitated, but finally she agreed. " Till two."

" You're going there now ? "

" I've got to pick up my luggage from Victoria, and then I'll go straight on."

He laid a note on the desk. " Take a taxi and get your stuff and drive back to Cunningham Road. Now remember, you're not going to ring anyone before two. That understood ? "

" Not anyone ? All right." She saw the stern face harden in exasperation and forebore further argument. It wasn't as though there was anyone to ring.

" Right. That's the door. Ring for the lift. And don't let anyone encourage you to go for a nice walk or anything, or start taking a bath. Just wait around till I call you. I daresay it won't be long. If it's all right, it's good-bye. If not, I'll be seeing you later."

Nora, a little dazed, gave the required promise and walked out of the room. It didn't, apparently, occur to Mr. Webster to open the door for her. In fact, he was already deep in cogitation. There was a good deal to be considered. The story she had told him was an odd one, yet it had the ring of truth. For the life of him, he couldn't see why she should invent such a situation. And if it was true, then a number of possibilities were opened up to him. He could immediately approach the police and state his dissatisfaction, but before doing so it might be as well to tackle the doctor in person. The girl appeared honest, but you could never be sure, and he didn't want to make a fool of himself, a cockshy for the penny press, particularly just now with the delicate matter of his new partnership in the balance. Besides, he argued, murder's just up Alfred's street, this sort of murder that doesn't involve blood and violence, and I happen to know he needed money pretty badly. Shady as a country lane, that was Alfred. Herbert had never trusted him from the start. He had known the fellow had married Adela for her money as clearly as if he'd signed a written declaration to that effect. Admittedly,

Adela hadn't always been wise. She was thirty-two at the time of the marriage, and was anxious not to be left. She didn't look a day younger than her age and she wasn't adaptable. There was about her a sort of slow obstinacy that would have infuriated a less touchy man than Alfred Newstead. Herbert had heard a number of stories about his brother-in-law's failings as a husband during the intervening years, yet when an opportunity—one opportunity after another, in fact —was offered her of shaking the fellow off she clung stubbornly to what she called principles and what Herbert called pigheadedness and Alfred, had his opinion been asked, damned dog-in-the-manger selfishness.

"All the same," reflected Herbert Webster, taking a watch out of his pocket and looking at it, "murder's a big step even for an outsider like Alfred to take. He seems to have laid his plans pretty well, if the girl's story's true and Adela may have convinced him at last she meant to take final steps to separate him and her fortune, which is the only part of her he ever cared two straws about. He reckoned without the girl, though, and he reckoned without me."

It wasn't in the man's nature to allow Newstead to get away with so appalling a piece of insolence unchallenged. Part of Herbert's indignation—it would be misleading to call it grief—arose from the fact that by a single bold stroke the worthless Alfred had virtually put himself in possession of £12,000, a sum he could be relied upon to squander.

"But a condemned man can't inherit," thought Herbert balefully. After a little further reflection he took up his telephone, called a certain Mr. Cradock with whom he was negotiating a partnership, following the death of his own partner by enemy action, cancelled a lunch appointment, called his secretary and said he had to go out and that he'd want the papers about his sister's investments put on his desk against his return, and if Mr. Cradock rang through again she could make an appointment for the morning.

Then he put on his wide black hat, took up a small briefcase, because he didn't believe in wasting time, not even on the shortest journey and turned towards the Underground station. He had to do a great deal in a short time, and the results of his actions during the next few hours might alter his entire life.

37

CHAPTER FIVE

What signifies me hear if me no understand ?
—ISAAC BICKERSTAFF.

As NORA, preceding Mr. Webster by about half-an-hour, turned her steps towards the Underground station, she realised that her uneasiness had increased. She realised, too, that she had been sub-consciously hoping that Mr. Webster would pooh-pooh her apprehension, would even be annoyed by her pertinacity in coming to see him. A little hard speaking would be far easier to endure than this feeling that she was walking into a darkness as impenetrable as last night's fog. She reached the Hostel in Cunningham Road without any lightening of her mood. There was a vacant room she could have, the secretary told her, adding that she had been lucky in getting an un-broken week end, hadn't she ? Nora said vaguely that she'd heard from matron, but the secretary, who had a cheerful horse-shaped face as polished as an apple, didn't take any notice and whistled her way back to her own office. Nora, who didn't like her much, decided that there was no point in saying anything further. If Webster decided to take action, then the whole story would come out, but if by some miracle his suspicions were allayed or he realised that he hadn't a chance of proving a murder charge, then she could put the whole affair behind her and go on to the next job which could be trusted to materialise without delay.

The secretary poked her head out of her room again to remark, " You're not going out, I suppose. Well, you'll find Weymouth in the lounge. There was a call for a nurse this morning and she got it. She'll be going after lunch."

In the lounge, that was really a common-room, a tall girl was sitting by the shabby fire, knitting a jumper in blue and purple stripes.

" Hallo, Deane, " she greeted the new comer. " Sunset and evening bell and one clear call for me. Pity you didn't turn up earlier, you might have got the job. And welcome. One of these heart cases. You know what they are. Nothing's ever right. If there are white roses in a blue vase they want blue roses in a white one. If they have faithful husbands then they

drink and they wish they were unfaithful, but if they're unfaithful, then they envy every woman in the country tied to a
sot who can't be persuaded to turn his attentions elsewhere.
I often think it would save a lot of trouble if doctors could
find some substitute for the heart."

She sighed deeply. Nora, like everyone else who had met
her more than once, knew that the speaker had been disgrace-
fully treated by a married man passing as single, and that she
had found out the truth " only just in time, my dear." Nora
had heard the story more than once and didn't want to hear
it again.

" I must go up and unpack my things," she said hastily,
making for the door.

Grace Weymouth stared at her, then burst into a great
guffaw of laugher.

" Well, you are an optimist. I didn't know there were any
left. What's the sense of unpacking ? You're sure to be off
again before night."

Nora smiled non-committally and continued her way to the
door. " See you at lunch ? " enquired Grace Weymouth
brightly.

" I—oh yes, I expect so."

" You don't seem too sure." Miss Weymouth sounded
roguish.

" I'm waiting for a telephone call," explained Nora.

" Ah—*now* we know." Afterwards Miss Weymouth said she
had had her doubts about the week-end right at the start, and
when she saw the state little Deane was in on her return her
suspicions crystalised.

" You mean, you appreciated that something was wrong ? "
she was asked.

" Well, I could see she had something on her mind," tem-
porised Miss Weymouth. " She wasn't quite herself at lunch
either. Of course, if she'd confided in me I should have
said, My dear, go to the police at once. Put the responsibility
where it belongs. But I'm afraid she's one of these rather
deep people, secretive, you know, like water flowing underground."

" I'm afraid I don't know," said her interlocutor, " but I
daresay it's not important."

Having ascertained that Nora had made no confidences his
interest in Miss Weymouth lapsed abruptly. That was the
time when everyone was talking about Nora and you saw her

picture in the papers, and the notorious Mr. Crook had been called in to find her. But that was some little way ahead.

Meanwhile Nora went up to the cell-like room that had been allotted to her but in which, as it happened, she was not destined to sleep, and fiddled about, because if she went down Grace Weymouth would be waiting for her and you could stop rain falling more easily than you could stop such a woman talking. And she didn't want to be cross-examined or inveigled into a conversation about the household she had just left, so she stayed where she was, despite the cold, until someone rapped sulkily on her door and told her she was wanted on the telephone—a Mr. Webster. As she hurried down Grace Weymouth happened to be crossing the hall.

" Your date's on the line, dear," she said. " Happy landings."

Nora took up the receiver, resentfully wondering why the telephone had to stand in the most public spot in the house.

" Is that Mr. Webster ? " she asked.

The voice came back deep and abrupt, a bit shaken yet masterful, dictatorial almost.

" Miss Deane ? Webster here. That matter we were speaking of this morning—you haven't mentioned it to anyone else ? "

" No. No, I haven't. Of course not."

" That's right. I don't know whether you'll be relieved, but I've made some enquiries and I've decided there's nothing to be done. I don't say I'm convinced, but I do realise my hands are tied."

" That's practically what the doctor said," murmured Nora.

" Precisely. And I can't feel it would do my poor sister any good to ventilate the facts of her death without more proof than I can hope to muster. As a matter of fact, I don't know that it wouldn't be doing you some dis-service into the bargain. You can never tell with juries. Speaking as a lawyer, I can assure you they're utterly undependable. They might say it was your duty to insist on seeing your patient at once, no matter what the hour."

" I do realise that," agreed Nora in a low voice, looking over her shoulder and half-expecting to see Grace Weymouth's head sticking out of the common-room door. " But there was the tea—I'm certain it was drugged."

" You've no proof, have you ? " The voice was deeper now.

" No—no, of course not."

" I'm afraid they'd simply say you put that bit in to excuse yourself. After all, you had gone back to your room."

" Yes. I had, hadn't I ? No, it wouldn't do me any good."

" And I daresay it wouldn't help me if people had an opportunity of saying that I was trying to get my brother-in-law hanged in order that I might inherit my sister's fortune."

" Oh, would you ? I mean, I didn't know . . ."

" It doesn't matter." The voice seemed hurried now, as if the speaker had gone a little too far. " The important thing is that, since it's obvious that no action is possible, whatever you or I may think, the less either of us speaks of this affair the better."

" I shouldn't be likely to speak of it," retorted Nora, a little nettled by his complete self-absorption.

" No ? Well, things slip out in general conversation. I'm only warning you because, if an enquiry were subsequently ordered, it might be awkward for you to have to explain why you'd said nothing at the time. What's that ? Did you speak ? "

" I ? No." She hoped that was true. What she was thinking was that Adela was perhaps fortunate to have escaped from the enmity of two men both of them so mercenary and self-seeking. " I suppose it's all right for me to ring the matron now," she added.

" What's that ? "

" You asked me not to ring the matron until I'd heard from you, in case you wanted me, but as you don't I suppose there's no reason to wait any longer."

" No, no." He didn't sound interested. " No reason at all. I daresay you'll find there's something waiting for you. By the way, if your matron asks about Mrs. Newstead it'll be sufficient to say she died of heart failure."

" That's all she'll want to know." Thank Heaven, the whole thing was off. She had been shaking with nervousness at the prospect of taking her place in the witness-box, should the affair have come to a trial.

" All right." She heard a click which showed that the receiver had been hung up. Slowly the girl put back her own instrument. You couldn't expect Mr. Webster to be exactly friendly ; possibly he did hold her more responsible than he would admit for what had happened. All the same, you could not pretend that he was heart-broken about his sister's death.

She was glad to be quit of the whole thing. By to-morrow she would probably be in another county and with any good luck she would never hear the name of Newstead again.

Feeling unwontedly depressed, she made her way back to the dining-room where lunch had just been served. Grace Weymouth was chewing her way through sausages and cabbage.

" Hallo ! Not gone yet ? "

" I'm not going."

Grace Weymouth arched her scanty eyebrows, whistled soundlessly as well as she could for the food in her mouth, swallowed hurriedly, and prepared to be sympathetic. She knew what had happened, of course. Little Deane had been led up the garden the way so many girls were. Providence, she said, as Nora unenthusiastically cut up a sausage, seemed to have a down on women. Otherwise it would grant them a sixth sense to warn when they were playing with fire.

" It isn't anything like that," said Nora wearily. " It's—oh, it's just that I don't like losing patients."

" Well, it's not your fault, dear. There's no need to look like a murderess."

" No, I suppose not. Don't you ever feel responsible, though, if a patient doesn't get over it ? "

" My dear," Weymouth sprinkled mustard on a sausage with an air that said, That'll teach you to lie down and keep quiet, " I'm a fatalist. People die when their hour comes. Nothing you or I do can make any difference. And you never can tell what they may have been saved. Perhaps they'd have had a tragic future if they'd lived." She dealt ruthlessly with the already dispirited sausage.

" How comfortable ! " said Nora. She got away as soon as lunch was over and telephoned to matron.

" Dead, is she ? " said Matron composedly. " When did that happen ? "

" Early this morning."

" You've been a long time in letting me know."

" Yes. I—I stayed for a bit—there wasn't anyone in the house except the husband . . ."

" I've told you before from our point of view the living are more important than the dead. I've a new case wanting a nurse at very short notice. An old lady just through an operation."

" On the danger list ? " Nora's heart sank. It didn't do a nurse any good to lose two patients consecutively.

" From all accounts she'll outlive her own grandchildren." Matron went into details.

" Am I to go this afternoon ? "

" I think you'd better. There is another nurse, but the old lady's the trying kind, wears out people half her age. I'll send a wire telling them to expect you. The other nurse will be glad, if no one else is."

Nora was given the address and the name of the patient and some necessary details and then rang off and went upstairs. She thought she might as well catch the next train. It wasn't too good a service, and experience had warned her that nurses are much more popular if they arrive in time for a meal, instead of disorganising the household by wanting a tray of tea at some inconvenient moment. Thank Heaven, she reflected, the fog had cleared completely. That was something to be grateful for.

" New job ? " asked Grace Weymouth eagerly, when Nora came down wearing her uniform coat. " Lady or gent ? Ah well, you like old ladies, don't you ? " She laughed. " Make the most of your opportunities, Deane." It was her little joke. She always said Nora put on her gentle manner in the hope of ravishing some elderly patient who would put her down for something handsome in her will. " Though it's more likely to be in his will," she'd say. " You can't get by with a woman very well. They know too much." and she'd droop one large while eyelid in a wink that Nora always found offensive.

Ministering angels, thought Nora taking up her case and turning towards the nearest underground station. She thought when she died and found herself in the Hereafter she'd ask the first spirit she saw the quickest way to the Underground.

" And I suppose they'd think that a poor sort of joke," she reflected drearily. The fog was gone, and a drizzle of rain had begun.

So she set forth on her momentous journey.

CHAPTER SIX

Pursuit of knowledge under difficulties.—LORD BROUGHAM.

AT ABOUT the same time as Nora went to the telephone to report to matron the young man called Sammy came striding down Askew Avenue and rang heartily at the bell of Number Twelve. He waited for a minute or two, then, when there was no reply, lacking nothing in determination and having a great deal at stake, he rang again. The next instant he walked out from the little porch to see whether he was being deliberately kept outside, whether some curious head peeped stealthily from a window, and it was then that he realised the blinds had been drawn in a room on the first floor.

"Dead, eh?" he reflected. "Did they anticipate that? What cursed luck. That may interfere with all my plans." He frowned as he pressed the bell for the third time. This piece of news had only strengthened his already powerful intention to see Nora Deane again, and though they might be "waking" the corpse he proposed to remain where he was until someone answer his summons. There were several things he wanted to know, and being a young man accustomed to getting his own way he didn't intend to budge until some at least of his questions were answered.

Whoever was inside the house, supposing it wasn't deserted, seemed to be in no hurry. Sammy lighted a cigarette and stepped into the drizzle. Round the monkey-puzzler he walked, round and round, oblivious to the rain, ringing the front door bell each time he passed, a tall, patient, purposeful young man waiting to achieve his own ends.

Mr. Newstead had been enormously busy since Nora's departure. He hadn't appreciated that his wife's death was going to involve him in so much activity. He saw Nora go with a sense of thankfulness. He had known real apprehension while the doctor hesitated about the death certificate; now that first stile was crossed he wanted to see the end of the doleful dangerous business as soon as possible. The sooner he could polish it off the sooner he could get away. No one would think it odd that he should want to leave the house where his

44

wife had died. He could say he had a war restoration job. Plenty of people were being retained in Government service to get on with post-war plans. Here, where everyone knew his whereabouts, he was too vulnerable for his own peace of mind. There was his brother-in-law, Herbert Webster, who would certainly make trouble when he knew what had happened. The more counties he could put between them the better pleased he'd be. Then, there was the inevitable woman. Unless he was much mistaken Herbert knew of her existence, possibly even of her identity. Adela had become very confiding of late. If ever an outsider could be held to have broken up a marriage, Herbert Webster had broken up his sister's. From the beginning he'd tried to plant a distrust of her husband in Adela's heart. At first he hadn't been successful, but presently Newstead had noticed that, when he proposed a change in investments, Adela would say lightly, charmingly, but quite definitely, " Oh, I'll just ask Herbert. He's so clever over money."

" And I suppose you think I'm a fool ? " he'd growl.

" Well, just not lucky. Herbert says some men are like that. Just the opposite of Midas who made everything turn to gold just by touching it . . ."

It had become harder and harder to obtain any control over her finances. And now, when he needed the money desperately she had refused outright to help him. The trouble was that she had probably told Herbert of the position. Herbert, who'd never forgiven him for marrying his well-to-do sister—as if money could ever do more for a woman than get her a husband and Adela was no chicken when they played The Voice that Breathed for her—and if he could work mischief now you could count on his doing it.

As if Herbert wasn't enough of a headache for anyone, there was also Harriet. Harriet Forbes was the last of his women, a fine full-bosomed creature with a bold rolling eye and a rollicking sense of humour. But whatever she might think Alfred Newstead had no intention of taking her to the altar.

" If Adela's taught me anything it is that marriage is a mistake," he reflected bitterly. " I'll never put my head into that noose again."

But though he might assert this to himself he was uneasily aware that Harriet might take a very different view of the position. That was another reason for clearing out as soon as possible. Harriet owned her little house and she wouldn't want to leave it. If he stayed away long enough she'd fix her changeable fancy on some other fellow. He'd told her earnestly that Adela was the religious kind who wouldn't give him a divorce whatever happened, but lately he'd wondered whether Herbert hadn't undermined her convictions in that respect. One or two remarks she'd let drop had started him prickling with sweat. He was no match for Harriet.

" You poor boy ! " she'd said. " No wonder you're antimarriage. Your Adela was born an old maid. But you wait— I'll show you . . ." She was plump and cosy and goodnatured, and you could have a lot of easy fun with her, but he'd never considered her as the second Mrs. Newstead. No, on all accounts it was a good thing he was leaving Charlbury. She could hardly, he reflected, come round to call before the funeral, and immediately afterwards he'd leave the place and later on give instructions for the house to be let furnished— or store the furniture and get a sub-let. Anything rather than ever come back here again. He drew a deep breath. He'd only got to keep his head for two or three days and all would be well. It had been a difficult time, and there had been unlooked-for complications—the girl's arrival late at night, for instance, Langton's doubts—but they were over now. He found himself remembering an old evangelistic hymn. One more river to cross, one more river. Only one more—the funeral—and then he'd be in the Promised Land. Always provided that Herbert didn't make trouble. He couldn't prove a thing, of course, and suspicion isn't enough, not even the suspicion of men like Herbert who wouldn't have trusted the Archangel Gabriel. But, say what you like about all men in England being innocent till they're shown beyond all reasonable doubt to be guilty, even an innocent man can have a pretty poor time of it if it comes to a jury. He thought of other men—Greenwood, Wallace, Mrs. Rattenbury—the sequel to their\ trials, and they'd all been finally acquitted, wasn't reassuring. The British public had a habit of looking sideways and squinting a bit when an unattractive wife died in her sleep just when her death was most advantageous to her husband.

He decided to arrange the funeral for Thursday and set out to visit the undertaker. As soon as he'd made the necessary arrangements he'd clear up Adela's desk—it was stacked with rubbish that was far better destroyed, and on Friday he'd get out. Any arrangements that had to be made about the house could be done by letter. All he need do was lock up one of the rooms, the dressing-room for preference, putting into it any personal possessions he wanted to safeguard, and then a reliable agent could put the house on his books and he, Alfred Newstead, need do nothing but take the rent as it came along. He looked forward to Friday as good men look forward to the millenium and saints to the Kingdom of Heaven, something that must be achieved because it was the only thing worth looking forward to. He had got the doctor's certificate and he shut up the house and went to see Jarvis and Jarvis, funeral upholders situated in the High Street. He saw the second Mr. Jarvis, and was told that their Mr. Hunter would be pleased to call during the day and make the necessary arrangements for the disposal of the corpse. Mr. Jarvis had a very good professional manner. You wouldn't, thought Newstead, have been surprised if he'd offered you a little sable buttonhole in token of his respectful sympathy. The clock was striking eleven when Newstead got back and the telephone began to ring before he had shut the front door. It was Harriet Forbes, and she said she'd just heard the news.

" It must have been a dreadful shock for you, Alfie, but I feel sure it was all for the best. I mean, it saves a lot of trouble, doesn't it ? "

He winced. " My dear Harriet . . ."

" Now, Alfie, don't go stuffy and conventional on me. You know Mrs. Newstead didn't really enjoy her life, and she was going to make things very difficult for us. I think it was very tactful of Providence, and if I believed there was such a thing I'd thank him."

" It was heart," he said desperately. " Langton says you can never be sure with hearts what to expect."

" You must be absolutely overwhelmed with details," said Harriet cordially. " Now if there's anything I can do . . ."

He was panic-stricken. " No, no," he exclaimed. " You must see that till after the funeral . . ."

" Perhaps you're right, dear," said Hattie obligingly. " People have such nasty minds, haven't they ? Still, if there should be anything . . ."

" I'm going to be choc-a-bloc," he told her. " My own affairs and winding up Adela's . . . She kept every paper she ever had, I believe."

" You let the lawyer do that," she told him. " What are lawyers for ? Well, be seeing you soon, Alfie."

He got the feeling that she wasn't really giving in quite so easily as it appeared. Her promise to give him a tinkle one day soon was anything but reassuring. He had just reached the foot of the stairs when the telephone rang again. It was another neighbour offering condolences. He remembered what he'd once heard someone say of the telephone—the bloodiest invention known to man. He was inclined to agree.

" Anything we can do to help ? " enquired the neighbour in a voice at once breezy and sympathetic, a combination he himself couldn't have managed to save his life. " I mean, the shock . . . I mean, care for a bed here ? Angela says I'm to tell you it's no trouble at all, and she's sure you shouldn't be alone."

He said quickly, " No," and then, " Very kind but it's quite all right." And then something about there being a lot to attend to and hung up quickly. That was Jenkins, a good fellow ; but he couldn't stand Mrs. J. One of those people who laugh heartily at the idea of women achieving equality with men in any field. Women aren't equal, she'd boom. They never will be in office life, and in homes they're superior. Nature knows what she's about. (Privately Newstead doubted that. If it were true she was a pretty treacherous old so-and-so.) Besides, she'd want to talk about Adela. The poor *thing* ! she'd say, and then, like Harriet, though she'd be furious if you told her there was any resemblance, she'd bleat something about it all being for the best. He put the thought of her out of his head and wondered about ringing up Herbert but decided to postpone it for a bit. He got upstairs and was just going to start on Adela's desk when someone came to the front door—another one who'd heard about Adela—and delayed him a long time, and there were two or three other telephone calls and the postman came with a parcel for someone else and a young boy shouted up did he want any logs ? He began to feel frantic. He'd never get away, he thought. He did a bit of telephoning on his own account and had a wrong number, and realised he'd never taken in the morning letters, which were all bills anyway. He didn't feel he could face lunch in that house of the dead and, with his nerves considerably shaken, he went down to the Bird in Hand and had two double whiskies and some sandwiches. They knew about his loss there and eyed him sympathetically, but no one spoke of Adela. On the way back he passed Hattie Forbes' house and, glancing up by force of habit, he saw her with her nose glued to the window watching him. He looked away hurriedly, pretending not to have seen. He supposed an enemy could make mischief even out of his going down to the public-house. As though anything he did could help Adela now !

He was glad when he came in sight of his own house, but he stopped, as if paralysed, when he saw a strange young man waiting purposefully for his return. His heart seemed to stop, too, and then ached suddenly with a hard determined pain that he didn't at first recognise as fear. He had never seen Sammy before, but he could guess why he was here. Langton hadn't been convinced, after all, and yet—how about the death certificate he had issued ? It wasn't possible—was it ? —for any fresh development to have taken place during the last hour that would turn his footsteps, in spite of all his precautions, in the direction of the gallows ? But his knowledge of what he had done filled him with terror. It is difficult to believe that a thing perfectly well known to oneself is not obvious or at all events a core of suspicion to the rest of the world. He remembered that he hadn't rung up Herbert's office yet. He must do that as soon as he got in, ought to have done it an hour or more ago. But a man can't think of everything. If he could there'd be far more successful murders than there are.

He opened the gate and came slowly up the path, saying as he came, " Were you looking for me ? "

" I guess so," said Sammy. " You own the house ? "

" I'm the tenant, but—who told you it was to let ? "

" No one," said Sammy, " and anyway I wouldn't be interested. I'm looking for the young lady."

Newstead experienced such a throb of relief it was like another pain. " The young lady ? " he repeated, vaguely.

" Miss Deane. I was to call for her at two o'clock."

" Indeed ? " Instantly his suspicions swelled once more. " I'm afraid I know nothing of that. As a matter of fact, she left some time ago, when it became obvious there was nothing further she could do," he added meaningly.

" Is that so ? Then maybe you could give me her address."

" I haven't got it," said Newstead swiftly. It was difficult to see what harm the girl could do in view of her own position and the doctor's certificate, but, as the Prime Minister liked to remind the country, it was in the last lap that races are won or lost, and though he didn't think he'd got to the last lap yet, he hoped most of his trouble was now behind him. " And in any case at such a time, with so much anxiety on my shoulders, you can hardly expect me . . ."

" Take it easy, brother," said Sammy. " I don't want to make things any worse for you, but I do want to contact Miss Deane."

" I've told you already, I haven't got her address," snapped the harrassed man.

" But the young lady was a nurse. You must know where you got her from."

He knew that all right, and that was another telephone call he ought to put through, or the matron would be charging him for more service than he had had.

" You must ask the doctor," he said roughly, pushing past the young man who stood there like a pillar of salt or something equally obtuse and impenetrable.

" Thanks," said the young man, " and who's he ? This really is important to me," he added.

Newstead began to panic again. He didn't want anyone nosing into his affairs ; it was too dangerous.

" As a matter of fact, she's gone on to another case. She happened to mention before she left . . . There's a great shortage of nurses, as you may know. She only got in late last night, unfortunately too late to be of any service . . ."

" Nasty night, wasn't it ? " agreed the young man imperturbably. " She and I . . ."

" Were you with her last night ? "

" Sure. Without me I doubt if she'd ever have got here at all. Broken her neck over a paving-stone or something."

Fervently Mr. Newstead wished that she had.

" And I arranged to pick her up at two o'clock," repeated Sammy.

" As I've told you till I'm tired, she's gone and I don't know where." And in a sense it was true. Most likely she had been posted to another case by now. " I daresay she'll get in touch with you in due course."

" She can't very well do that," objected Sammy. " She doesn't know where I am."

" If she's your young lady or whatever you call it," Mr. Newstead began, and Sammy told him tranquilly, " Well, not exactly. That is, she is, but she doesn't know it yet. I'm giving her a trial run."

He had moved up and was standing quite close to his companion, tall and cool and enquiring, as though there wasn't death and terror on the other side of the door, as though neither death nor terror could touch him.

"Lord Galahad or something," reflected Newstead, whose literary education was not very profound.

"You see, she doesn't seem to have many friends," continued Sammy in the same enraging voice. "And that's bad for a girl."

"After what you've told me, let me assure you that if I knew her address I wouldn't pass it on," said Newstead in savage tones. "Your kind better keep away from young girls." Suddenly he lost his temper. "I don't know who the hell you think you are coming here at a time like this and asking questions I've already told you I can't answer. Haven't you any sense of decency?"

"Parker's the name," said the young man patiently. "Sammy Parker. And you don't understand. I've got to meet that girl again. It's a matter of life and death."

"That's melodrama."

"Well, I suppose life is melodramatic sometimes," the young man conceded. "Still, I don't want to make things worse for you, and since I can see you'd prefer my room to my company, I'll git." He sketched a faint unsmiling salute and went off.

Newstead let himself into the house and stood panting in the cold hall. Had he made a false step, antagonising a young man who looked about as likely to be turned from his course as a young tank? Still, a man in his (Newstead's) position couldn't afford to take risks. He wouldn't really breathe freely till after the funeral when, with everything settled, he could get away and start afresh, unhampered by the past.

As a matter of fact, if it was favourable to his plans that Sammy should not contact Nora Deane, the luck was with him, for Dr. Langton, also anxious that a number of awkward questions should remain unasked, was quite unhelpful and Sammy was left to seek the truth up some other avenue.

CHAPTER SEVEN

Now does my project gather to a head.—THE TEMPEST.

ALFRED NEWSTEAD went into his house feeling very much perturbed. He thought life gave a good many people a pretty cheap deal. He had been up against enough as it was, before

Sammy's arrival, and he had reached the state where he no longer believed that anything that happened to him was fortuitous, it was all part of some diabolical scheme working for his ruin. Feeling slightly intoxicated, thanks to the double whiskies and the fact that he had eaten nothing but a sandwich all day, he went upstairs towards Adela's room. There was probably any amount of papers and letters to be destroyed. Adela was a natural hoarder ; she hoarded letters, she hoarded bits of material and odd sheets of paper, just as she hoarded trifling sums of money. Adela would always stop for the last halfpenny of her change ; you could depend on that just as you could depend on her never cheating the bus company out of even a penny fare. She'd ride on to the next stop and walk back, waiting for the conductor.

Pausing on the stairs to light a cigarette Newstead wondered whether she'd kept any of Herbert Webster's letters. That there had been a considerable correspondence during the past few months he was convinced, though his attempts to wean her from her brother's noxious influence had proved unavailing. All the same, he wanted to be sure that her letters were satisfactorily dealt with in case even at the eleventh hour, awkward questions should be asked.

He hated the idea of going into the room where she lay dead, though common-sense told him that she couldn't do him any harm now, not at all events by her physical presence. It was odd to think that never again would she lift the receiver and have one of those long confidential conversations with Herbert in which he knew she indulged when he was out of the way. Herbert acknowledged it by saying, " Adela has been telling me . . ." this or that. He wondered if they knew about Harriet. Adela had suspected something was wrong, and for Adela to suspect a wrong was to create it, he told himself savagely. There had been trouble enough in the past—Alice Holmes, for instance. Adela had flown to Herbert for counsel then, though her husband had assured her there was nothing in it at all. If women only knew, he reflected, pausing on the half-landing and looking out of the window at the garden, looking grey and autumnal in the afternoon light, they were really responsible for giving body to these affairs. If they had the sense to ignore them, why, they'd just die away like a flower in a button-hole. Naturally it had suited Herbert's book to make the most of these minor matters. He wanted to rouse Adela's suspicions against her husband, gain influence himself and finally establish complete control over Adela's finances. He had been urging her to get a divorce, though Alfred asserted angrily that he had no proof. There had been a stormy scene in the morning-room.

" If my marriage goes to pieces I've you to thank," Alfred had said furiously. " From the outset you were resolved to ruin things."

" I was antagonistic, certainly," agreed Webster, " and with ample justification. I knew, if Adela didn't, why you married her in the first place. You married her for her money, and you've spent all your time since then trying to get it into your hands."

" You can't talk," shouted Alfred, " you've been playing precisely the same game. Adela wasn't a suspicious woman till you made her one. Do you think I don't know you're trying to separate us altogether . . ."

And Webster said suavely, " I'm only thinking of her happiness."

" You mean you're thinking what a lot you could do with her £12,000 if it came into your hands," retorted Newstead bitterly. " You're a bachelor, so perhaps you don't understand about marriage being a partnership."

" In a partnership each side contributes something," Webster assured him. " I'm contemplating a new partnership myself, but naturally I shall be expected to put up my share. Your notion seems to be that one side—Adela—does all the giving, and the other (yourself) does all the taking. I admit that marriage is a partnership, and wives help their husbands over rough places, true, but I repeat I can see absolutely no justification for your spending my sister's money on other women."

He had looked so righteous, so inhuman, so sure of himself, that there had been murder in his brother-in-law's heart. One of these days, he thought, Herbert will go too far, and if anything happens he'll only have himself to thank. He'd let me starve or swing or rot in prison for years without a qualm.

Thinking of Herbert made Newstead remember that he hadn't yet telephoned to his office, and he went quickly down the stairs and into the dining-room.

He rang Herbert's home first, but the housekeeper who answered the telephone said he wasn't there.

" What time do you expect him back ? " Newstead enquired.

" I don't think he'll be back to-night. Who's that speaking ? "

" This is his brother-in-law, Mr. Newstead. There's news about his sister."

" Oh dear," said the woman pleasurably. " I hope she's no worse."

" I'm afraid the news isn't good. Are you quite sure I can't get him at his home to-night ? "

" He's gone on one of his Government trips," explained the woman.

" It's very odd he shouldn't have telephoned me before he went."

" He didn't expect to be going till the morning. That I do know. But he rung up not long ago to say his plans was altered."

" Is that all he said ? " Newstead sounded impatient.

" That's all." In her turn, she sounded offended. He reflected that the servants of bachelors, women servants, that is, were nearly always insolent, like men-servants in women's clubs.

" When's he coming back ? He must have told you."

" He don't generally know himself. He has my home address and he sends me a card when it's time to open up the house. I don't sleep on the premises when he's not here," she added ungraciously.

" Oh, I didn't know that. Very well, I'll try his office. He must have left a note of his whereabouts somewhere."

He got through to the office and on to Herbert's private secretary or some haughty piece who gave herself that title.

" I'm afraid Mr. Webster's not available," she said. " If you will tell me your business, I daresay I can help you."

" That is quite out of the question," he replied in his most cutting voice. " I am Mr. Webster's brother-in-law and I wish to speak to him urgently on a private matter. Will you please tell me where I can get in touch with him ?"

" I really couldn't say," drawled the secretary. " I'm sure we expected him back this afternoon, but we had a telephone call to say he'd had to change his plans and would I cancel his booking at his hotel."

" Where was that ? "

" The Grand, Wolverhampton."

" And you've cancelled it ? "

" Oh yes."

" But," his voice sounded strained beyond endurance. " he can't have left things in the air just like that. Did he say he wasn't coming back to-night ? "

" He sounded in a fearful hurry, and he just told me what I've told you—to cancel his room and he wouldn't be coming back."

" Where the devil can he be ? " muttered Newstead.

" You might try his home address," said the girl.

" They don't know anything. I've tried."

" Well, then, p'raps he had a message from the Ministry."

" Which one's that ? " he barked. " I always forget."

" Goods and Chattels," said the haughty piece in a drawling voice as if she couldn't understand how anybody could not know that.

" I could try them," he agreed, " but—look here. Is there no one in the office who could help me ? He's got partners I suppose ? "

" Not since Mr. Smythe was killed in a robot raid. There's Mr. Anstey, of course, but he wouldn't know anything."

" If he wouldn't know anything there's no sense my wasting time talking to him," snapped Newstead. He hung up the receiver, and stood scowling by the instrument. Hadn't Herbert given anyone a hint of where he was going ? He was what the present generation called " cagey," but all the same it wasn't business-like . . . And then he remembered about the telephone messages saying his plans had been changed. It didn't seem to him there was another thing he could do. Slowly he mounted the stairs, hesitated a moment outside the door behind which his wife lay awaiting the last reverent attentions of Mr. Hunter of Messrs. Jarvis and Jarvis, and at last opened the door and went in.

As he had suspected, there was enough evidence to hang a man, if behaving like a snake in the grass was a hanging matter, as, thought Alfred Newstead savagely, it should be. Herbert stood out from this correspondence as a viper without a single redeeming quality. He opened the drawers methodically one after another. In the bottom one he found a hypodermic syringe and a supply of morphia. That shocked him till he remembered that two years ago he had suspected Adela of using drugs, and had indeed attributed her suicide attempt to this cause. He wondered whether she'd used it at all recently. Langton had never spoken of it, but he began to wonder if he could trust even Langton . He slipped it into his pocket. It might be as well to throw that away. But he didn't make up his mind immediately. It might be that it would come in useful later on.

Presently the front door bell rang and he jumped up, the thought " Herbert ? " leaping into his mind. Then he calmed down. He was letting himself get panic-stricken. If only he kept his head everything would be all right. Again he tapped the pocket where the death certificate lay. The bell rang again. He muttered angrily, " The Englishman's home is his castle—what nonsense ! He has no privacy at all these days."

Standing on the step was Mr. Hunter, looking discreetly sympathetic. He was wearing deep mourning, in spite of years of clothes rationing, but then probably all the clothes he possessed were black. He looked like the bereaved widower, thought Newstead sardonically.

" I hope I have come at a convenient moment," said Mr. Hunter looking modestly at the carpet, as if he expected that to turn black under his gaze. He walked, with downcast eyes, to Adela's room and became gently professional. He produced a form and asked a number of questions.

" Now, about hymns, sir," he said. " What had you thought ? "

" I don't want a choral service," said Newstead bluntly. " My wife wasn't given to a lot of church-going. I want things done very simply—properly, of course, but without a lot of trimmings. A service in the mortuary chapel at the cemetery is my idea and would have been hers."

" Er—cremation, sir ? " insinuated Mr. Hunter. " A lot of gentlemen prefer it these days."

And so would he, he thought, but that meant another medical signature and he couldn't afford the risk.

" My wife had strong feelings about that," he said. " No, an ordinary service is what I want. And I don't want a lot of fal-lals put up over the grave later on, either. A plain stone with her name and the date of her death—that's all that's necessary."

Mr. Hunter thought him a typical husband but more outspoken than most.

" How about the time of the funeral ? " asked Newstead impatiently.

" We suggested Friday morning," began Mr. Hunter.

" Nothing of the kind. I said Thursday afternoon."

" Well really, Mr. Newstead." Mr. Hunter caressed his

moustache, which was as black as everything else about him. "That's hurrying things rather." His voice said it was a pity to hurry anything as important as a funeral.

"Do you mean they can't manage it ? It's plenty of notice surely."

"We—ell, business, as you might say,. is booming, Mr. Newstead. I've been looking up our commitments . . ."

"If you can't do it," said Newstead brutally, " I'll try another firm."

He hoped he didn't look as shaken as he felt. Every hour he spent in this house was a nightmare Thursday was the last day he could stand having Adela here, and on Friday morning he'd get away. Thank Heaven, the time was gone by when the authorities could requisition your house for refugees if you left it empty for more than about a week. He knew a feeling of blind impatience. Time couldn't go fast enough till the hour of the funeral. It had to be on Thursday. Then on Friday, early, he'd be off, begin a new life. He need never come back here again. There were all the hours till the time of the funeral to fill in checking books and papers. Soon he might get a little car. He'd always felt lost without one. The garage had stood empty too long. He drew a deep breath. It was easier to get petrol now. Herbert, he reflected bitterly, had been able to get petrol all through the war, by virtue of his Government connections.

He was suddenly aware that Mr. Hunter was standing patiently beside him.

" I quite see your wishes, sir," said Mr. Hunter soothingly, when he realised that he had regained his companions attention. " I'll see if we can possibly make it Thursday. It'll all very upsetting, I'm sure. And the weather—so cheerless."

Newstead muttered something about shock and Mr. Hunter said in the same voice something about a pick-me-up.. Newstead wondered if that were a hint, but he felt there was something incongruous in drinking whisky and soda with a man in black gloves with a black handlebar moustache that surely owed more to foresight than to nature in a man of Mr. Hunter's age, so he offered no invitation, and seeing that nothing was likely to eventuate the undertaker's representative left, practically walking backwards, as though in the presence of Royalty. He always did that as a mark of respect for the bereaved. He thought they liked it. Newstead reflected savagely, " What's the matter with the fellow? Does he think I'm going to put a knife in his back if he turns round ? "

After the man had gone he went into his own room and began to look through his clothes. He wanted to fill in all the hours, make sure everything was left in order. But he soon tired. He wanted to say good-bye to all his past. The clothes could be given away to one of these organisations that looked after the down-and-out, if there were any down-and-outs left. But if there were none now they'd come along all right after the war. They always did. He didn't approve of indiscriminate charity, but this was different. He'd have to take something, of course. Clothes were still in very short supply. He found himself remembering how he and Adela had sat over the fire one night examining patterns for a summer suit that had moths in it now. It had been one of the happy interludes. It was a good thing when you were young you couldn't look forward and see what lay ahead. The disillusion would be too cruel. He'd never dreamed that one day he'd find himself in an empty house—a house empty of life, that is—remembering an isolated evening and facing—what ? He didn't know. For a moment he could almost envy Adela lying in bed across the corridor, cold and never to be hurt again, in her last senseless sleep.

He glanced at his wrist-watch, held it to his ear, because time seemed to be crawling so. The watch had memories, too. Adela had given it to him to mark the first anniversary of their marriage. He wished he needn't spend the night in the house with the body, but it hadn't been possible to suggest her being taken to the mortuary, and he couldn't face the thought of spending the night in anyone else's house. It wouldn't be for much longer. He had finished in Adela's room at last, and he went back to his study sorting papers of his own. He found a box of old envelopes, carefully re-conditioned, to save paper, that had proved an extravagance in the end, since they were destined never to be used. He had a sudden fear that Hattie would ring up again, or even come round. At nine o'clock he unshipped the telephone and put the bolt on the front door.

He put on a small table-lamp and sat there, ears astrain for something—he couldn't say what. But more than once he got up and opened the door and looked up the staircase, though he knew, of course, that the dead can't move, can't speak. Commonsense told him he was terrifying himself unnecessarily and for once commonsense was right.

The days went by slowly enough and Thursday came. Hardly anyone attended the funeral, the afternoon was cheerless, the clergyman, as usual at funerals, had a cold. On Thursday evening he went round leaving things clear, and on Friday morning, as soon as the bank opened, he went out and drew a hundred pounds. He drew it in single notes. Now he had plenty of cash to carry on for the time being. On the way back he saw Hattie crossing the street to speak to him and stood his ground, warning himself that he'd attract attention by trying to avoid her.

" I didn't write," she said, " I knew you'd understand."

He nodded. " There have been enough letters anyway."

" Going to have a bit of a holiday ? " she enquired.

" Just a spell."

" Don't forget to come back," she said warningly.

He achieved a ghastly sort of grin. " Not likely. Back in about a month, I expect." He wouldn't be, though. He'd never come back. The whole place was tainted for him.

" Bit done up, aren't you, Alfie ? " said Mrs. Forbes in a kind tone.

He confided suddenly, " Had a letter out of the blue from my brother-in-law. He's coming down here at ten o'clock."

" Left it a bit late, hasn't he ? " Mrs. Forbes suggested. " Mean to say, the funeral was yesterday. You'd have thought an affectionate brother . . ."

" Oh, he's been away, I think," said Newstead vaguely.

" But why's he coming back now ? " she insisted.

Newstead had to say he didn't know.

" Unless it's to ask me how I dared to let Adela die of a weak heart."

" I know that kind," said Mrs. Forbes. " Every time John had a stomach-ache his sister 'ud say to me, I daresay you'd poison him, if you could. Not that I ever took any notice, of course. Poor thing, she was a spinster and they're not really responsible."

CHAPTER EIGHT

Plain truth will influence half a score of men at most in a nation,
while mystery will lead millions by the nose.
—LORD BOLINGBROKE.

NORA DEANE'S new patient was an elderly woman, as viva-
cious as a cockatoo, and with a voice almost as shrill. The nurse
already installed came to greet her, saying, " Well, thank
goodness for two of us. Though that one could wear out a
Zoo."

Nurse Turner was a bouncing woman in the late thirties,
with red cheeks and a lot of black hair ; you'd have said nothing could wear her down, but Mrs. Trentham could have worn
down an entire S.S. battalion. She was a skinny little creature,
about 70, with scant grey hair knotted back severely, a big
dominant nose, a parchment skin and the chin of a witch.
" Thank Heaven you're not another of these Amazons," she
said when she found herself alone with Nora. " That woman's
appetite—and if I say anything she tells me it's glands."

Nora knew Mrs. Trentham had been desperately ill, but
nothing quenched her spirits. Rather surprisingly she had
been a welfare worker at one time, labouring in the East End
of London, and her persistent plaint was that life had lost its
sparkle when it became secure.

" Because it is more secure in spite of wars and air raids,"
she assured the astonished girl. " They're only passing events
and when they're gone life settles down to its pre-war drab-
ness. But in those days every morning you woke not knowing
if you'd be dead by night."

She was full of horrific stories about alleys where the policemen had to patrol in pairs and even that didn't always save
them, and fights with knives between women in Ratcliffe
Highway. Life, according to Mrs. Trentham, was one long
thrill when you got as far as East India Dock Road.

" Chinatown really existed then," she said disdainfully.
" Nowadays the coloured men all wear European clothes and
even if their shops have got Chinese names over them, all the
notices in the window are in English. Cup of tea tuppence.
Pineapple chunks—a bargain line. As for the newspapers—

all uplift and the new economic order." She dismissed these as unworthy of consideration.

"It's better than all war news," suggested Nora.

"When I was a gel," retorted Mrs. Trentham, "we had real news in the papers. Jack the Ripper—Charlie Peace—that man in the last war who went one better than Henry VIII. Had six wives and drowned most of them by hand. That was a case." A smile crept over her little withered countenance. "Bang in the middle of the war," she said, "I don't think there ever was a more popular case. Took people's minds off horrors, see—and there were plenty of horrors in 1915. Oh yes. I've always remembered *noblesse oblige.* Mr. Smith may have been a murderer several times over, but he was unquestionably a benefactor to thousands of people feeling choked and disheartened by the news of the war. We had some bad setbacks in 1915." Her mouth tightened at the recollection. Then she cheered up. "It was one of Marshall Hall's most striking cases. He didn't get his man off, but that wasn't his fault. I remember him conducting the defence. Really a terrible man." It was obvious that by this she meant Smith, not his defending counsel. "But so enterprising. And one can't help feeling that a man who can attract so many women must have something good about him. Nowadays we never get a story like that, and if there is a murder one of those ridiculous Government Departments hushes it up, as if we were a lot of children who didn't know anything about life. I call it wrong. Taking away what little entertainment old people like myself can look for . . ."

Mrs. Trentham was a lively old lady who slept far less than any nurse could appreciate, and when she wasn't talking she liked to be read to. Nora would go through all the newspapers looking for something sensational. Mrs. Trentham's nephew, Roger, was a crime reporter on the *Daily Post*, and she used to say though she knew he was fond of his Auntie May he'd be fondest of all of her when she was found with her throat cut.

"That's why I admire my nephew so much," she told Nora robustly. "He wouldn't let any sentiment stand in the way of his ambition. Of course, I'd like to help him all I can—but not to the extent of having my throat cut. Though he's always told me he'd be sure to run the criminals to earth. He says," added Mrs. Trentham impressively, "I'd be worth at least two columns a day to him while the case lasted."

" He must be lovely company for you," suggested Nora politely.

" He's best of all when he's on a case. The trouble is we don't get these good cases any more. Nowadays, of course, people get divorced so easily there's no need to resort to murder. It's what I've always said. Take religion out of daily life and what's left ? I'll tell you. The sort of the news we get in the papers nowadays."

Each morning, therefore, Nora combed the press for anything that held out prospects of developing into something sordid and violent. Presumably butchers were still murdering their wives and unhappy spouses putting arsenic in their husbands' tea, but in the general rush of daily life such people were overlooked.

" Or else people have had their fill of killing since September, 1939," said Mrs. Trentham in disappointed tones. " I can understand the soldiers, of course. But what about the civilians ? Haven't they any spirit left ? "

One morning, when she had been about a fortnight in her new employment, Nora spied a paragraph at the foot of a column in the *Daily Post* which looked rather promising. " BODY FOUND IN PIT " it read. She looked up.

" This sounds hopeful," she suggested.

" I daresay it's only a legpull. You'll find it was a rabbit or a prehistoric man or something," returned Mrs. Trentham resignedly. " Never mind. Read it out, dear. It might lead to a murder. We mustn't look on the black side."

Nora began to read : " The body of a man named Alfred Newstead—Alfred Newstead . . ." She paused.

" What's the matter ? " demanded Mrs. Trentham. " Go on."

Nora pulled herself together. " I'm so sorry, Mrs. Trentham.

" The body of a man named Alfred Newstead was found by some boys in a quarry known as Lone Pit, at King's Wyvern, near Charlbury, yesterday afternoon. It had apparently been lying there, under a quantity of gravel and some large rocks or boulders, for some two or three weeks. Owing to the dampness of the situation a large degree of decomposition had set in. Facial and other injuries had been inflicted by the rocks, and efforts to conceal the dead man's identity had been made by the removal of tailor's labels from the suit. The deceased, however, was wearing a handsome gold wrist-watch inscribed inside the case : Alfred with Adela's love.

" Lone Pit, as the name suggests, is in a solitary part of the country on a site originally selected by the Ministry of Aircraft Production for a factory. After a year's work had been done, however, it was found that the soil was too damp for the purpose, and the site was abandoned at a total loss of six figures, according to reports from authoritative quarters. The buildings themselves, however, were later removed and set up elsewhere for the benefit of the Women's Land Army.

" The discovery was made by one of the boys noticing what appeared to be a human foot lying at the bottom of the quarry and subsequent examination revealed the body. But for the accident of the boys playing on what is known to be a dangerous site the body might have gone undiscovered for months.

" Police authorities are considering the possibility of foul play."

" Our wonderful police ! " sighed Mrs. Trentham ecstatically. " No one else would even consider any other possibility. Do they really think a man puts himself at the bottom of a quarry then rolls boulders down on himself to make sure he can't get out ? My dear, I wouldn't be surprised if Roger wrote that piece himself. I think I must ring him up. Isn't it exciting ? " And she clapped her little hands with delight.

Nora was looking so pale that her employer noticed it. " My dear, what is it ? Surely you're not going to be squeamish ? Here have we been longing for a good murder and now we've got one you look as washed-out as though you've come out of your coffin just for a visit and intend to go back as soon as the clock strikes."

" It's rather horrible," suggested Nora, speaking with some difficulty.

" Nothing of the sort. Everybody has to die, and I daresay he wasn't a very pleasant person. Have you noticed that murdered people are hardly ever nice, unless they're political and then one can't help feeling there's probably something to be said for the other side. But you may just as well provide some interest for your neighbours by the way you die as go off with all your relations singing hymns at the bedside, the way my grandmother did. Is that all it says ? "

" That's all."

" It's either money or a woman," said Mrs. Trentham. " A man from Scotland Yard told me it's always one of those two reasons. I hope it's a woman. It's always more interesting when it's a woman. I wonder if Roger would be in if I rang him up now. He probably knows the very latest developments."

Nora sat with her hands clasped over the paper and wondered what she did next. She found herself trembling at the thought of being involved. She couldn't, she argued, help the police. They knew who the man was, and doubtless they would eventually trace the criminal. All she could do, if she came forward, was inform them of her visit to Herbert Webster, and allow them to draw their own conclusions.

Mrs. Trentham, who was an autocrat to the tips of her old-fashioned bead-embroidered slippers, made no bones about telephoning her nephew, but she got no satisfaction.

" I daresay he's down at the scene of the crime," she gloated. " Perhaps he'll discover a bloodstain or something. They say, you know," she prattled happily, " even an experienced murderer leaves some clue. Well, of course, he must or how would the police ever solve crimes at all ? Oh dear, it's all very exciting. I can hardly wait till to-morrow."

Nora could hardly wait either, but in her case it was not excitement but apprehension that moved her. Up in her room that night, after one of those endless days that never seem to move from one hour to the next, she reviewed the position. It all fitted together too dangerously well. Webster's declaration that he would see his brother-in-law and take action ; his message, sounding urgent in its insistence on her silence, to say that after all he would do nothing, that there was indeed nothing he could usefully do ; his demand for her silence, twice repeated.

" I don't like it," she whispered to her reflection in the mirror. She didn't much like what she saw in the mirror either, a pale small heart-shaped face, big troubled eyes, too little colour, a general air of strain. Mrs. Trentham was nobody's fool ; she'd notice any change of bearing and leap, with diabolical swiftness, to the true reason.

" Once she knew that I'd been in Mr. Newstead's house she'd broadcast it to the world," Nora told herself. " But I daresay I'm making mountains out of molehills. In to-morrow's paper we shall hear that he's come forward—Mr.

Webster, I mean—and can prove he had nothing to do with the crime. He's a lawyer, he'd know you can't commit crime and hope not to be found out."

She powdered her face and took an aspirin. Anxiety wasn't becoming, she decided.

The next morning Mrs. Trentham ramped like a too-fresh mare until the paper arrived.

" Quick, quick ! " she told Nora. " Never mind about measuring out my medicine so carefully. The doctor puts on a long face and pretends its tincture of gold, and so it ought to be considering what he charges me for it, but I know it's just bicarbonate of soda coloured to look like something else. What doctors would do without bicarbonate of soda I can't imagine. Well, is there anything else in the paper ? "

Nora looked. The Lone Pit Mystery had a column to itself on the front page. There was nothing very startling, though the enterprising Roger had made as much as he could out of an interview with Mrs. Harriet Forbes, the last person but one to come forward and admit that she had seen Newstead alive.

I saw Mr. Newstead when I was on my way to the shops on Friday morning, she had told the reporter. Yes, I remember the day particularly because it was the day after Mrs. Newstead's funeral. I thought he was looking a bit washed-out, but that's only to be expected. She led him a rare dance and everyone knows it. He told me he was going away for a holiday, about a month, he thought. No, I'm sure he had no idea in his mind of leaving Charlbury for good. He had told her he was going to the bank and that his brother-in-law, Herbert Webster, was coming down to see him at ten o'clock.

It is anticipated, wrote Mr. Trentham cheerfully, that Mrs. Forbes' evidence will be very valuable. So far the police have not been able to contact Mr. Webster, who is a well-known lawyer connected with the Ministry of Goods and Chattels.

Another theory, he continued, is that Mr. Newstead was a victim of foul play on account of a sum of money that he is known to have drawn from the bank on the morning after his wife's funeral. The amount was one hundred pounds, and he explained to Mr. Davies, the cashier, that he would be going away for at least a month. The police are following up a report that a shabbily-dressed man was seen to emerge from the bank just behind Mr. Newstead and to turn in the same direction.

65

" That, my dear," announced the delighted Mrs. Trentham, " is what Roger would call a snip. Of course, it's perfectly obvious that the shabbily-dressed man hasn't anything to do with it. Unless he was hand in glove with the widow."

" I don't see that his being murdered would help her," protested Nora. " I mean, she doesn't come into any money or anything and if you mean, as I think you do, that she was— she was in love with him, then he must have been much more use to her living than dead."

" My dear," Mrs. Trentham leaned over and rapped her sharply with a blue knitting-needle, " you're so young. But even you can't be so innocent as you pretend. They say nurses see all the sordid side of life. Suppose he'd been—well —philandering with her and she'd hoped to marry him, and now he tells her there's nothing doing ? He said he was only going away for a month, but a hundred pounds is a lot of money."

" And you think this Mrs. Forbes may have murdered him ? But how did she get him up to the Lone Pit ? "

" I never knew a site the Government had rejected that someone else didn't find convenient for his own purposes. I daresay that place was quite a well-known rendezvous. Well, there aren't so many spots where you're safe from Government interference these days."

Nora considered. It was a new idea and she wished she could believe it was true. If only Herbert Webster would come forward !

Other people were saying the same thing. Her fellow-nurse said it.

" He's a fool to lie low now," she announced. " Mrs. Forbes has given him away completely. We know he was coming to Charlbury and his brother-in-law was expecting him."

" He may not have heard the news," murmured Nora weakly, but she knew that wasn't so. If the police want to contact a man they use every channel at their disposal, and even if Webster hadn't heard their message over the radio someone else would and tell him. No, it was difficult to combat the suggestion that he had his own reasons for lying low.

The press certainly thought so. The *Daily Post* came out with a great headline :

66

WHERE IS HERBERT WEBSTER?

MYSTERY OF MISSING
BROTHER-IN-LAW IN LONE PIT MURDER

And there were pictures of the two men on the front page. Oh, it was jam for Roger Trentham, who was a newspaper man to his fingertips, and knew that what interests THEM isn't political reaction to the Government's White Paper but the true story behind the discovery of the headless bathing belle of Margate. It specialised in headlines, too.

IT MIGHT HAVE BEEN YOU

it said of the bathing belle and showed a row of pictures of nondescript young women to whom nothing so interesting as murder was ever likely to happen.

" I believe you're right," said Mrs. Trentham, who was loving her blood bath, as Nurse Turner put it. " It is the brother-in-law. Of course they might both be murdered and then you couldn't blame him for not coming forward, but that seems to me too good to be true. No, I believe he did it, and he's hiding somewhere. Think of it, nurse. You might be coming back from the post one of these dusky evenings and someone spring out of a bush, a little figure like a monkey, with hands like steel. I really don't think it's safe for you to be out after dark till this man's found. Nurse Turner's different. She wouldn't let herself be murdered."

" But why on earth should he jump out at anyone ? " demanded Nora.

" He's probably a homicidal maniac. If you could see him you'd probably find he had a film over one eye, that's always a sign of insanity . . ."

" But he hasn't," exclaimed Nora desperately. " He's perfectly ordinary."

She stopped and half-rose from her chair. Mrs. Trentham was eyeing her with a determination as pitiless as the glance of the Gorgon.

" What did you say ? Do you mean to tell me you've met this man and you've never said a word about it ? You deceitful creature ! Have you been to the police behind my back ? "

" No," exclaimed the girl. " It wouldn't be any good. I couldn't tell them anything."

" When did you see him ? "

" The—the morning after Mrs. Newstead died."

" Did you *know* Mrs. Newstead ? "

" I was sent there as a nurse. It was that very foggy night before I came here. I arrived very late and she was half-asleep. She just said she wanted to get in touch with her brother and I said I'd get him, meaning to get him in the morning. But in the morning she was dead."

If Nora had been Mrs. Trentham's private employee she would unquestionably have got a rise in wages on the spot. To say that the old lady was pleased would be absurd. She was delighted, she was enchanted, she was enthralled.

" And you've kept this up your sleeve all this time ? " she exclaimed incredulously. " I don't know how you could. If it had been me, I'd have wanted to proclaim the story from the housetops."

" I haven't anything to say," Nora protested. " I mean, I don't know anything."

" Know anything ? You may be the last person to have seen this mysterious Mr. Webster."

" How can I be ? I saw him on Tuesday morning and Mr. Newstead wasn't murdered till Friday at the earliest."

" That's true. Now tell me some more about this woman who died, Mrs. Newstead. What were they like ? A loving couple ? " Mrs. Trentham drew down the corners of her malicious old mouth.

" I've told you I was only there a few hours. Mrs. Newstead died before dawn next day."

The old lady looked dizzy with delight. " Foul play ? " she hissed.

" The doctor said it was heart failure."

" If you were to put strychnine in my broth to-night it would be heart failure. Don't try and gammon me. What did she really die of ? "

" I've told you. The doctor said . . ."

" I'm not asking what the doctor said. I'm asking what you think."

" How can I have any opinion when I only saw her about two minutes ? All I did for her was give her a glass of water."

" Plain water ? " Mrs. Trentham reminded the girl of the dog in the fairy tale whose eyes were like mill-wheels.

" Yes, of course."

" Did you pour it out yourself ? "

" Certainly."

" Ah, but where did you get it from ? Out of the tap ? Or a bottle by the bed ? And who filled that bottle ? My dear, I've often thought that the opportunities offered a man with a sick wife are legion. I never meant to give my husband the chance. I took care to keep in good health until he died. Why, he doesn't even have to give her the stuff himself."

" That's slander ! " protested Nora weakly.

" Fiddle ! " scoffed the old beldame. " It's the most interesting conversation I've had with you since you arrived. Tell me—did you know this husband before you went on the case ? "

" Of course not."

" What did you hear about him afterwards ? "

" Nothing. That is . . ."

" Well ? "

" Well, it was obvious there wasn't any love lost between him and his brother-in-law, but . . ."

" Just what I suspected."

" But if we all went round murdering people we didn't like —I mean, it just doesn't happen."

" How do you know ? I daresay it's happening all the time. I had a parlourmaid some years ago who died very mysteriously. She and the cook had been at daggers drawn about a widower who made up to both of them, and I always suspected the cook of putting her rival out of the way."

" But you didn't say anything to the authorities ? "

" Of course not. You don't take that sort of risk when you've got a cook as good as that one was. Was there an inquest ? "

" No."

" Didn't the doctor suggest one ? "

" I—I——"

" He did ? "

" He said there was no proof . . ."

" That means he thought there was some hanky-panky. And I daresay Herbert Webster thought the same. Did she have any money ? "

" I really couldn't say."

" It was either the widow or money—it's always one of the two. And it's more likely to be money. Widows are three-a-penny to any personable man, but money doesn't grow on bushes. No, you wait till my nephew hears this story."

" But—you can't tell him ? " Nora was appalled. " I mean . . ."

" Not tell him ? I never heard anything so selfish. Here's a wonderful chance for him to get in on the ground floor as they say, and just because it might be a little inconvenient for you you don't want him to have that chance. Roger's a young man with his way to make. A thing like this will be very helpful to him. I'm going to ring him up to-night, and I'm going on ringing up till I find him."

CHAPTER NINE

Joy rises in me like a summer's morn.—COLERIDGE.

IN THE MEANTIME the police were following up such clues as they could procure. They, like Roger Trentham, had interviewed Mrs. Forbes and had come to the conclusion that she could tell them very little that was helpful. They had called at Webster's office and seen his secretary, and learned from her of Mr. Webster's intention to link up the fortunes of his firm with that of Mr. William Cradock of Austin Friars. She told them she understood that no definite agreement had yet been signed. Mr. Webster had said that he would be fixing things up within a few days. He had not been seen in the office since the date of his sister's death. He had not spoken of this event, but had gone out soon after 11 and had intended to return that afternoon. Something had caused him to change his mind, however, and he had telephoned to have his room at Wolverhampton cancelled. There had been no opportunity to ask him further questions, as he had been very abrupt and had rung off at once.

" Should you say he sounded different from usual ? " asked the police official, and the girl said, " He sounded as if he was speaking under some terrific strain."

The police also went to see his housekeeper but she again was unable to throw any light on his disappearance. They went over Alfred Newstead's house with a tooth-comb, and it seemed obvious that he had left it at very short notice and without an opportunity of leaving things in order. Except in Adela's room everything was in a chaotic state, china left on the table, food in the larder, furniture scattered about, table-drawers open, as though someone had ransacked the place. A number of unopened letters lay on the mat. Only in Adela Newstead's room was everything quiet, finished. Officials examined Newstead's wardrobe, but they were hampered in their inquiries here since no one could be certain what clothes he had possessed or how much luggage. It was shown, however, that his sponge and tooth-brush were in the bathroom and his hairbrushes on the dressing-table. There was a long black overcoat hanging in the hall, but that wasn't absolutely conclusive, since no one knew how many coats Newstead had possessed.

The Post Office clerk, who was later interrogated, said that the dead man had given no instructions about re-forwarding his letters which were still being delivered to Askew Avenue. The milkman said that he had been told not to deliver milk after the Friday, and so there had been no reason to suspect anything wrong because, as so often happens in the storybooks, a long trail of milk-bottles stood on the step. The curtains in the front living-room were drawn over the windows, but they were drawn back in the dining-room. If Newstead had intended to leave the house on the Friday morning he probably would not have troubled to draw the curtains in a room he did not mean to use.

Various neighbours were seen by the police, but none of them could help. Charlbury was a busy suburb on the outer fringes of London, and most of the residents went out to some form of work. They hadn't time to linger at street corners watching the movements of their neighbours.

Mr. William Cradock also received an official visit, and agreed that the last word he had had with Mr. Webster was on the telephone on the Tuesday that Adela Newstead died. Mr. Webster had rung up to cancel an appointment for lunch for that day and had said that all would be well and he would be ratifying the agreement in the course of a day or two.

" He seemed to me to be a little anxious in case I should change my mind," said Cradock drily. " And indeed he had cause. I cannot abide shilly-shallying and for some time it seemed that Mr. Webster could not make up his mind. He was havering about this and that, and I had told him I could find other partners if he couldn't come to a decision."

" And he was afraid that you would be annoyed at his cancelling an appointment at such notice ? "

" He was most apologetic," acknowledged Mr. Cradock

grimly. "And he was what I'd call an autocrat as a rule. I told him I would wait till the week-end."

"And of course you expected to hear from him ? "

" I'm still waiting," said Mr. Cradock ironically.

" No doubt he will attempt to get in touch with you," urged authority. " This partnership means a good deal to him, and if he wishes to carry it through . . ."

Cradock looked shocked. " There could be no question of such a thing," he announced in severe tones. " For one thing, I am not accustomed to being kept dangling for weeks and for another—you must excuse me speaking bluntly—there has been too much talk about Mr. Webster in connection with his brother-in-law's death for me to welcome any further association."

" You haven't told him that ? " intimated the police.

" I have had no opportunity. For myself, I can think of only two reasons why he should not have come forward when requested to do so. He may have become involved in an accident and be lying stupefied in some hospital or he may know more of the matter—I only say may, it is a possible supposition offered without prejudice—than he cares to reveal. In either case, he would be valueless as a partner to me."

The police, who privately agreed with Cradock, did not press the point any further. They had received information that the missing man's car had been traced to a garage at Weyland, in the Midlands, where it had been left on the day of Adela's funeral. The garage proprietor, a stolid man with hair combed in bars across a bald scalp, said huskily that he'd only just got to know that the police were looking for it, gentlemen, and that was the truth so help him God. A gentleman had left it, but he personally hadn't seen him. One of his sons, enlisted for the duration, had been on leave and had taken in the car. There hadn't been any reason to suppose there was anything fishy about it. He'd said he was staying at one of the local cottages for a week or so and would come back for the car later. But he never had. The police tried to get a description of the man, but one middle-aged male looks much the same as a thousand others and that enquiry got them no further. An examination of the car revealed no dropped buttons, torn bits of paper or bloodstains, nothing to indicate that it had played any part in a crime. " And yet," said Vereker grimly, he being in charge of the case, " it was used to take Newstead to Lone Pit or I'm a Dutchman. Then it was brought up here . . . Wonder if this chap really was staying at one of the cottages."

" They'll remember him if he was," said his colleague, Dobbie. " They've got civil service evacuees plastered on 'em here like flies on a fly-paper. A holiday-maker would make a nice change."

But, as Vereker had anticipated, no amount of enquiry got them anywhere. The mysterious car-owner had apparently vanished into space.

" More likely to have hooked it to Manchester," said Dobbie. " There's a good train service, and you could look for a month in Manchester without finding your man."

" Or he might have come back to London, though I suppose as he's better known there he might have qualms. Still, you know as well as I do, men generally hide in familiar surroundings. Less likely to give themselves away—or so they think. And as for being recognised there's such a thing as make-up, and if this chap's a lawyer he ought to know all the ropes."

The police were gradually working backwards in their conduct of the case. They had one certain fact—the murder ; they had reason to believe that the dead man and his brother-in-law had met on the day of the former's disappearance, and now they began to search for a motive. Why, they asked, should Herbert Webster cherish hard feelings against his brother-in-law. ?

Mr. Webster's housekeeper gave them the answer to that. She said they were about as friendly as a couple of bucks. The reason was Mrs. Newstead. She went into a long rigmarole about Adela coming to see her brother and telling him she couldn't bear it any longer, and Herbert had said, " It's infamous that you should. Why should our father's money be squandered on your husband's light-o'-loves ? "

" Did he really say light-o'-loves ? " asked Vereker respectfully.

" His very words, sir. I couldn't help hearing because I had to bring them in some tea for which he'd rung. And she had been crying in a ladylike sort of way. That was her trouble, I always thought."

" Crying ? "

" Being so ladylike. You need a bit of go to keep a marriage exciting enough to hold a man's interest, and Mrs. Newstead never knew that. Being a lady isn't enough and so I could have told her."

She went on with her story. Apparently divorce had been
mentioned and Adela had said that she didn't believe in
divorce on religious grounds and how about a separation ?
Herbert had said that a separation was never satisfactory,
you were married and yet not married. A clean break was
better.

" I knew what he meant," said the housekeeper. " There
was something a bit soft in a way about Mrs. Newstead, and
Mr. Webster was afraid that sooner or later her husband
would get round her again."

" So he thought in Mrs. Newstead's interest that the
marriage should be dissolved ? "

" Well, partly that, I daresay, but—you know it was all
her money, and Mr. Webster was careful about money, as a
rule, that is."

" What does that mean ? "

" He always took plenty of money with him when he went
on these Government investigations. Of course, it didn't
come out of his own pocket, not his expenses, I mean, and as
for the rest—well, he was a bachelor and entitled to his bit of
fun like the rest of us. I'm sure he never let himself go when
he was in London."

" Dear me, what a vivid imagination you have," said
Vereker smoothly, and to Dobbie he said, " If all her sup-
positions are true Webster may have been knifed by some
irate female who disliked his stinginess. You know, I don't
like this at all. The only reasonable explanation for Webster
holding back would be if there was a third party involved
who was deliberately restraining him, and there's no third
party that I can see, and he doesn't sound to me the sort of
fellow it would be easy to restrain."

He and Dobbie entered Webster's house with a search-
warrant and examined his papers. They found two letters
from Adela Newstead bearing on the problem of her future.
Both were short, both were painful. The first read :

MY DEAR HERBERT,

I agree that if I find further evidence that Alfred is
untrue to me I will institute proceedings at once. Anything
would be preferable to the humiliations I have to endure at
present. Unfortunately I am not well and so cannot be a
cheerful companion for my husband. This helps to drive
him out in the evening. However, I am a little better

to-day, and shall make one more effort to keep my marriage afloat."

ADELA.

That was dated July of the current year. The second letter was almost three months later and had, in fact, only been written a short time before her unexpected death.

MY DEAR HERBERT,

I broached the subject of a divorce to Alfred to-day and I found him most distressed at the notion. I know that I agreed to take this step if I had further evidence that he was unfaithful to me, and I agree that I do now possess such evidence. I know, too, that you will say my money is the main consideration in his mind, but I am not prepared to accept this. I cannot forget that he is my husband whom I took " in the sight of God and of this congregation for better, for worse," and so long as he is ready to try to make amends I feel I have no right to cast him off. He tells me that it would spell ruin for him in every sense if I did so. So I shall give him one more chance.

Your affectionate sister,

ADELA NEWSTEAD.

On the bottom of this sheet was pencilled a note in what was shown to be Webster's handwriting, reading, " Telephone call from A. Alfred has actually had this woman to the house. Petition to be filed without delay. Evidence ? "

" It's an odd thought that if Mrs. Newstead had taken her precious brother's advice the three of them might still be alive," commented Vereker with a twisted grin. " I like the look of this less and less. It seems to me there was plenty of ground for a quarrel that might easily have had fatal results. Who gets Mrs. N's money now Newstead's out of the way ? "

" Herbert Webster," said Vereker, " and it doesn't look as though it's going to be much good to him either."

It was at this juncture that Mrs. Trentham took a hand in the affair and did her best to precipitate yet another murder.

She was one of those people who assert sweepingly that Government Departments are inefficient, police are corruptible and doctors are an ignorant lot who care only for their fees, so it was natural that she should go to work through her nephew on the *Daily Post*. Roger Trentham had not, to date, been particularly impressed by the murder. It had none of those features that make a crime fascinating to the general public. There was no boy-meets-girl element, no passionate drama—because even if he could work up the theme that Alfred Newstead was in some way responsible for the death of his wife, and this sort of thing had to be carefully done, since even newspapers are liable to the law of libel, you couldn't ask the country as a whole to mind much because an obscure middle-aged wife had been put to sleep by her equally obscure middle-aged husband—no titles were involved, there was no hope of society, such as it was, being shaken from top to bottom by the personalities concerned, in short, as a crime it was as near a flop as any crime can be. There wasn't even much mystery about it.

" The Lone Pit affair " ? he said to his aunt on the telephone. " Well, that's nothing to shout about. What I want is a beautiful girl, abducted if possible, and a young Apollo Belvedere—or possibly an elderly but charming seducer. . . ."

" What a horrid mind you have, Roger," said his aunt. " And how you do talk ! I wonder you ever find time to do any work. I've got your beautiful girl, and for all you know she may be abducted before the affair's over. In fact, I shouldn't be a bit surprised. As for the young man—well ! " she cackled.

" This is business, not a parlour game," said Roger severely.

" Marriage isn't a parlour game either, as you'd know if you'd tried. Anyway, she's just what you want—petite, feminine, ravishing violet eyes. . . ."

" Where does she come in ? "

Mrs. Trentham told him. She was rewarded by a long whistle over the line.

" He put in his thumb and pulled out a plum," he said. " Auntie May, you're a wizard. I might have known that if there was a secret element in the case you'd have it up your sleeve. You know, you missed your vocation. You should have been a conjurer."

" And you've missed yours. You should have been that man on the halls who talks three hundred words to the minute."

" Has she been to the police ? "

" No. I told her she ought to, but she says she doesn't know anything that they don't."

" She will by the time I've finished talking to her," said

Roger in a prophetic voice. " Can I get down to-night ? No, I've got a job on hand. Besides, I don't suppose there's a train. I'll be along in the morning, though."

" She says she remembers the watch," went on Mrs. Trentham, who was prepared to talk all night. " If ever I commit a murder I shall take your advice first. It must be very difficult to think of everything."

" Any sporting criminal has to give the poor bloody police a hand," said Roger. " Besides, it's damned difficult not to make a slip. And he didn't expect the body to be found for months and he had to be sure it would be recognised when it was—found, I mean."

" Was that so important ? "

" Well, of course. He comes into the dead woman's money, if the husband's out of the way."

" They might still suspect him."

" They might, but it's going to be a hell of a job pinning a man down to something that happened months back. Clues grows old like coffee if you leave 'em standing too long. There's something to be said for the Malthusian theory from a criminal's point of view. If those boys' parents had been Malthusians they couldn't have found the body."

" The worst of being a journalist is you can never talk King's English," complained Mrs. Trentham. " I shall be having a fowl for lunch to-morrow, Roger."

" I shall be there," her nephew promised her and rang off.

" Now Roger's on the track things will begin to hum," smiled Mrs. Trentham as she came away. " In fact, I wouldn't be surprised if Herbert Webster ended his days in some quarry or other, too."

Thus is many a true word spoken in jest.

CHAPTER TEN

The devil hath the power to assume a pleasing shape.
—HAMLET.

WHEN the doctor came next morning he told Mrs. Trentham
her health showed such an improvement that he thought she
could now dispense with the services of one of her nurses.
Nurse Deane, for instance. . . . Mrs. Trentham instantly
threatened a relapse.

" It's entirely due to Nurse Deane's cheerful influence that
I am not now being measured for my shroud," she announced
firmly. " If you must take one of them, you're welcome to
Nurse Turner. But Nurse Deane is my mainstay and I will
not have her removed."

" You play your cards well and you can retire at the end
of this case," said Nurse Turner jovially to Nora about an
hour later. " Yes, I've got my orders to quit. Well, I can't
say I'm sorry. Old ladies never were my cup of tea and you
can't call this a very lively case. No fun and no prospects.
And the doctor's nothing but a stick. I believe they wind
him up every morning to keep him going during the day."

" I shan't be here much longer either," returned Nora, with
more truth than she knew.

" That's what I'm pointing out. Even old battle-axes like
this one can't last for ever, and she's taken a fancy to you."

" Only because I've met this man who's been murdered,
and that can't go on for ever."

" Nor can she. Or perhaps you'll manage to get involved
in another murder."

Nora shivered. " I hope not."

" I've often thought of committing a murder," reflected
Miss Turner, " but I realise it's not so easy as it sounds. One
thing about nursing, you do see things from the inside. And
doctors are such nosey people. Of course, that's as it should
be. If it was easy far more people would be doing it, and
nobody I know has ever committed a murder, though goodness knows most of 'em have had provocation enough." She
went off with a toss of her fine head to pack her things, with
no regrets at leaving her colleague to the pickling of the
ruthless old lady.

78

Nora went into the hall to collect the *Daily Post*, which arrived late in the country and carried it into Mrs. Trentham's room.

" I heard you gossiping," said Mrs. Trentham instantly. " What was it ? "

" Nurse Turner was telling me she was going. That's all."

" H'm. What about the paper ? Anything new ? "

She didn't mean anything new on the Far Eastern front or in the world of science or politics, she wasn't interested in research or education, she didn't care a button about anything but the Lone Pit murder. Nora shook the paper open, glanced at the headlines and stood dumb and rigid with mingled resentment and fear.

" Well ? Do you hear me speaking to you ? On my soul, I'm not sure I didn't make a mistake when I told Dr. Grant to let the other one go. What on earth's the matter, child ? "

Nora lifted her head ; her face was chalk-white, her eyes looked almost black.

" Mrs. Trentham, what did you tell your nephew yesterday —about me, I mean ? "

The old lady's eyes danced with pleasure. " You mean, there's something in already ? He is an enterprising boy. When I saw him as a baby I said to his father . . . Don't look like that. Don't you want to help the police to solve the murder ? "

" I don't want to have anything to do with it," said Nora.

" I never heard of anything so un-British. It's the duty of every citizen to help the police, and in your profession you oughtn't to dream of shirking your duty. Now read me out whatever is making your eyes pop out like a frog's."

" I suppose you told him all this—about me, I mean."

" Now don't be selfish, my dear. Roger's got to earn his living the same as you have. And he did his job in the war, too. Out in the Middle East till 1942 and retired with the Military Cross. This is what is known as a scoop for him. He's coming down to lunch, by the way."

" Not to see me," said Nora.

" Don't be so conceited. To see his aunt."

" Then it won't matter if I'm not here."

" Of course it'll matter. Anyway," she added comfortably, " you won't be able to resist Roger. Girls never can."

White with rage and alarm, Nora read out the startling paragraph that occupied the place of honour on the front page.

LONE PIT MURDER
STARTLING DEVELOPMENT
MYSTERY NURSE'S STORY

" Our Crime Reporter last night made a startling discovery that may well throw light on the mystery surrounding the death of Mr. Alfred Newstead, the Charlbury stock-broker whose body was found in an advanced state of decomposition in a pit on the Sandham Site a few days ago. He is to-day to interview a young nurse who was actually in the house at Askew Avenue when Mrs. Newstead died and who carried the dying woman's last message to her brother, Herbert Webster. As readers of the *Daily Post* are aware, the authorities have been seeking news of Webster since the discovery, so far without success. It is believed that the nurse can throw light on the situation that has to date baffled the most acute brains of the police force."

" I call that very handsome," said Mrs. Trentham in her candid way. " The bit about acute brains, I mean. So far as I can see, any sort of brain would have got as far as the police have, in this affair."

" There's only one thing, you'll have them playing ring-a-ring-of roses round the house any minute now," prophesied Nora savagely. " In fact, I can't think why they haven't arrived already."

" Because they don't know where the house is, and they don't know where you are. Trust Roger for that."

" They'll find out," Nora assured her. " Anyway, I'd rather talk to the police than the press."

" Roger will be down for lunch, perhaps earlier. I've got a chicken and I want you to make me another of those delicious things you made for a sweet the day before yesterday. Roger loves sweets. My cook has a heart of gold, but her puddings have the consistency of gold, too. And touchy! The last time she made me a steak-and-kidney pudding I asked her if she thought she was raising a funeral monument to her worst enemy, and do you know she actually gave me notice ? It took a whole day's cajoling and the most ridiculous rise in wages to make her withdraw it."

Nora agreed to make the sweet. At least it would take her away from the old lady's room for a bit, give her a chance to collect her thoughts. In the hall Nurse Turner was at the telephone.

"Just my luck," she said hanging up the receiver. "I've been on to Matron and told her the news and she's got something else for me at once. I did think I might have time to get my hair permed. Oh, and she says someone's been asking after you, but I told her you were booked here till Kingdom Come. What's up with her ladyship?"

"She wants me to make something special for lunch."

"There's one thing, Deane. If there's ever a slump in nursing, you'll be able to go out as a cook. Far better conditions and no comparison in wages."

"Oh, I don't think so," said Nora. "By the time Mrs. Trentham's through no one would dare engage me. They'd be afraid I'd put arsenic in the soup."

"So long as it wasn't their soup I daresay they wouldn't mind. Well, here's hoping. Hoping for a rich widower with a short tenure," she added. "I've always thought I was cut out to be an old man's darling, for a strictly limited period."

Nora watched her go, her heart full of envy. Then she went down to the kitchen. It was while she was here that the first telegram arrived for her. Mrs. Trentham unscrupulously opened it, saying later, "I thought it was addressed to me. These Post Office people write such shocking hands."

The message was brief and unsigned. It said:

Be careful. You are in greater danger than you know.

"Just like a film," exulted Mrs. Trentham. "You must be sure to keep that to show Roger. It probably came from the murderer." "More likely to be your nephew's sense of humour," said Nora acidly. "He likes things twopence coloured, doesn't he?"

"But he likes other people to do the colouring."

"Anyway, it doesn't prove a thing, even if he does want to reproduce it in his paper to-morrow morning."

"At all events it proves that whoever sent it is a reader of the *Daily Post*. You know, I'm glad I've got Roger in on this. He'll look after you."

"You don't mean that," Nora told her. "You know quite well Roger would sell me up the river any time for half a column in to-morrow's *Post*."

"He has his work to think of, naturally. As a matter of

fact, I think it's an excellent thing he is coming down. He can advise us . . ."

The second telegram arrived about half an hour later. This time Mrs. Trentham allowed the girl to open it.

"Well," she said, almost before Nora could finish reading the message. "Is that another warning?"

"Not exactly." She stared at the slip of paper, which read:

You've led me a nice dance never say die meet me Market Place Holt Cross 12.30 to-day for lunch always your servant Sammy

Automatically she smiled as she read it. Sammy! The mysterious young man she had forgotten all about in the rush of events that had followed her late arrival at Askew Avenue. Now for the first time she remembered his parting words. See you to-morrow at two, he'd said. She wondered if he had really turned up. Presumably he had and Newstead had given him the address of the hostel.

"Of course," she exclaimed just loud enough for Mrs. Trentham not to be sure of the words. "Nurse Turner said someone had been asking Matron—that's it, of course. He's read the *Daily Post*, too."

She felt a rush of warmth for the absent Sammy. He was at all events more faithful than she, who hadn't given him a thought all these weeks. He had awaited his opportunity. He realised she was in danger, and she wondered if he was also the author of the original wire.

"He could be," she thought. "Perhaps he would feel I wouldn't meet him if I didn't think I was in danger." From what she could remember of Sammy she felt it was quite in accord with his temperament first to create a situation and then to offer to solve it. Suddenly she laughed. "Why, I haven't laughed for days," she reflected.

Mrs. Trentham broke in on her thoughts. "Another warning?" she demanded.

"No. A—a lunch invitation."

"For to-day? I suppose you sent that to yourself to escape meeting Roger. But you can't go. I won't allow it. You're my nurse, here to look after me."

"I couldn't have sent it to myself," pointed out Nora reasonably. "I haven't been out all the morning and I haven't been near the 'phone."

" You might have got that Turner creature to send it."

Nora felt anger beginning to rise in her. " How could I ? It comes from London. Look at it." She held the slip of paper out.

Mrs. Trentham, who had been aiming at this, took it and read it with interest.

" Who's Sammy ? "

" He—he's a man I know."

" Thank God you don't say boy, like the modern young vulgarians. Well, I didn't think you meant the Zoo Polar bear. What I did mean was—what's he to you ? Your fiancé ? "

" No, oh no."

" You seem very certain. Now then, my dear, tell me the truth. Is he married ? "

" No. That is . . ." she stopped. The fact was she didn't know, but surely if he were married he wouldn't have sent that telegram.

" Do you mean he's divorced ? Or going to be ? "

" No."

" Then he's married. My dear girl, I thought you had more sense. I don't blame you in the least for getting mixed up in a murder, because that might happen to anyone, though most people don't have the luck. But there's no excuse at all for getting yourself involved with a married man. Such a copycat thing to do, falling in love with somebody some one else has already picked."

" It isn't like that all," said Nora.

" You're not secretly married ? "

" No. He—he's just a friend and he's seen the *Daily Post* and he wants me to have lunch with him."

" You'll have to wire back that you can't."

" That's impossible. I haven't got an address."

" You must know something about him."

" And he'll have left London by now. I shall have to meet him anyway, even if I can't stay for lunch."

" Why should he be interested in the murder ? "

" I think he's probably more interested in me, but—well he was there that night."

" Where ? "

" At Charlbury."

" Do you mean, he was in the house ? "

" Oh no. But he showed me the way and was coming the

next afternoon, only of course I wasn't there, and I suppose
he's only just discovered my address."

" Wouldn't that matron of yours tell him ? "

" Oh, I shouldn't think so. Anyhow, I can't keep him there
all day. I must meet him, even if I can't stay for lunch."

Mrs. Trentham was thinking rapidly. How would Roger
view this latest development ? He might be angry if she
refused to let the girl go into Holt Cross, because after all
Sammy did seem to be connected with the murder, and he'd
been complaining of the lack of male interest in the case.
Mrs. Trentham didn't know what Sammy was like, but he was
presumably young—and lunch was no great matter.

" If I let you meet him for lunch," she stipulated, " you'll
come back on the 2.15 bus ? "

" Oh yes, Mrs. Trentham."

" Then I suppose you'll have to go. But don't be a selfish
girl. Don't forget Roger has to earn a living as much as you
have. And I'm only letting you go, mind, because it may be
important for you to hear what this young man has to tell
you." She paused. The girl looked incredibly young, incredibly defenceless. " I suppose you do know what you're
doing," she said slowly. " I wouldn't like any harm to come
to you while you were under my roof. I didn't mind about
Nurse Turner. I'd be sorry for any man who pitted himself
against her. But you're different. I'd like you to be safe."

" I'm not going to elope, if that's what you're afraid of,"
said Nora gently.

" Anyone could tell you were a spinster. When I say I want
you to be safe I don't mean I want to see you married. Marriage
can be as wild as the jungle. I ought to know. I sometimes
wondered if I'd married the original Tarzan. Still, as your
need is so shall your strength be. And you'll find out the
same."

Nora went away and upstairs to change her frock. If she
was to meet Sammy at 12.30 there wasn't too much time, and
the bus service was apt to be erratic. Changing her dress she
began to wonder if he were her friend or no, if she was running
her head into a noose by accepting his invitation. But when
you're up against things as she was—for she was convinced
that Mrs. Trentham would gladly use her as a pawn in Roger's
game—you take risks. You have to. And one Sammy seemed
less alarming than a combination of Mrs. Trentham and Roger
and the police.

It was a drizzly kind of day and she put on her blue oilskin and the little blue oilskin hood that matched it. That way you didn't need an umbrella. She reached the bus station in time to secure a seat and they jolted off. At each stop they took on more people. She soon had to give up her place to a girl carrying a baby. A small boy, crushed against her by the crowd, said indignantly, " Well, at least sardines are dead before they're packed," and that roused a gale of laughter. As usual, she got into conversation with a woman standing next to her, and at Holt Cross a number of passengers alighted, for this was a market town of some pretensions. Nora had wondered how she could be sure of recognising Sammy again, since she had never really seen him, or how he would know her. She had had the forethought, however, to bring the telegram with her, and she meant to stand by the War Memorial that had been erected in the middle of the Market Square and wave it like mad till someone came up and spoke to her.

CHAPTER ELEVEN

Let us have a quiet hour, let us hob and nob with death.
—TENNYSON.

THE RAIN had thickened during the journey and it was coming down quite heavily as she alighted from the bus. There was no one standing by the War Memorial, though the usual hawker with fruit and cut flowers was in his place by the kerb. Drawn up near him was an unobtrusive black car with a man at the wheel. She approached hesitantly. Now that the instant was upon her she felt less certain. But as though as he had been watching her, the man leaned forward and opened the passenger door for her to enter. He didn't speak and she remembered the words of the first telegram—You are in greater danger than you know.

" Is it—Sammy ? " she whispered.

" Yes. Get in quickly. Don't talk but look through the window at the back as I move off and tell me if we're being followed." His voice was low and urgent.

" Followed ? Do you mean . . . ? Then there is danger ? "

" Of course there's danger. It's always dangerous to know

85

more than other people. My only hope is that no one has recognised me. I wore this ridiculous theatrical hat . . ." and she saw that he had pulled a wide black hat over his face. " It's pretty obliterating, isn't it ? " he went on, taking a narrow path to the left and making a good pace. " Well ? "

She stared through the window, watching the houses, patient and narrow, besieged by the rain.

" I don't see anyone."

" Good. I may have shaken him off."

She turned back and began to untie the strings of the oilskin hood.

" Why did you send me that telegram ? "

He laughed. That laugh startled her. It wasn't friendly, casual, amused.; it wasn't tender or forbearing. It was scornful and cruel.

" Why, Sammy," she began, and he turned and looked at her, and she broke off. " But—I don't understand—Sammy," she began again.

" I'll answer your question," he told her. " You know too much. Little girls who know too much have to be kept quiet."

She put a hand towards the door of the car. " I shouldn't do that. We're going at a good pace. You'd almost certainly be killed."

" What did you mean when you said I knew too much ? "

He asked coolly, " What made you interfere ? You were safely out of it, weren't you ? Why didn't you have the sense to keep your mouth shut ? " And then he added more angrily, " I believe I had an intuition that first night when I saw you looming out of the fog. I felt you were going to be dangerous to me. A mystery, you know, is like one of these special locks. There's only one key and only one person can open the door. In this case, you're that person, and—that door mustn't be opened. Couldn't you have seen that without my having to show you in this rather drastic fashion ? What about the sixth sense that women possess that. we hear so much about ? Didn't that warn you, come shouting at you in the dark : Don't open the door ! Don't open the door ! "

" But—but . . ." She broke off helplessly. It was difficult to believe that this was really happening to her. It always is. Murder's a word in a printed book, an act on the stage, an incident in a film, but not a thing that happens to you. She was certain in her own mind that Adela Newstead had been murdered, and that had been followed by an unquestioned murder at Lone Pit, but in neither had her own life been in danger. Now she knew she was in deadly peril. She said again, her voice shaking, " I still don't see why you're doing this. Oh, I suppose I was mad to have come. But Sammy—I have to keep saying Sammy because I don't know the other name. . . ."

" That's all right," he said. " Sammy'll do very well."

Then he jammed the hat back over his eyes and gave himself up to the task of driving. But before he got really under weigh he leaned across and locked the door on the passenger side of the car. "'Pity to spoil the ship for a ha'porth of tar," he said. " It's lucky for me I read the *Daily Post*, isn't it ? "

Thereafter for a while the car ran in silence. They were outside the thirty mile limit once they had left the shops and the little residential houses behind them. The lights that had been snapped on in many windows to counteract the gloom of low sky and driving rain shone like so many jeering stars. In the rooms the illuminated people sat sewing or talking or writing letters, doing all the ordinary things that people do in the course of the ordinary day. Perhaps they said to one another, How tame life is. Nothing ever happens. Perhaps they wished something would. And all the time, without their knowledge, something frightful was going on. Even if they looked out and saw the car they wouldn't guess. What was there to warn them ? A man and a girl driving through the dark afternoon. Some of them might even envy the girl. her escort—they wouldn't know. Perhaps they'd never know.

She fought down the rising waves of hysteria. With every passing moment her danger increased. Soon they would have left the residential part of the town behind them. Already the houses were thinning out, while ahead, through the clouds of rain, she could discover all the dank unpopulated country-side, where he and she would be the only living creatures.

She caught her breath on the thought. The only living creatures ! The phrase started a train of reflection that made her shiver, ringing in her mind like some sombre, ominous bell.

" You know," she heard her companion remark, " most of the present trouble is your fault. You're only reaping where you strawed. It's poetic justice really that this should happen to you. Why couldn't you keep your mouth shut ? "

She said wearily, " Oh, this doesn't make sense. Can't you see what you've done ? If you'd stayed in the dark I couldn't have really hurt you because I didn't know enough. The

ANTHONY GILBERT

police hadn't any evidence to lay hands on you, you might
have got away for years, for ever. Don't you understand ? "

" It doesn't matter," he said indifferently. " In any case,
it makes no difference now."

" No difference ? " She repeated the words like an
automaton.

" Well ? " He sounded impatient. " How should it ? "

" Where are we going ? " she wanted to know as the car
took another turning, and the last sign of human life was
blotted out.

" Somewhere safe," he assured her.

" Safe for you—or me ? "

" Which do you suppose ? "

" But why—oh why are you doing this ? "

" I give you three guesses."

She put it into words then. " You mean, you're going to
kill me ? " She still couldn't believe it, in spite of all the
facts, just because these things don't happen to oneself. She
repeated it over and over again.

" Well, put yourself in my shoes," said her companion.
" What would you do ? "

" But it won't help. Because the police will make enquiries
. . . Mrs. Trentham will go to them."

" And what happens then ? You showed them the
telegram ? "

" Mrs. Trentham read it. She didn't believe it came from
London."

" That was thoughtful of you. When she goes to the police
she will be able to tell them that you went off to lunch with a
young man and haven't come back. In the circumstances,
they won't think that so odd. The young man from the *Daily
Post* was coming down to-day, wasn't he ? Well, perhaps you
had your reasons for not wanting to meet him."

" But sooner or later they'll start looking," she persisted.

He smiled. " Do you know how many girls disappear every
year and are never traced ? Oh, believe me, the police don't
worry very much. They have an answer ready."

Her helplessness almost choked her. She could only say
once more, " They will ask questions, all the same. They'll
know there's something wrong. Why, I didn't even bring a
sponge."

He took another turning. It was getting quite dark now.
She wondered if this was going to be another night of fog. It

would be easy to stage an accident and then disappear, and by the time the police got on the track the trail might be cold. Anyway, it wouldn't help her if her assailant did eventually swing.

She said, " You've been very foolish and you will be caught. They know too much. Besides, you've really signed your own death-warrant, because if you hadn't staged this meeting I couldn't have told anyone anything of value. But now if I'm asked questions. . . ."

" You won't be asked questions," he said simply.

She quivered away from him, looking at him sideways as though she longed to discern some sign of softening there ; but the face might have been moulded from iron.

" Yes, I suppose I knew that really," she whispered. " I suppose you haven't any choice."

" I'm glad you see that."

Then she felt quiet, as though she had at last accepted her fate. Because he was right, she couldn't escape. She couldn't leap from the car because the door was locked, she couldn't hope to overpower him ; it wasn't likely he'd give her a chance to defeat him by subtle means. It was queer how the small things governed your destiny. There had been a minute or two on the night of that appalling fog when she had hesitated about completing her journey, when she'd thought even Matron couldn't blame her for waiting till the morning, and if she had she wouldn't have found herself now in what Roger Trentham would be certain to call the car of death. But she had persisted and now she found herself racing towards some unknown destination. She shivered again. Unknown ? She knew it well enough. She was racing towards her grave. It made it seem lonelier than ever to realise that no one, except her companion, might ever know where her bones would lie. He didn't look the sort of person who would do things by halves.

The car seemed to have been running for a long time. She had lost all sense of the hour, and the premature darkness made it difficult to guess how near the day was to its close. The fog she had apprehended was becoming denser. Everything, it seemed, favoured the criminal. In a fog it's much easier to make a get-away. She thought, becoming a little light-headed—Sammy. Sammy What ? Will anyone ever know ? He wouldn't tell me. I wonder why. Surely it wouldn't matter my knowing, because I've got to die. She weht on saying the words over and over again. I've got to die. How absurd I am to think there's any way out. I'm much too dangerous now. Of course I've got to die.

She wondered a little what Mrs. Trentham would do when she didn't arrive. Roger Trentham must have come hours ago. Would Mrs. Trentham believe that she had deliberately engineered this disappearance because she knew something about the Newstead case she didn't want to reveal? What steps would Roger take? Or would he simply regard every development as fuel to his fires? And what steps would the police take? After an instant it occurred to her that this really didn't matter, since it was hardly likely she would be able to take any interest in them by the time the enquiry was got under weigh. She recalled various novels she had read and films she had seen where the beleaguered heroine had performed acts of unequalled heroism, somehow contriving to send telephone messages so that the villain on arrival at the place of destruction, found himself confronted by a cool, eagle-eyed hero who proceeded to overset all his vile machinations and carry the heroine away, apparently without turning a hair. She thought, " If anybody had asked me who the hero was I'd have said—have said . . ." Suddenly she began to laugh. She laughed and laughed till the tears ran down her cheeks.

" It won't help you to get hysterical," said her companion, brutally.

" I c-can't help it," whispered Nora. " Did—did you see that cow looking over the hedge at us? Did you see its face? Isn't it lucky for you that cows can't talk and tell the police later on that we came this way and . . ."

" Is this another of your acts? " the man demanded.

" I don't see why you should mind me laughing when I have so little time left. It's better than crying all over your car, isn't it? "

" What was it you were going to tell the *Daily Post*? " he asked casually. " Or was that just a journalistic stunt to attract the reader's interest? "

She made for that frail hope like Noah's dove making for the olive-branch.

" I shan't tell you."

He didn't seem impressed. " Please yourself. You won't tell anyone else either."

" It—it was something the doctor said."

He laughed. "What value do you think that would have ?
It's the Lone Pit Murder the authorities are interested in."

"I can't believe you know what you're doing," she burst
out desperately. "However clever you are, when they find
me. . . ."

"You won't be found. You'll never be found."

Now she could not prevent the fear from sounding in her
voice. "Then—you have a plan?"

"Oh yes," he told her mockingly, "I have a plan."

"You'll have to be quick." The colour had drained out of
her lips. She put one hand to her throat, where it closed over
a small old-fashioned trinket she wore, a moonstone set in
fine filigree silver on a delicate chain. The strength of her
clasp broke the chain's fine links and she remained as she was,
stiff with the effort to preserve a courageous front, clutching
the locket in her fingers. "There are others besides Mrs.
Trentham who'll be interested to know what has happened."

He laughed again. "Meaning the enterprising nephew will
turn private detective?"

"He might. I think most certainly he might."

Again she remembered the book heroines who drop hairpins
in a steady trail from the fatal stairway to the murderer's
lair, or the men in the Chestertonian romance who had spilled
soup and broken windows to leave evidence of their passing.
Only had one ever really believed those stories? They didn't
happen in real life. Detectives looked for something more
subtle than a trail of hairpins, and anyway two plain brown
combs and a kirbigrip wouldn't make much of a show. She
tried to believe that already the virile Roger Trentham was on
her track, but it was too good to be true. She'd be found, of
course. People always are found, even if months passed before
their skeletons were recovered, but they weren't often found
alive. She realised that she was shivering.

CHAPTER TWELVE

*'Tis a naughty night to swim in.—*KING LEAR.

TIME, it seemed, had stopped, or at least it was no longer marked by minutes and seconds on the hands of a watch, but by the steady revolution of the wheels of the car. Presently she realised that time was slowing down. The driver was keeping a sharp look-out and muttering something to himself. "These damned deserts," he muttered and then, "Am I the first motorist they've ever seen?"

Nora tried to see the time by her own sensible silver wrist-watch but the fog was now dense enough to make the whole surrounding countryside dark.

"It's a little after four," said her companion in a grim voice. "Maybe soon we'll stop for tea."

She couldn't believe him. Only four o'clock? It seemed like yesterday at least since she had first met him.

"Are we stopping?" she whispered, and he answered clearly, "The damned woman whose car I pinched hadn't got her tank properly filled. I reckoned we'd have enough to make the coast."

"The coast?" She drew in a sharp breath. Now she was beginning to understand not merely what lay ahead, for that she knew already but the shape it would probably take.

"That's what I said. Considering how long the coast was barred to sightseers you might be glad of the chance."

She found herself thinking, "He's mad. That's the answer. Only mad people do what he's doing, laugh as he's laughing." Which might be a sound conclusion but didn't help her much. Besides, he wasn't madder than any other murderer. She looked out of the window at the cheerless landscape. It looked as though no human creature had passed that way since the end of the first world war. The countryside was lonely and untenanted and although a zealous Minister of Agriculture had done what he could in the national interest between 1939 and 1944 even he hadn't found much land hereabouts fit for ploughing-in. Even if the order had been made and complied with the grant that accompanied it would never have been earned. The first crop would have been water-logged, black-

92

ened, sterile, on such a soil. The car dropped a little more pace and turned a corner. Then they came upon new signs of life. By the side of the road stood a public-house, not much better than an ale-house, the man suspected, and beside it were a couple of pumps.

Nora's heart beat so loud it was deafening. Here it seemed was Providence offering her a last chance. She didn't know who would answer their summons; it might be only a boy, or one of these slow-witted yokels in whom the sight of the Loch Ness monster would scarcely arouse curiosity, but at least he would be a human creature like herself. She had a moment's terror lest her companion should try to gag her before he stopped the car, but he made no such move. Only he was careful to see that all four doors were locked before he moved up the little path leading to the inn. It was called the Blue Boar and an aged sign of some shapeless beast who might once have been blue hung over the entrance. She saw the side door of the inn open in response to the driver's summons, saw him begin to explain. The inn-keeper was a stolid laconic man, no fool but a man who didn't want to get mixed up in other folks' troubles. He'd had troubles enough in his time ; now he wanted a quiet life and no interference. To Nora, however, he appeared in the light of an ally, the only ally she could hope to find. Somehow she must attract attention, convince him of the truth of her position. Tearing off one shoe she slammed it desperately through the glass window nearest her. The lunatic action aroused both men. They came hurrying down the path. She heard an exclamation, " My God ! " and then both men were standing looking down at her as though she were a criminal. The inn-keeper observed severely, " Now then, what do you think you're doing ? Don't you know tyres are in short supply ? And if you go spreading great jagged bits of glass all over the road you're making a bad position worse. It's murder, that's what it is."

To her horror she felt a laugh bubbling up in her throat. " That's funny," she said, half-choked by this ill-timed mirth, " Oh, that's very funny. Because, you see, that's just what it is—murder, I mean." She was appalled at the sound of her own voice, so cracked and shrill. He'd think her demented, and suddenly she understood that that was what he was intended to think. That, of course, was what *he* had been saying at the door of the inn.

" Don't take any notice of my passenger," he must have said. " She's crazy. I have to lock her in the car." And she had played straight into his hands by smashing the window and then going into peals of insane laughter.

" Now then," said the inn-keeper in a severe voice, as before, " that's enough of that."

" You don't understand," she screamed. " He's a criminal. He's going to murder me. He got me out here by a trick, he's taking me to the coast, he's going to—to . . ."

The man intervened. " Now Moira, I warned you, you can't behave like this. I've warned you what will happen if you're not sensible. You know perfectly well that sane people don't break windows."

" I suppose now you're going to pretend I'm mad, that's why I'm locked in the car. It's not true." She turned fiercely to the inn-keeper. " Can't you see it's not true. But I'm dangerous to him, that's why I've got to be put out of the way. Dangerous ! "

She saw the two men exchange glances. " Crazy as a loon," said one glance.

" Mad as a coot," agreed the other.

Nora's mood changed. The hysteria left her, to be replaced by a worse form of fear. She understood that, if she wasn't altogether a fool, a man risking his neck isn't a fool either. The landlord wasn't going to believe her, because the ground of his mind had already been prepared. He was going to fill up the tank—he put in two gallons—and let the car drive on. He wasn't going to help her, call the police, ring up Mrs. Trentham and verify her story. . . .

" You don't understand," she said desperately. " He's a murderer. He's a murderer. . ."

" Two gallons, sir," said the man. " You want to go back about three miles and take the left fork. Lestingham's six miles on. Can't think how you came to miss the turn."

" This damned fog ! " He shivered. " D'you often get them as bad as this on the coast ? "

" You're some way from the coast yet. Oh well, sometimes. We get used to 'em."

" That's more than drivers ever do."

" We don't get a lot of cars round this way, not once the summer's over. They come for the caves during the season. The charabancs do a roaring trade. But now we're pretty quiet till Easter." Nora saw that they were going to pay no attention to her. She said again, " Will you let me use your telephone ? There can't be any harm in that, just telephone to Mrs. Trentham . . ."

" Now then, Moira, we've had enough of that," said her would-be killer in tones that sounded more weary than annoyed. " You go round ringing up non-existent people or people you've never met. You'll do it once too often."

" You listen to what your husband says," the inn-keeper joined in.

" Husband ? He's no husband of mine." Again she saw the exchange of glances, and impulsively she thrust her hand and arm through the hole she had made. The jagged edge of the glass caught her wrist, drawing a little blood.

" I'm not wearing a wedding-ring. You can see that."

" Look what you've done," said the inn-keeper in vexed tones. " You've cut yourself. Have you got a handkerchief ? "

She pulled one out of her pocket. " That'll prove it," she screamed triumphantly. " N. D. And he called me Moira"

" There now, you've been at it again. If I've told you once I've told you a hundred times, Moira, one of these days you'll find yourself in trouble with the police. This time it's only a handkerchief, but one day it'll be something valuable, and I shan't know how to pull you out. Give that to me." He took it from her and thrust it into his pocket. " Have you got anything else that doesn't belong to you ? " he demanded. " And where's your wedding-ring ? Have you tried swallowing that again ? "

" I never had a ring."

" Don't be ridiculous. What's that you've got in your hand ? " He forced her fingers apart and revealed the little locket on its broken chain.

" What made you break that ? "

" It was an accident," she panted.

He took it roughly from her and put it into his waistcoat pocket. " You're not fit to be trusted with anything," he said. " Look at that glass. The fog will come in and you'll get one of your throaty colds." He turned back to the inn-keeper. " Do you think it would be possible to give my wife a cup of tea ? In this fog it's going to take us a little while to get to Lestingham. We have rooms there and the appointment with the doctor is in the morning."

" It's all lies," shouted Nora. " All lies. There isn't a word of truth—oh, why won't you let me use the telephone ? "

" I'll ask the wife," said the landlord, moving away. The other moved with him.

"'I don't want any tea," Nora called after them. " There'd be poison in it."

" That's no way to talk," said the inn-keeper whose name was Blackman. " We don't serve that sort of tea here."

She saw the two of them go into the house and knew that her last chance had gone. Whatever the woman was like, she would have been warned that she had a crazy girl to deal with, a girl who didn't even know she was married, who wouldn't wear a wedding-ring, who stole other people's things and broke windows and accused her husband of murder. The driver came back after a minute with the news that the tea would be brought out to them.

" And don't repeat what you've just said about its being poisoned," he instructed her. " If I poisoned you I should be hanged."

" People aren't always hanged," said Nora. " Sometimes they're clever and get away." She thought of Adela Newstead. " Oh, you think you're very clever, don't you, but when the hunt begins and questions are asked, these people are going to remember we came here. . . ."

" And you think they'll link that up ? Not they. It's foggy, remember. They'd be hard put to it to identify us even to-morrow, and each day the memory of us will become fainter. Besides, they'll be looking for a nurse. . . ."

" Not a madwoman who doesn't recognise her own husband ? Oh, I understand. In a way, you deserve to succeed. You think of so much."

The door of the inn opened again and the Blackmans came out. Mrs. Blackman was younger than her husband, a sensible-looking woman in the middle thirties. She brought a tray with a pot and two cups on it and a plate with some buns.

" I've explained that you'd rather not leave the car," said the man. " I'll hand you your tea through the door."

" I shan't drink it."

Mrs. Blackman came up alongside. The tray was a black japanned one with a pink rose in the centre, the teapot was black and there were gold roses at the bottom of the cups. She poured out two cups of tea, handed one to Nora and the other to her companion. There was no deception whatsoever.

" It was just a trick," Nora decided. " He meant to back up his original impression that I was mad by asking for tea so that I could refuse to take it. Then he'd get the woman on his side as well as the man. All right. I've played into his hands once already, but I won't do it again." She lifted the cup and drank the hot tea. It was strong and very sweet ; it made her feel better.

" They've come out of their way," Blackman was saying to his wife. " Missed the fork. They were making for Lestingham."

" I don't know this road very well, you see." Nora leaned back and watched her betrayer earnestly explaining his mistake. " And the fog's thicker down in the valley than it is here. It's funny because though it was wet this morning there was no sign of any mist."

" We often get them here," said Mrs. Blackman. " Will your wife have another cup of tea ? "

Nora said " No, thank you." She felt this was her last opportunity, but lassitude was stealing over her. It didn't seem worth bothering any more. She remembered something she had once read, about horses in the Great War that had raged from 1914-1918. They had been caught in the rivers of mud in Northern France during the last two appalling winters and had sunk gradually in a sea of mud, and had to be hauled and coaxed by their drivers. And again and again a moment would come when the beasts themselves lost heart, gave up the struggle, refused to co-operate, and there was no alternative for their drivers but to abandon their efforts and watch the heart-breaking spectacles of fine and splendid animals sinking to an appalling death, because they'd lost the will to live. She had seen it, too, in sick-rooms. People seemed to have turned the corner, be on the road to recovery, and suddenly there would be a relapse for no physical reason, but just because the spirit had lost the power to fight. So a similar sense of failure, of the helplessness of everything, now assailed her. Sooner or later, she thought, this man was bound to succeed. She hadn't a chance. It was like being a disembodied spirit standing beside the car watching a girl called Nora Deane throw away her last chance of life. It was less trouble. She could still hear the conversation going on amid the fog-wreaths.

" I'm afraid it's hereditary," the man was saying. " Naturally I didn't know that. But I still have hope that with proper treatment. . . . You can do so much with the young." He got into the car. " They come in fits and starts. She'll be normal for quite a long time and then she'll start thinking everyone's against her and making the most wild accusations, hardly knows who she is."

Mrs. Blackman said politely, " We had a case like that down in the village. An old man, who thought he was King David and went round plaguing the girls something cruel. A bull got him in the end. He was so daft seemingly he couldn't tell a bull from a young lady. . . ."

" The B.M.A. ought to have that one," observed the murderer, starting his car and backing towards a convenient spot for turning. The girl didn't speak any more. She seemed to have sunk back and be half-asleep.

" I do call that sad," said Mrs. Blackman to her unresponsive husband as they re-entered the Boar. " Quite a pretty girl, too, so far as you could see. I wonder what was the real cause. A miss, I shouldn't be surprised. My sister, Susan, had to be taken to the County Asylum after her miss. . . ."

Joe Blackman, who had known his sister-in-law before this disaster, said with feeling that Susan's husband had been saved a lot. Mrs. Blackman retorted, " Whom the Lord loveth He chasteneth " and Joe said irreverently that it would take someone like an apostle to think of a thing like that. Mrs. Blackman said, " Give over, Joe " but for the rest of the evening she looked more cheerful. It often bothered her that she had no children, but thinking of Sister Sue and the young lady of the afternoon she realised that blessings are like cuckoo's eggs—you find both in the most unexpected surroundings.

A little while later she went up to her room, taking her thankfulness with her. She was engaged in putting things to rights, whatever that convenient phrase might mean, when she heard the sound of a car coming up the road. It was travelling slowly and she thought, " Coming here ? Two in one evening. That's queer " and the notion flashed into her mind that the two cars might in some way be connected. That was the first time it occurred to her that perhaps everything wasn't quite right. She went to the window and pulled back the curtain. The fog hadn't lifted at all, but it didn't seem any denser than it had been. You didn't get the pea-soup variety here, more like a thick mist coming up from the sea. As she looked out the car accelerated suddenly and was gone.

She came back to the room with the sense that there had

been something wrong. It wasn't till she was sitting at supper with her husband that she realised what it was.

" Of course," she exclaimed, " lights."

" What are you talking about ? " demanded Joe, a man of few words.

" That car that came this afternoon—no, not the one with the young lady in it, but the other."

" There wasn't any other."

" There was, a bit later. It didn't stop here. I felt at the time it was odd, but I couldn't think why. Now I know. It didn't carry any lights."

Joe, who believed in minding his own business in the hope that in consequence no one would interfere with him, said shortly, " It's no concern of ours, anyway."

He couldn't have been more wrong.

CHAPTER THIRTEEN

Life is a series of surprises.—R. W. EMERSON.

WHEN NORA failed to return on the bus that reached Green Valley at three o'clock Mrs. Trentham was furious.

" I thought she was to be trusted," she fumed to her nephew, who had come down cool and charming and entirely at his ease in excellent time for lunch. " She promised . . ."

" Oh come, Aunt May, have a heart," he protested. " How about love's young dream ? "

" Two o'clock in the afternoon is no time for it. Besides, she told me . . . Roger, you don't think she's eloped ? "

The newspaperman in Roger Trentham was instantly uppermost. " What a story ! Don't you see, Auntie, it would show she knew something she was afraid of anyone finding out ? This chap may have been her accomplice."

" Anyone could tell you were a human vulture," said Mrs. Trentham witheringly. " Though I'm quite prepared to believe this Sammy is dangerous to her. I wouldn't be in the least surprised to hear he is married, whatever she may say. She hadn't got the honest open look I want from a girl who's respectably in love."

" Is she supposed to be in love ? "

The old lady looked exasperated. " How do I know ? Girls

don't do any of the things they did as a matter of course when I was young. They call it old-fashioned to fall in love with an eligible bachelor and get married. We thought it was our duty."

"Maybe they're not in love with duty," suggested Roger.

"If she's not back by four I shall telephone the police," said Mrs. Trentham decidedly.

"The laugh will be on you if you do. A girl isn't missing in the official sense because she goes off with her young man and isn't back to tea." Roger, it will be understood, didn't want to be made to look a fool either.

"I'm going to make sure she didn't take anything with her. She was most peculiar about you, my dear. I got very suspicious. She definitely didn't want to meet you. I hope she doesn't mean to let me down after all the kindness I've shown her. That would be most ungrateful."

Roger grinned. "Didn't you know gratitude's gone out with duty?" he enquired.

An examination of Nora's room showed that she had taken nothing but her handbag. Her sponge and toothbrush, her hairbrush, slippers and pile of clean handkerchiefs were all in their usual places.

"So she can't have gone off with him," Mrs. Trentham concluded. "He may be the most generous young man in the world but no man's generous enough these days to present a girl with a whole new outfit. Coupons won't run to it."

"Who is the chap anyway?" Roger wanted to know. "Can't you give me any sort of line on him?"

"I can only tell you I'd never heard her mention him till the telegram came. The second telegram, that is."

"The second?" Roger pricked up his ears.

"Yes. She had one, unsigned, telling her she was in danger and had better look out."

"And I've been here all these hours and this is your first mention of it? Auntie May, I'm shocked at you."

"I didn't think it was important. That isn't the one she went to meet."

"It's news," he insisted. "Where is the telegram?"

"I think she dropped it in the basket."

Roger scrabbled through the basket like a dog looking for a bone. "Here it is," he said, smoothing out the crumpled ball. "You are in greater danger than you know," he read. "This is a find. Where's the second?"

" She took that off with her."

" That's a pity. Still, this is something. We could reproduce this on the front page. Have you got a photograph of the girl ? "

" She was polyfotoed the other day to please me. She gave me one or two. They're in that drawer there. No, on the right hand side. Don't upset everything."

" She's a nice-looking wench," observed Roger. " Wonder if she has eloped ? You know, it'll make a grand story."

" That's all you think of," snapped his aunt. " No concern for me at all. As a matter of fact she was very—what's that word all you young people use nowadays—cagey about this Sammy. She didn't even seem to know whether he was married or what he was up to."

" It could be that she wanted to miss me." Roger's voice was dreamy. He didn't mind about the girl. He was seeing the headlines in to-morrow's *Post*.

" What's that got to do with it ? An honest girl has nothing to hide."

" You do make the virtues sound so darned unprepossessing," murmured the young man. " You know, it's all beginning to fit together. She gets this scare telegram, which properly puts the wind up her. Then her young man comes riding out like young Lochinvar and carries her off. . . ."

" Young Lochinvar married his girl."

" You mustn't be old-fashioned. Besides, perhaps he's going to."

When the five o'clock bus came in and there was still no sign of Nora the old lady waxed furious. She ramped and she raved until Roger told her soothingly that now he wouldn't need to go to church on Sunday, he'd had his sermon in the middle of the week.

" I shall ring up the matron and tell her to send me someone more reliable," she threatened.

" Now, don't do that. You'll blow the gaff completely. This is my scoop, remember. If you won't play ball with me one of these days you may have me on your hands as a down-and-out."

" I'm not surprised the newspapers are so fantastic if you're typical of the people who write them," was Mrs. Trentham's swift retort. " Oh, I'm furious. I know what they say about still waters running deep. This girl looks as though butter wouldn't melt in her mouth, and don't say that with the present ration, it's not likely to have the chance. You'd have said she was such a nice quiet girl. . . ."

" The sort you'd like your nephew to marry. I know."

" And now she's got herself mixed up in a disreputable murder case. . . . Oh, I don't blame her for that. I daresay nursing's a very monotonous life. But I can't help thinking that if everything had been above-board she'd have gone to the police direct."

" That's the trouble with murder, it hardly ever is above-board. And you'd be the first person to complain if it were. Anyhow, if you knew anything about the police you wouldn't say that. It's like having small-pox, the patient may be cured but the scars never completely disappear."

The six-thirty bus came and went and Roger began to talk of getting back to town. At six-forty-five the telephone rang.

" I'll take it," said Roger. " It's probably for me anyway."

" Why on earth should it be for you ? " grumbled Mrs. Trentham. " You young people are so conceited. Nobody knows you're here. . . ."

" My paper does." He lifted the receiver. " Hullo ! "

" Is that Mrs. Trentham's house ? " enquired the masculine voice. " I'm speaking for Miss Deane. She asked me to ring up."

Roger drew a bow at a venture. " Is that Sammy ? "

" Yes. Who are you ? The reporter chap ? "

" You're so quick off the mark," sighed Roger. " Has Miss Deane got a message for me ? "

" For Mrs. Trentham."

" I'll take it."

" Well, she's very sorry to cause any inconvenience, but she won't be along for a few days."

" She'll have trouble with her Trade Union, won't she ? Any special reason ? "

" She's in danger."

" That's what the telegram said, the first one, I mean. P'raps you know who sent it ? "

" I could guess."

" Well ? "

" The chap who killed Alfred Newstead. The fact is, Miss Deane knows too much to be safe without an escort."

" And you're her escort ? Stout fellow ! Why didn't she go to the police ? "

" She's safer with me." The voice sounded grim. " She

didn't appreciate her danger till to-day, but I've made her realise just how considerable it is." And that at least was true.

" You couldn't give me a hint, I suppose ? " pleaded Roger. " Something for the front page. I've got the original telegram, the anonymous one. . . ."

" That's enough to be going on with, surely ? "

" Nothing's ever enough, but if you aren't going to open up it'll have to do. Where are you speaking from, by the way ? "

" A call box. You'll pass the message on to Mrs. Trentham ? "

" Any idea how long Miss Deane proposes to stay on vacation ? "

" Till I think it's safe for her to come back."

" And that'll be ? "

" When the police have located this fellow Webster."

" I hope she remembered to bring her ration book," commented Roger politely. " Where exactly do you come in this ? "

" I'm her big brother—to date. Well, poor kid, she's got no relations, no one at all so far as I can make out."

" Known her long ? " asked Roger.

" Long enough to know my own mind."

" You know all the answers, don't you ? Thanks a lot. By the way, one last question."

" Well ? "

" What's the rest of it, besides Sammy ? "

" Wouldn't you like to know ? " There was a short laugh and the caller rang off.

" Well, well, well," murmured Roger, going to rejoin his aunt. " That was Sammy."

" I knew it," exclaimed the old woman. " Did he say when that girl will be back ? "

" When it's safe."

" And when does he imagine that will be ? "

" When the police have found the real murderer. He's right, you know. She could be in a spot."

" I don't understand your ridiculous slang. And may I ask who is going to look after me to-night ? "

" How about that sourpuss you've been keeping all these years as a pet—Ellen ? She can cope for a day or two, can't she ? "

"I shall ring up the matron at once," announced Mrs. Trentham in steely tones, and could not be deflected.

"All I beg of you is don't break my bag of tricks right open. Can't you wait till morning?"

"Certainly not." She obtained her connection and was put through.

"Mrs. Trentham? Oh, I hope there's nothing wrong with Nurse Deane."

"She's quite a satisfactory nurse, if that's what you mean. But she's had to give up the case for a few days."

"Give it up? Why, only this morning Nurse Turner was telling me . . ."

"I'm really not concerned with what Nurse Turner told you," interrupted Mrs. Trentham with unpardonable rudeness. "The plain fact is that I'm ill and I've no nurse here. Nurse Deane had a telegram this morning and had to go off in a hurry."

"She should have informed me," said Matron icily.

"Perhaps she's writing."

"How extraordinary!" exclaimed Matron in a different tone of voice. "Mrs. Trentham, I'm extremely sorry about this. I do hope that Nurse Deane has been quite straightforward with you."

"What does that mean?" demanded Mrs. Trentham, sounding like a snapping turtle on its day.

"A rather peculiar thing happened this morning," said Matron slowly. "I can't say I thought very much about it at the time. One's busy and so forth. But someone telephoned —a man—asking if Nurse Deane was at liberty. I said, of course, that she was in a post and I expected she would be there for some time. He said that his wife had had her once before, and was very anxious to engage her again. I told him we had another nurse, but he asked if there was any likelihood of her being free in the near future. Naturally, I said I couldn't tell him anything definite about that."

"Did you happen to mention she was with me?"

"I can't be certain." Matron sounded a little guilty. "I may have mentioned the address, but. . . ."

"So that's how he found out? I see. You may be hearing more of this."

"Really, Mrs. Trentham . . ."

Mrs. Trentham, however, hadn't been an autocrat for sixty years for nothing.

" Have you got someone else you can send me in the interim ? " she said. " Someone bright and young ? "

" I'm afraid at the moment there's nobody. Did Nurse Deane give you no indication of her plans."

" I've had a telephone message—not from her—to say she'll be away for a few days. A few weeks is more likely in my opinion. However, if you read the *Post* to-morrow you'll probably hear all about it. It won't be my nephew's fault if you don't."

And without giving the discomfited woman any opportunity for further questions Mrs. Trentham rang off.

" And now, Roger," she observed in stately tones, " perhaps you would like to instruct Ellen in her new duties."

" Pleasure is mine," said Roger. " Ring for the old dumb-bell, will you ? "

In spite of her anger, Mrs. Trentham couldn't help chuckling a little. It would be pleasant to see Ellen meet her match.

" Oh Ellen," said Roger with the cheerful insensitiveness of the young male dealing with domestic situations, " my aunt's just had the most romantic news about Miss Deane."

" Yes, Mr. Roger ? " said the gaunt, unsmiling woman, looking about as interested as if he'd told her he'd brought twopennyworth of fish for the cat.

" Her young man's appeared in a whirlwind like the prophet in the Old Testament and swept her off. He doesn't think she's safe here."

Ellen bridled. " I'm sure I don't know. . . ."

" There was a mysterious death at the last house she was in," remarked Roger solemnly.

" I didn't know." He wouldn't have thought it possible for her to look more disapproving than she had done on arrival, but somehow she achieved it. " In that case, it may be as well she's gone."

" Ellen, I'm shocked at you if you think she had designs on my aunt. No, no, hers is a delightful story and I'm only sorry we haven't got a picture of the devoted young man to pair off with the one Mrs. Trentham's given me of her. Doesn't young love move your heart, Ellen ? "

" I'm sure Nurse was safe enough here," returned Ellen, totally unmoved.

" Lots of people have thought that, till they've found themselves murdered, and then it was too late."

The woman nodded conclusively. " I'm sure Madam doesn't wish to get mixed up with a murder," she observed.

" You're a fool, Ellen," snapped Mrs. Trentham. " You know quite well there's nothing I should adore more. I shall never forgive that girl for going off and keeping all the fun to herself."

" She had a flighty look," commented Ellen inaccurately.

" Of course, my aunt is the main sufferer. No one in the house to do a thing for her, in the way of nursing, I mean. Nurse Deane was clever. . . ."

" I'm sure I can look after Madam," said Ellen scornfully, as he had known she would, " as well as any young piece like that. And what's more, it's to be hoped she's not coming back."

" I shall certainly look forward to seeing her again," was Mrs. Trentham's forceful comment. " I want to know more about this young man. Besides, even as a girl, I always liked to be in at the kill."

" I'm afraid you have a bloodthirsty nature, Aunt May. Well, I shall have to be getting back. Don't forget to ring me the minute you have any news. This story's going over big, or my name isn't Roger Trentham."

" It proves one thing," said Mrs. Trentham in absorbed tones to her elderly attendant, as that long-suffering and not very skilful creature prepared her for bed. " Don't pull my hair, Ellen. You may not believe it, but it is actually attached to my head. As I was saying, it proves she did know something. I wish I knew what it was. Life's very unfair, Ellen."

" Yes, Madam," agreed Ellen stonily, handing her employer the little shawl she always wore over her head at night. She had had a hard life herself, but she had long ago adopted the convenient doctrine that suffering implies virtue in the sufferer and this maintained her through all vicissitudes.

" Here's this girl, who doesn't appreciate it in the least, mixed up in a murder and I, who'd give my eyes for the chance . . ."

" You may have it yet," returned Ellen in her uncompromising way. " And you can say what you please, Madam, but murder's like the doodle-bug. Where they've been once they come again. If you ask me, it's a good thing Nurse has gone, and if you take my advice you won't have her back here, not if that's the kind she is. You know cook's weakness—

faints at the sight of blood. She tells me it's nothing but will-power makes it possible for her to cook a juicy steak."

" She can't have to exert much will-power these days," returned Mrs. Trentham unsympathetically. " I suppose that's why I always get this insipid white meat for my ration."

Even X. might have found it difficult to get the better of Mrs. Trentham. On the whole, it seemed a pity there was so little likelihood of their meeting.

CHAPTER FOURTEEN

How cheerfully he seems to grin, how neatly spreads his claws
And welcomes little fishes in with gently-smiling jaws.
—LEWIS CARROLL.

THE MORNING after Nora Deane's dramatic disappearance from Green Valley, Sammy Parker was up early. He collected his *Daily Post* from the doorstep before he had his bath, and the first thing he saw was his name sprawled all across the front page.

LONE PIT MURDER
NEW ROMANTIC DEVELOPMENT

and then in letters that looked as though they demanded neon lighting :

WHO IS SAMMY?

Roger Trentham had certainly spread himself on this affair. Half-fascinated, half-appalled—because great efficiency in other men is apt to have that effect on the inefficient—Sammy digested a feast more stimulating than a 1945 breakfast.

I was after all unable to interview Miss Deane, the young nurse in attendance on Mrs. Adela Newstead of Charlbury, whose husband, Alfred Newstead, was recently found foully murdered in a remote quarry, for when I reached the house where she was employed yesterday afternoon it was to learn that she had received a mysterious telegram signed Sammy and had already left. Miss Deane, it is believed,

107

had evidence of vital importance that might have assisted the police to solve the Lone Pit Mystery, evidence of such weight that " Sammy," who has so far refused to reveal his identity, has carried her off " for safety."

I spoke to Sammy on the phone last night.

" I am sorry to disappoint the public," he told me, " but my first duty is to Miss Deane who is, I believe, in serious danger. I have persuaded her to put herself in my care until I am satisfied that it is safe for her to return to her work—i. e. when the police have apprehended the murderer of Alfred Newstead."

This development adds one more mysterious factor to a case that is already teasing some of the best brains of the Force. I pressed Sammy to tell me his full name, but he only laughed.

" I guess Sammy'll do to go on with," he said. He is understood to have met 'Miss Deane recently in romantic circumstances.

" I intend to look after her until I am convinced that her peril is past," he wound up. " And by that time I hope she will be convinced that I may be counted upon to look after her for ever."

" Did I really say all that ? " Sammy reflected, throwing the paper on the floor and picking it up again to look at the photograph of the missing girl. " Well, I'll hand it to this fellow—he earns his pay."

All the same, he was disconcerted and distressed. Life, it seemed, was always on your heels, and not content with catching you up, overtook you and put down obstacles over which you were pretty certain to take a header. There wasn't, he realised, an instant to lose. That paragraph spelt danger in capital letters, and not only to Nora Deane. The *Daily Post* advertised a reading public of about a million and a half, and all of them would be gulping down this morning's instalment and waiting eagerly for the next. When life's at stake a man has to go carefully, but he can't afford to waste time or run unnecessary risks.

" I've got to come into the open," Sammy decided, getting to his feet, " and that means I'm ripe to be shot at. Still, the press will hound me out if I don't make the first move."

He considered the matter during the fastest bath and shave on record, then raced down the stairs of his apartment house, saw a crawling taxi, snapped it up under the nose of a party of American officers and was driven to 123 Bloomsbury Street, where Mr. Arthur Crook held a watching brief for all and sundry, including those who feared, with justification, the too keen interest of the police in their activities. It appeared, when he had mounted the 180 stairs, this being one of the frequent days when the lift was out of order, that Mr. Crook had not yet arrived.

" Gone on the 40 hour week campaign, I suppose," snapped Sammy, walking up and down like the proverbial caged lion and reviewing the story he had to tell.

After a comparatively short time what appeared to be the last of the rocket-bombs came shooting into the office with such velocity that the visitor would scarcely have been surprised to see the furniture fall apart from blast.

He said as much.

" It wouldn't surprise me either," said Mr. Crook. " I could make better stuff than this out of an old packing-case and a penn'-orth of tin-tacks. Well, well, soldier from the wars returning, while we kept the home fires burning—what can I do for you ? I've got a nice line in forgeries at the moment."

" Not interested, I'm afraid," said Sammy, in a dry voice. " Have you by any chance seen the *Post* this morning ? "

" Not by chance," said Crook. " I always see the *Post*. Never know when I may not be called in, one side or t'other."

" Then you've seen this charming story about me and Miss Deane."

" That kind of yarn always rings the bell with me," said Crook enthusiastically. " Galahad can always be backed for a place. What am I supposed to do ? Give the bride away ? "

" Quit fooling," said Sammy. " Crook, I know no more about that telegram than you or any other reader of the *Post*."

" Which telegram ? " demanded Crook. " There seem to have been two."

" Oh, I don't mean the one they reproduced. I mean the one signed Sammy."

" Well, well," said Crook with the air of one offering consolation, " more fellows know Tom Fool than Tom Fool knows. It's clear someone knew the girl would fall for a line like that. How well did you know her, by the way ? "

" Well enough to want to know her better."

" And how long did that take ? "

Sammy hesitated.

" Come on," said Crook.

" I met her once," returned Sammy with an air of defiance, " but . . ."

" I know," said Crook, " I know. Whoever loved that loved not at first sight. But you take my tip, Sammy boy, loving at first sight's all right if you don't let it go any further. A lot of these fellows don't take a second look till after they're tied up, and that's how the trouble begins."

" I meant to see her the next day," pursued Sammy doggedly. " I told her I'd call for her at two. But when I got there she'd gone, and that old—Newstead—wouldn't give me her address. Said he didn't know it. If you ask me, he didn't want any enquiries made about the late Mrs. N."

" It could be," agreed Crook, " it could be. Still, you didn't let a little thing like that stand in your way."

" How would you find a girl whose name you knew and the fact that she had violet eyes and a small mouth and whose voice you could recognise but whose face you'd never seen properly, if she disappeared into the blue overnight ? " demanded Sammy interestedly.

" I don't answer questions like that unless I'm being paid for it. But I tell you this. If I'd given up heart the way you gay Lotharios do I'll still be on the bottom rung of the ladder of fame."

" Instead of standing dizzily at the top liable to come a cropper any minute," Sammy sounded disagreeable.

" So you didn't know where she was."

" What's more," growled Sammy, " no one can prove I did."

" Well, you know best," agreed Crook, pushing his billy-cock on to the back of his head, a sign that he meant business. " I take it, by the way, your interest in this case is purely romantic."

" You could," suggested Sammy, " say I'm as interested in self-preservation as the next fellow. I've been making a habit of it for years. . . ."

" Quite so." Mr. Crook sounded soothing. He'd fought in the first World War himself and he knew what a lot in the way of self-preservation a war can teach you. " Well, what are you afraid of ? "

" Isn't it as plain as the nose on your face and can I say plainer than that ? " demanded Sammy, rudely. " Someone had his own reasons for wanting this girl out of the way. He sends her a telegram signed with my name. . . ."

" Knowing that'll bring her."

" Well, I guess so."

" You guess quite a lot, don't you ? " said Crook. " The girl doesn't seem to have shown any wild interest in you to date. She could have left a note for you at Askew Avenue."

" There was no knowing that I'd get it. Besides, she was probably upset, didn't think of anything but how quickly she could get out. Anyway, however pig-headed you are, you'll agree that if she has disappeared something pretty bad has probably happened to her by now."

Crook took off the billycock hat and slammed it on the table. " If you're asking me, Sammy, the whole thing has a phoney ring about it. Now, you're prejudiced. I don't say it's not natural, but it makes a difference."

" What's phoney about it ? " asked Sammy, hotly.

" It don't strike you as queer that a girl you'd only met once should come out in the rain to meet you, like a bird ? "

" Remember, she'd had one telegram warning her she was in danger."

" Unsigned. I remember. Sammy, suppose she knew who'd sent that wire ? "

" Then she wouldn't have left Mrs. Trentham's house ! "

" Why not ? Every girl who disappears ain't been abducted or sandbagged or ravished and left in a ditch for dead. Some of 'em drop out because it suits their book. Now, try and see this thing sensibly. This girl seems to have known something she didn't pass on. Some writing chap announces that he's goin' to interview her. Well, we hear a lot about the power of the press, and we all know a hell of a lot about the power of the Home Secretary, and what's a copper but the Home Secretary's representative ? If she didn't want to hide whatever it was she knew she wouldn't have gone dashin' out into the storm anyway. Now, you've admitted yourself you don't know anything about this girl. You met her one night in a fog—what were you doing there, by the way ? "

" Over-ran my station and had come up for air."

Crook surveyed him critically. " Oh well," he said, " I daresay it'll pass. I ain't doin' the prosecutin'. Now, suppose that telegram was a code between the pair of them ? "

" The pair ? "

" Wake up ! " said Crook, impatiently. " She met some-

one, didn't she ? And it's common sense to suppose that that
someone also knew a bit about the Lone Pit affair that he'd
not care for the police to learn. It's goin' to be dangerous to
her and maybe death to him. He's safer at the minute than
she is. For one thing, she may give the show away without
meanin' to, she may be trapped into it or terrorised into it.
He knows that and he's not taking chances. Well, then, he
sends her this wire to get her away from the house."

" And hides her somewhere ? How do you know it won't be
in a cemetery ? That's the safest place there is."

Crook shook his head. " You're not much of a murderer,
Sammy. Oh, it's easy enough to whack someone over the
head, but it's not so easy to explain afterwards just how it
happened, and explain it in a way that'll satisfy the police.
And they use your name because, if there is trouble, you're
to hold the baby. After all—get this, Sammy—if she's on the
level why hasn't she been to the police on her own account ? "

" Would you ? " Sammy's retort was savage in its
simplicity.

" Well, maybe not, Sammy boy, but then I'm a hardened
case. I know the police. If she's as innocent as you think
she looks, she wouldn't know."

" Then your suggestion is they're in on this together ? "

" I only say it could be, Sammy, it could be. Be able to tell
you more about it in a few days."

" But what on earth would Nora Deane get out of it ? "

" Depends how generous X. is. You know what they say,
Sammy, the heart is deceitful and desperately wicked. Now,
forget she's your dream-girl for a minute and see things
straight. She's young and she's working for a living, and
nurses ain't paid all that much. And it's a wearin' life and
unless you can persuade some senile old dodderer to put you
in his will, and even if you do everyone talks, you're liable to
be left hangin' on to life by the skin of your teeth by the time
you're about fifty. Well, she's got no friends, no relatives, only
herself. Oh, I daresay she came innocently enough to this
job. Then something happens, something a bit out of the
way. A woman dies in suspicious circumstances. She can't
pit herself against a doctor, but she goes to see this Webster
fellow. Now why, why not let things alone ? "

" Perhaps Mrs. Newstead had asked her. Oh hell, I know
what you're going to say. That she only had an infinitesimal
chance of talking to her, but it is a chance."

112

"**And suppose** she did ? You really think the girl would carry on the case after Mrs. Newstead was dead ? Why ? Unless she saw a chance of making a bit on the side."

" You've got the instincts of a vulture," exclaimed Sammy angrily.

" Just tryin' to see things straight," Crook corrected him. He didn't take offence. He said that no wise man allows himself to feel insulted in business.

"" Besides, it would take a lot of guts for a girl like that to go to the police. Newstead would have raised hell, and suppose she couldn't prove anything ? She's got to consider her future."

" My point exactly," agreed Crook, folding his hands over his comfortable paunch.

" You mean, you think she'd stoop to . . ."

" Now then," warned Crook hastily, " no hard words. Say the girl saw a chance to put by a bit for her old age. Now, just suppose Herbert Webster is mixed up in this affair, and bein' sensible chaps, the pair of us, we damn' well know he is, and he puts the position to her that it's goin' to be damn' unpleasant if she starts bein' questioned by the police—well, what would you do ? "

" Lie low and say nuffin ? She didn't seem to me that sort of girl."

" It could be a bit uncomfortable for her. It's the duty of every citizen to support the police force—you know that one, Sammy—and every good citizen simply sits like a frog in front of a fly, eyes bulgin' and tummy all aquake, to do this duty. Besides, there's such a thing as accessory after the fact."

" So that's the attitude you're going to adopt ? "

" No, no," said Crook quickly, thinking he wouldn't much care to be the fellow that Sammy didn't like. " I never said I wasn't ready to take chances. Matter of fact, they're meat and drink to me, as well as bread and butter. Only remember chance plays both ways, and if you should find your girl isn't Florence Nightingale and Nurse Cavell rolled into one, don't blame me. Now, you go and have a Turkish bath or something and leave this to me."

" What are you going to do ? " asked Sammy cautiously.

" What you're payin' me to do. Show that whoever abducted this young woman it wasn't you."

" I don't like it," said Sammy abruptly. " I don't like it a

113

bit. Why did he suggest Holt Cross for the meeting ? There
are other places round there much bigger and more likely for
a couple who don't want to be noticed. The only road out of
Holt Cross leads to the cliffs, and what the hell's anybody
doing on cliffs at this time of the year ? "

" I could make a guess," said Crook unemotionally. " If I
wanted to make a getaway I'd get my girl to come to some
godforsaken place, and be as noticeable as possible. Then
they'd start lookin' for me there."

" And you'd have slipped up to London or something ?
My God, if only the police were efficient this sort of thing
couldn't happen."

Crook didn't attempt to answer anything so silly as that,
and Sammy had the grace to blush.

" You going down to Green Valley ? " he suggested.
" There's a good train in twenty minutes."

" There's a good one in two hours and twenty minutes, too.
I've got to do a bit of ferreting first. Spade-work, you know."

" And by the time you're through with that I daresay the
local authorities will be doing a bit more spade-work on the
girl's account."

" If she's still alive she's in no special danger," Crook
pointed out. " If she isn't, it's too late to do anything. But
I promise you one thing, we'll find her, dead or alive. Remember, Crook always gets his man—and that goes for women,
too." He banged a little bell on his table and Bill Parsons
came in.

" Meet Mr. Parker," said Crook. " His name's all over the
papers—that is, Britain's Most Dashing Daily."

" Interested in the lady ? " murmured Bill. You couldn't
get him either elated or cast down. " Interesting case."

" Interesting my foot. You might be a lot of damned
curators in a bloody Museum the way you talk. This girl
is . . ."

" We know, we know." He nodded to Bill and Bill contrived, without seeming to do so, to get the young man away.
At the door Sammy turned and said, " Sure you won't be getting that train ? " and Crook smiled and said he was quite
sure.

" And you trust your Uncle Arthur," he said. " He's like
that brand of suspenders that never let you down."

After the door had closed behind the young man, Crook sat
for some time deep in thought. He didn't like the position at

all, and the more he considered it the less he liked it. He had, of course, kept a file on the case, with notes of police enquiries and results, and this he now consulted. He noted a number of points, frowned over them and shouted again for Bill.

"That chap who's just gone," he said, "he might be difficult."

"I gathered you thought that," agreed Bill.

"These chaps are all the same," Crook continued, rather unfairly. "They wait till a position's practically hopeless and then they call in the doctor. Who am I to do the police's job for them? and who's going to thank me if I do? And if it's the other way . . ." He fell silent, his big stubborn chin in his big freckled hands. "Were you ever in the wrong, Bill?" he asked after a pause.

Bill frowned. He walked across to the window and he limped a little as he went. In the days before he was on the side of the angels he had been up against the authorities professionally, and even now he knew more of the whereabouts of certain famous jewels than the police did. But a bullet in his heel some years earlier had put an end to all that. You can conceal a lot of things if you know how to but a limp isn't one of them.

"I shouldn't have run that night," he said slowly. "Then I might only have got five years. As it is, I got a life-sentence."

"My good angel was on the look-out if yours was having a quick one," returned Crook heartlessly. He sometimes, though not often, acknowledged he didn't know what he'd do without Bill. "Nice to know you're wrong sometimes, even you," he went on. "Bill, I have a feeling I'm going to come an unholy mucker over this, or else end by finding something I'd rather not know.'

"I thought it might be that way," said Bill. "It beats me why people pay so much to learn the truth when the other thing's so much more comfortable and about a quarter the price."

Crook settled back in his chair. He outlined the plan he had already formed. He told Bill what he himself intended to do and what Bill was to do. He said they'd better look out in case Sammy, with an eye to the best, threw a spanner into the works. He said it was a pity the police didn't trust him, because they might have been quite helpful just now.

Bill said, "Maybe they're sorry you don't trust them," and Crook with a sudden grin, said it was like Private Enterprise

115

against the Community Undertaking, he being private enterprise. Then he clapped on his billycock and went round to the garage and fetched out the little red car known as the Scourge and got down to it.

CHAPTER FIFTEEN

The lucrative business of mystery.—EDMUND BURKE.

EVER SINCE morning the telephone and front door bell at Mrs. Trentham's house at Green Valley had been ringing. The new development in the Lone Pit Murder appeared to have attracted as much attention as even Roger Trentham could have anticipated. Mrs. Trentham, who began by being excited and thrilled, presently became bored and later resentful. This, she felt, was Roger's particular pigeon. She didn't mean to give anything away to the representatives of rival publications. When a servant came in and said that a Mr. Crook was asking for her, she snapped, " I can't see anyone else. I'm tired '

" It's me or the police," said a voice from the threshold.

She looked up to see a rather stout gentleman clad in a ginger suit, with a bright brown billycock in his hand.

" Are you the press ? " she demanded.

" Lady ! " Mr. Crook sounded hurt. " Do I look like the press ? "

" Then who are you ? "

" I represent Sammy."

" The one who sent the telegram ? "

" The one who didn't send the telegram."

" What's that ? " She faced him with spirit, a spirit of complete antagonism, he understood.

" I said he didn't send it."

" But it had his name on it."

" So it had. And quite a lot of my clients present cheques with names on them that were never written by the owners. It's an art."

" Are you drunk ? " asked Mrs. Trentham bluntly.

Crook looked hurt again. " At this hour of the day ? "

" Then what do you want ? "

" Sammy wants me to find out what happened to the girl."

She stiffened more than ever. " Roger—my nephew—is doing that."

" Even Scotland Yard has its Big Five," said Crook. " Your nephew's middle name may be Northcliffe, but he can't have the whole field to himself."

" If you do find her you won't give the story to another paper first ? "

" It's all odds if I do find her I'll call the police right away," was Mr. Crook's grim retort.

" You mean, you think something's *happened* ? "

" Well, what do you think ? She gets a fake telegram and disappears and you get a fake message. Does it sound like good clean fun to you ? "

" I told her she didn't know enough about this man."

" Considering she's met him once and in a fog at that—he told me he'd recognise her voice again but he never really saw her face—I'd say she was a pretty fast worker."

" Anyway, I want her to meet Roger. I don't think this Sammy person can be much use if he lets other people use his name and abduct his girl."

" You're a daisy," said Crook approvingly. " If Roger's half the man you are he'll go a long way."

" And what do you think I can tell you ? " enquired Mrs. Trentham suddenly realising her opportunities and becoming cosy.

" What she looked like, what she wore—got another photograph you can give me ? "

" I might," conceded Mrs. Trentham. " But there was one in the paper. That was the best. Roger said so."

" Roger ever seen the girl ? "

" No. Of course he hasn't. He would have done, but . . ."

" I know," said Mr. Crook. " Who's afraid of the Big Bad Wolf ? Well, I am, for one. What your Roger means is it's the nicest pin-up picture of the lot. Which is the one that's most like her ? "

Mrs. Trentham, revelling in the situation—she was one of those single-minded women who don't allow themselves to consider more than one aspect of any matter at a time—pored over the pictures and finally selected one.

" I think that's as good as any."

Crook took it with thanks, inwardly reflecting that by the time he and the girl met it very likely wouldn't matter which of the pictures he'd taken, she'd be so unlike any of them. He gratefully accepted one for the road and departed with enough backfiring to scare any enemy parachutist who might have landed that morning. He had taken the precaution to bring a map with him, and from this he deduced that Holt Cross was practically a cul-de-sac. The only road leading out of it, in addit on to the one he was on, seemed to go for miles over uncultivated countryside as far as the coast, with one branch road forking south to Lestingham. Lestingham was best known for the big lunatic asylum there, that had been erected ten years earlier. The residents had objected to the plan, but had been overruled by the Town Council, who saw its possibilities. And the Town Council had been justified. The asylum had put Lestingham on the map. Now it was a flourishing resort. Crook supposed that the lunatics' relations had started the fashion of going there, or else were taking stock of their possible future surroundings. Whichever it might be Lestingham was now popular and well-to-do. It seemed to him that the spurious " Sammy " of the telegram might well have taken this road.

Before he followed his example, however, he made a few enquiries. It seemed to him obvious that a car had been used, and though the hope was not a very strong one he began to nose round on the chance of finding some spectator who had noticed a car hanging about round Market War Memorial or perhaps a girl wearing a light blue oilskin hood dashing across from the bus stop to enter it. It was one of his theories that many murderers and indeed criminals of all kind are brought low by some event against which it was impossible to guard. It was the woman walking her dog, the invalid watching life from an upper window, the street hawker, the professional beggar, who often supplied him with the necessary clue.

And so it was in this case.

He found it was generally safest to grasp your nettle boldly and at all events make a show of putting your cards on the table. (This mixture of metaphors was typical of him, as a good many people had observed.) There was a man selling fruit and flowers by the kerb and he made for him direct. He bought some of the fruit and while he waited for the change asked casually, " You here yesterday ? "

" I'm always here," said the man. " Wet or fine. The day I'm not here you'll know I'm in my coffin—or it's the end of the world."

" Happen to notice a car standing by the Memorial about midday ? " asked Crook.

The man was instantly suspicious. " What business is that of yours ? " He broke off to serve someone else with some flowers.

" I'll tell you. There was a chap waiting here yesterday to meet a girl—and he met her. I represent the girl's family. They want to find that couple before it's too late."

" You mean, before she . . . ? "

" You don't want me to tell you what I mean. They weren't going off to get married, if that's what you're thinking. And we want to get that girl back."

" Maybe he did marry her," said the hawker, counting threepenny bits and dropping them into a little canvas bag.

" That don't seem very likely. Of course, the girl was a fool to come, but she'll be worse than a fool if someone doesn't stop it."

" I remember the fellow," said the hawker. " Asked me if it was all right to park here. Well, the car park's down behind the Dragon, but it was raining a bit and the police weren't so up-and-doing as usual. Now I come to think of it, he said he had to meet someone off the bus."

" That's the chap," said Crook. " If this were a novel you'd have noticed the number of the car."

" I can tell you that, too," said the hawker calmly, " a bit of it anyhow. There was a dame came up with a kid, and you know the game these kids play, counting the numbers of cars. You begin with 1 and then you wait till you see a car numbered 2 and so on. Well, this kid had her eyes all over the place and suddenly she screamed out, ' Look, there's a 29. Now isn't it lucky we came ? I wish we could see 30 before we go back ! "

" You ought to be in the Force," said Crook, " and I'd buy some flowers if I knew any girl who'd take 'em. Went east, I suppose ? "

" That's right."

Crook nodded and went off. He had been lucky, but not luckier than he had anticipated. He said luck was a matter of desert. The people who deserved it got it. He generally did. There was only one alternative to the cliff road and that led to Lestingham, but he didn't think the car had gone that way. If, as he suspected, the car was a stolen one, there might be too many people about in a biggish town for the driver to take the risk. Besides, sooner or later the girl must recognise her peril and she might do her best to attract attention—any girl who wasn't a complete gumph would, and though she'd been a fool to drag Herbert Webster into this affair it argued a certain amount of courage and character to take the chance —and the murderer wouldn't want that. So Crook took the left road and bumped over a very poor path that might, reflected Crook grimly, be all very well for cattle for whom it had presumably been made, and presently found himself on a better road and decided to stop at the pub that was marked on his map—he chose his map because it was one of a series that marked all the pubs even the little ones—and see if anyone there had seen the car. There wouldn't be many coming by in this weather and with no destination in view suitable to any honest man.

He looked at his watch. It was the least promising time to arrive at a pub. A little after four. He doubted whether there was much to be done this evening, and the Boar didn't sound the sort of place that would make you very comfortable for the night. Still he cherished the belief that pubs are the places for ambitious men to collect information.

" I don't give a damn for a teetotaller in our line of business," he would tell Bill. " They're cutting off their income to please their conscience. The things I've picked up in pubs. Pubs are the common denominator. Each man's as good as his neighbour provided he can pay his whack. Y'know, there are times, Bill, when I believe I was cut out to be a lay preacher."

So to the Boar he went, and, as usual, his faith was justified.

Mrs. Blackman was a firm supporter of the *Daily Post*. Living in a remote spot with a taciturn husband, she found in its pages the company, the colour and some of the excitement her individual life lacked. It was because the *Post's* owners understood the temperament of people like Maggie Blackman that they could proudly advertise a rising circulation, and if it hadn't been for the unsportsmanlike action of the President of the Board of Trade in limiting paper supplies they'd probably be near their third million by this time.

On the morning after the visit of the strange couple she came down very thoughtfully, secretly very anxious, though she was too wise to confide her doubts to her husband. Most of the night, lying sleepless, she had seen against the darkness the frantic face of the girl as she thrust her arm through the broken glass of the car window, crying, "I'm not married. You can see I've got no ring."

Taken by surprise, accustomed to yielding to her difficult, disillusioned husband, influenced by a natural disinclination to put herself in trouble's way, she had taken no action, and indeed even now, she reflected, sweeping out the sitting-room behind the bar, it was not easy to see what action she could have taken in the circumstances. All the same, she was uneasy. The man's story didn't ring true, and if the girl was in her right mind, then the position didn't bear contemplating.

"There was something wrong," she told herself wretchedly, stooping to collect the paper. "We shall hear more of that couple," and she looked at the front page as if she expected to see their history blazoned there. What she did see was the picture of a girl, with a charming gay face smiling back at her. She stood very still. At first she thought she was the victim of an illusion, but when she looked again there they were, the small irregular features, the youthful independence and buoyancy. . . . She had been distrait yesterday and no wonder—but though she longed to deny the fact, *this was the same girl.*

"It's her," she muttered and bent her head to read the letterpress.

"Miss Nora Deane, the young nurse who disappeared yesterday in the company of her fiancé, Sammy."

And then "Exclusive to the *Daily Post*," and underneath that the reproduction of a telegram.

"That wasn't any fiancé," Mrs. Blackman told herself, horror informing her face. She remembered how the man had called the girl Moira and how she had protested, holding out her handkerchief with the initials N. D. on it.

"If that was Sammy he was up to no good," she assured herself. "What ought I to do? Tell Joe? The police? He'll never stand for that. He'll say it's no affair of ours. I thought it was queer at the time. Even in a fog it 'ud be hard to miss the Lestingham road."

And she recalled, too, the car that had slid past so stealthily later in the evening, with every light extinguished.

Joe came in a few minutes later, while she was still trying to make up her mind what should be done, and said, "I'm going out for a while. What's the matter?"

She said, " It's this bit in the paper. Look."

He shook his head impatiently. " I've no time for papers this hour of the day. Nor, for that matter, have you."

The face she turned to him stopped him halfway to the door. " You don't understand, Joe. It's a matter for the police."

He scowled. " Not for me, thank you. It never does a public any good getting mixed up with the police."

She said in a whisper, grey as crumbling ash, " It's murder or something like it."

He said harshly, " There's nothing like murder. Either it is or it isn't what are you talking about anyway ? " all in one breath without a pause between his sentences.

She held out the paper towards him and this time he took it. " What is all this ? "

" That's the girl who came last night, the girl who's missing."

He read the caption. " Well ? It's nothing to do with us if a girl goes off with a chap."

" She wasn't going off with a chap and well you know it. She was terrified, that's why we thought she was mad. I daresay she was mad—with fear."

" She was mad, all right, mad as a coot."

" You'd be mad if someone was taking you away to murder you."

" Where did you get this idea of murder from ? It's my belief you're a bit mad yourself this morning."

" He was taking her away against her will, and she told us she was going to be murdered."

Joe shrugged. " That kind of thing's not evidence. Lots of women talk about murder, without meaning a thing."

" Oh, you know I'm right, but you don't want any unpleasantness."

" You're dead right, I don't. I've had enough for one life-time." He'd been one of the men who hadn't been so lucky in the gas warfare of the first Great War, and he'd bear the scars, physical and mental, for the rest of his days. He skimmed through Roger Trentham's column. " This isn't a case for the police. They won't thank us for butting in. This is just a stunt, the sort of thing a newspaper runs to send up its sales. Some young fellow thinks he can go one better than the authorities and he stages a special interview. . . . Why, it wouldn't surprise me if the whole thing were a put-up job, girl and all. Probably they're counting on you dragging the police in. If it were what you think, would they have called here ? "

" If they ran out of petrol they'd have to. They'd probably count on the bad weather preventing us recognising them again."

" Which it would. I wouldn't swear to either of them and I'll tell the world so."

" I'd know the girl, I'd swear to her anywhere. Besides, there's something else—Joe, after the car had turned back for Lestingham last night, it came back."

" Came back here ? "

" Yes, it went past, with all its lights out."

" If it had its lights out you can't possibly have seen if it was the same car."

" How often do cars go past here in the winter when there are no excursions ? They're as rare as butterflies in December. That car went past in the direction of the cliffs ; you know this road goes nowhere else. That fellow never meant to get to Lestingham any more than he was ever married to the girl."

Joe Blackman was stubborn. " We didn't do anything but sell them some petrol and give them a cup of tea. . . . '

" Joe ! " Her face was deathly white. " I hadn't thought of that. He made me put a pellet in her cup, said it was a sedative the doctor had given him for her if she got violent. And I swallowed it—his story, I mean. For all I know it was poison."

" When they find the girl's body you can start having hysterics," said Joe coldly. " And if it was poison it's not likely he'd give the pellet to you. Have some sense, Maggie. You should be ashamed, a woman of your age, behaving like a girl at the pictures."

" That road to the cliffs goes by the caves," said Maggie dully. " Perhaps that's where she is at this minute—in the caves."

Joe lost his temper. " And I suppose I take the car and go after her "

" It's too late," said Maggie in the same dull voice. " He'd need to know the path down, though . . . How was the tide when they came yesterday ? "

" Too high to get into Big Hole. If he knew about the path he could make Little Hole, I daresay," acknowledged Joe grudgingly. " But there's no sense putting her there."

123

" Who's likely to look in those caves for weeks to come ?
The tourist season's over now till Easter. By then there'll be
no telling how or when she died or even who she was. Joe, if
this is murder . . ."

" Even if it's murder it doesn't do a publican any good,"
repeated Joe stubbornly. " I've had enough of the limelight.
All I want now is a little peace and quiet." He dashed the
paper down and brushed past her.

Maggie sighed. It was no good arguing with him in this
mood. She remembered his wound, his period of imprisonment
in an enemy camp, his attempt to break out and subsequent
recapture, the penalty exacted for his insolence in trying to
get away—you never altogether got over that, it seemed.
All he wanted these days was to be allowed to exist unnoticed,
left to his own devices. That was why he'd insisted on coming
to this solitary place. Crazy—that was what Susan said about
him. Lucky not to be shut up, she said. When you've been
through what Joe has you can start talking about being crazy,
Maggie stormed, and even from herself she concealed her fear
of this quiet, moody desperately stubborn man. Now she was
torn between a desire to do what she believed to be the right
thing and fear of consequences to herself and her husband if
she did. It wouldn't do a man with Joe's troubled mind any
good to be dragged into the witness-box, hectored perhaps. . . .
All the same, it wasn't any sense trying to persuade herself
she was hunting an imaginary hare. She knew the girl she'd
seen the day before was Nora Deane !

And when later on the young man came down asking
questions she was more convinced than ever.

After that things happened thick and fast, fast, that is, for
so quiet a place where you hardly saw a stranger once in a
month. . . .

About four o'clock someone rang the side door bell and
when she opened the door she found a thickset man in a
ginger-coloured suit with a ginger-coloured hat on the back
of his head, and a voice as ginger as the rest of him.

" Any chance of a cup of tea ? " he asked. It was best to
begin that way with a woman. Later he might see the landlord
and contrive to have one on the house.

The woman stepped back and was about to admit him when
a door opened down the passage and a dark surly man looked
out.

" We don't serve teas," he announced in a short voice.

" You'll have my death on your conscience if you don't,"
said Crook, and could have sworn that the woman started.

" I've told you, we don't serve teas."

" Whose car's that ? " enquired Crook conversationally,
pointing to a car that stood in a little yard at the side of the
pub.

" It's the young gentleman's, Joe," said the woman quickly.
" And as we're serving one tea, though my husband's right,
we don't do it as a rule, we might as well serve two."

" That's the ticket," said Crook, entering briskly.

There was a young man having tea in the sitting-room
behind the bar, a cheerful spruce young man whom Crook
had never seen before but whom he recognised at once. Mrs.
Trentham's sitting-room had been full of photographs of him.
Roger Trentham equally recognised Crook. In his line, he
said, you have to know the pro's. Crook waited till his tea
had arrived and then said, " Did Auntie put you on to this ? "
and Roger Trentham said, " She flew for the telephone the
minute you were gone. You know, it's a pity Auntie May
wasn't a newspaper man. She's so public-spirited she'd have
committed a murder herself sooner than leave the paper
without news."

" Any luck ? " asked Crook.

" So Sammy says he didn't send that wire," reflected Roger.

" So he came to see you ? I thought he would."

" Breathing tongues of flame, swearing he'll have the paper's
guts. He's got it badly over that girl, hasn't he ? "

" You know what I think of amateurs givin' their opinions
and buttin' in on the professionals' preserves," returned
Crook, " and I'm the amateur here, but since you ask me, I'd
say he minded like hell what happened to her."

" Better and better," said Mr. Trentham blissfully. " Only
thing is—we've got to hurry. One chap's got here before me
now—not sure who he is yet."

" Aren't you ? " Mr. Crook looked astonished. " Well,
after this morning's para. there's only one person it's likely
to be. . . ."

" Like that, is it ? " Mr. Trentham nodded.

Crook took most of the jam on his knife. " Get anything
out of mine host ? "

" He's very cagey. *She's* terrified he'll find out she rang
up."

" Rang you up ? "

" Rang the paper. Said she thought she had news. That was just after Auntie May. I came down hell-for-leather, got a puncture and had to change the tyre and lost about an hour."

" Whatever is is best," quoted Crook cheerfully. " If you'd got here earlier we'd have missed one another. What did she tell you ? "

" It's a damned odd yarn, too odd for her to have invented it."

Crook listened attentively to the story. " I suppose she didn't notice the number of the car."

" Have a heart," urged Roger.

Crook drummed his thick fingers on the tablecloth. " That was about twenty-four hours ago. And she thinks it was one and the same car going and coming. She's probably right, you know. And it was heading straight for the cliffs. And the girl had had a drug or something of the sort to keep her quiet. It may be a good story for you, Trentham, but it's no jam pudding for my man." He paused. " I knew I'd pick up something here," he said. " There's no place like a pub. If M.P.s and Cabinet Ministers really wanted to know the way the country was feeling about any particular trick they were plannin' they'd do well to spend less time in Parliament and more in pubs. Since they don't it proves they're either teetotallers which don't augur well for the future of the nation, no Strength through Joy movement, if you get me, or else they don't really want to know, because then they might have to do something about it."

" Well, come on," said Roger. " I've told you all I know. Suppose you give me a line now."

" Such as ? "

" Can I take it you're getting ready to pull your man in ? "

" I'm not a policeman," Crook pointed out.

" And I haven't escaped from a mental home. No, you haven't got a warrant in your pocket, but you won't need one. You never do, do you ? When you get into Who's Who you'll be able to put Catching Criminals Red-Handed for your favourite indoor sport. You know who he is, I suppose ? "

" Oh yes," agreed Crook. " I know who he is."

" Confided in the police ? " ventured Roger, ringing the bell for more hot water.

" The police don't need to learn to play ball with me. No, as a matter of fact, I didn't tumble right away. And seein' he practically put the card into my hand, that's odd. But I daresay I'm growing old. Not so limber in the joints as I used to be. And it's still 'vantage in," he added buoyantly, " because he don't know I'm on his trail. Boy, is he goin' to look surprised when I walk in some day and say, ' And how's the trade in corpses this morning ? "

Here Maggie came in with the hot water and Crook put a few questions on his own account. She said regretfully that she hadn't noticed the number of the car, but it was an Austin Ten, black, rather an old model.

" You're a daisy," said Crook. " Didn't think of getting in touch with the police, I suppose ? "

" My husband doesn't like the police," Maggie explained.

" Who does ? " enquired Crook sympathetically, " always excepting old girls who've lost a pekinese and think the police are Maskelyne and Devant."

" He won't find it too easy to get away with you and me on his tail," said Roger encouragingly.

" How green was our ally," commented Crook in his rude way. " You know, it's a funny thing about murderers. They're like dipsomaniacs. Never know when to stop. Probably there's what that chap Shakespeare calls a tide in the affairs of men—you know that bit, I daresay. Probably quoted it a dozen times. Anyway they come to a fork in the road and one path goes to safety and the other to ruin, and nine times out of ten they choose the road to ruin. Their trouble is they want to be too clever. If only they could commit their crimes and stay put, but no. They want to be sure they're safe. If this chap had lain low I daresay he'd have been secure till the end of time—his time, anyhow. . . ."

" Not with you on his track surely," suggested Roger politely.

" Shouldn't have been on his track. Now he's come into the open and we're after him and we'll get him as sure as the path of the righteous leads on to the eternal day." Crook had these poetic moods sometimes. He said it usually meant he was going to do something pretty good. " May as well be getting on," he said. He crossed to the window. " Praise the pigs, the fog's gone down. You know, one way and another there's been a lot of fog in this case. Began in one and may even have ended in one so far as the girl's concerned. But our Mr. Murderer ain't goin' to be so lucky—if you get me," he added hastily, feeling that might have been better phrased. " Well, no luck in getting one on the house, I suppose."

" I'm sorry, sir," said Maggie regretfully. " If Joe were out—but he's not, and what's more he won't be so long as he knows there are customers in the place."

" Ah well," said Crook, " I just thought it might be our last. Still—How can man die better than facing fearful odds ? Who said that ? "

" Horatius," said the better educated Mr. Trentham. " Ancient Roman," he added explanatorily.

" Oh, an Eye-tie." Crook looked disappointed: " Well, who was the other chap who saw a bright light on a road going from some place to somewhere ? "

" Another Roman," replied Roger, correctly supposing that Crook was referring to the Apostle Paul on his journey to Damascus.

" No ancient Britons ? " enquired Crook incredulously.

" *They* wouldn't have made a song about it," Roger consoled him.

" No more they would," said Crook. " How about leaving your bassinette here and coming along in the Scourge, these roads would break the heart of any decent car, but the Scourge knows what's expected of her."

So they agreed, and set out together on their perilous last lap, Crook driving and thinking pretty hard—there was about one hour of daylight still, he reflected, and about four hours' work to do—and Roger proving his worth by conscientiously doing an interview with Crook for to-morrow's edition of the *Post.*

CHAPTER SIXTEEN

It's dogged as does it.—ANTHONY TROLLOPE.

JOE BLACKMAN was more sullen that evening than ever. 'He hardly had a civil word even for the regulars. Not that that was any great change. He never welcomed strangers. Experience had made him wonder whether they spelt trouble. That was all the legacy that remained to him from four years' service overseas. The regulars, who were accustomed to him, didn't mind, though now and again one more sensitive than the rest would wonder how Maggie stood it. But not often. Sensitiveness was not one of their more notable characteristics.

" Those chaps coming here won't do me any good," growled Joe after Mr. Crook and his companion had departed. " I'll be surprised if we don't hear more of them."

The next thing they heard came from a man called Willis, who arrived on his bicycle in a state of considerable excitement soon after the bar opened and wanted to know if he could use the telephone. They knew him at the Boar as one of a gang working on local roads, a little fellow like a cock-sparrow with enormous ears. Joe looked doubtful as he always did whenever anything even remotely out of the common occurred.

" What is it ? " he said.

" Chap stopped me by the cliff road, said a car had gone over the side and he wanted the police. Give me half a crown to come back on the push-bike and put a message through."

" Did he tell you to come here ? " growled Joe.

" He did. Said he couldn't speak for the beer, as he hadn't had any, but you served champion tea."

" I told you what would happen," said Joe, unsmiling, but he led the way to the telephone just the same. " What was this chap like ? "

" Town chap, brown suit, fat as a hog. . . ."

" Well, one thing," said Joe. " I won't have the police here."

" That's awkward, Mr. Blackman. You see, I'll have to go back with them to guide them, like."

" They can come to the side-door," said Maggie quickly. " It's getting dark, no one will see."

" And if they do it won't matter," said Mr. Willis sturdily " When this story gets round it'll bring custom. They say an accident's always lucky to someone."

" I don't want that sort of custom," returned Joe in a surly voice, going off to serve some new-comers higher up the bar. Mr. Willis went ahead to telephone and then came a little nervously back to the bar. Maggie leaned across as she gave him his order.

" Mr. Willis " she said, " was there anybody in the car ? "

Willis looked up at her out of his faded blue eyes. " I don't rightly know," he said. " The chap didn't say. Daresay he didn't know, come to that. Or what he was doing there. Oh." His eyes brightened. " Maybe it was his car. Only that was standing on the cliff."

" A little red car," amplified Maggie.

He looked perplexed. " No. Not red. This was dark blue."

129

" Then there's someone else there." She caught her breath.
That car last night, she was thinking, that was a dark car.
Could he . . . ? After all, the *Daily Post* had given the matter
enough advertisement to attract the dead from their coffins.

" But cars don't go over a cliff of theirselves," continued
Mr. Willis, who had a single-track mind. " Mind you, this one
didn't go right over. Got stopped by that ledge just below
the Point. Lucky, if there is anyone in it."

" Lucky for her," agreed Maggie under her breath.

" Nasty sort of accident," continued Mr. Willis.

" If it was an accident."

" Why, but—mean to say, you think some chaps . . . Why,
Mrs. Blackman . . ."

" Supposing you had a car and the police were after it,"
said Maggie rapidly. " And suppose there was someone in the
car you didn't want the police to meet. . . ."

" Cor stone a crow ! " whispered the little man. " What do
you know, though ? "

" There was a couple here yesterday—take care, I don't
want Joe to hear all this. You know how Joe is, don't like
strangers—but this man said they were married and the girl
was daft, and she said she wasn't. . . ."

" Then maybe she was daft," said Willis. " I've heard of
plenty of females calling themselves married without their
lines, but not one that was the other way round."

" Maybe he wanted them to be married and she wouldn't."

" And he drove the pair of them over the cliff ? " Willis
sounded disgusted. " Danged if I'd do that for any female.
But maybe the gentleman came from London. They're a mad
lot there."

" I wish the police would come," said Maggie uneasily. " I
wonder if the driver knows the car is stuck on that little
platform. He may think it went down on to the rocks."
She shivered as she spoke. Just below Dead Man's Point
were some sharp black rocks, cruel, ruthless, known as the
Witches' Teeth. No hope for any car that got impaled on
them.

" Not likely. And if he did he couldn't hope a car caught
that way 'ud be fit even for scrap."

" How'll the police get the car up, Mr. Willis ? "

He wagged his head. " Easier said than done. Thanks,
Mrs. Blackman, same again. There's that path down the cliff-
side, the one they say the smugglers used to use, but whether

the soil 'ull stand up to a crane, and nothing short of a crane 'ull haul the car to the cliff-top, well, I don't know. The whole lot might come down. It's a pesky job." But he brightened at the thought that it would be the police and not ordinary citizens, human beings like himself, who would be involved.

Joe suddenly put in an appearance. " Don't you encourage her in her fancies," he said forcefully. " Any car might go over the side with the state most folks' tyres are in now and the ground like a marsh."

" Oh aye," agreed the old man. " Only what would any sensible chap be doing up on the cliff after dark ? There's safer places if he wanted to do a bit of canoodling. . . ."

Then the police did arrive and Willis went to explain the position and to say that he'd never met the gentleman in the brown suit before and it warn't no use threatening him but the police might be grateful to a chap doing half their work for them—finding the car, he meant.

" If I find this is a practical joke," growled the sergeant, but Willis said, " Give me half a crown, he did. That's no joke, I tell you."

When Crook caught sight of the car lying half on its side on the shelf of rock halfway down the face of the cliff he was instantly convinced that this was the actual vehicle for which he was searching. There were two roads along the cliff, an upper and a lower. He had taken the lower as being less strain to the overworked springs of the Scourge. But he saw that he wasn't first on the scene. There was another car—a small dark blue one—already parked on the cliff-top.

Roger Trentham was frankly dismayed at the sight. " If that's some other chap jumping my claim," he began, but Crook, in his dryest voice, returned, " Stay around a while and you may make history for your paper before morning."

Roger looked round uneasily. " It's gettin' damned dark."

" I know. And even if it wasn't the tide's wrong—for getting down the cliff, I mean."

He drew the invaluable map from the pocket and flashed on a pencil torch.

" There are two caves in the side of the cliff," he announced. " One of 'em's flooded at high tide, and the other isn't. The second one used to have another entrance, from the cliff-top, but that was stopped by the authorities a considerable time ago, so now you have to go down by the path, the sort of thing only a goat could hope to do successfully at this time of night, and come in crawling on all fours. You've started quite a thing, you know," he added to Trentham but without sounding particularly pleased about it. " Heaven only knows how many deaths there'll be before we're through."

" We've got two to date," observed Roger.

" A possible three. We don't know if there's anyone in that car. I'd say that if there isn't there ought to be."

" Whose car's that ? " demanded Roger, indicating the dark blue car standing above them.

" I give you three guesses. Oh, after all that stuff in your paper this morning I guessed he'd come down. Wouldn't be able to stop away. Well, this reminds me of the last war. Over the top, boys."

He trudged, a sturdy little figure in an absurd brown suit, to the place on the cliff where the precipitous path ran down to the ledge.

" I wonder if there is anyone in it," speculated Roger.

" I could make a good guess as to how many occupants it had when it went over the side."

" One ? " suggested Trentham.

" One," agreed Crook.

" Female ? " hazarded Trentham.

" Female," confirmed Crook.

" And the chap who owns that car ? "

" I may be wrong," said Crook modestly, " but I think this is a matter of life or death to him."

Trentham looked round as if he expected a murderer to materialise from the misty grey air of evening.

" He's somewhere round here still ? "

" I think he came down this path, too."

" Might have pitched into the sea," said Roger, not sure whether this would be a good development from his point of view or not.

" We might join him," acknowledged Crook grimly. " Y'know, if I'd known we were goin' to enjoy ourselves like this I'd have brought my skis. You only want to take one false step and you're done for."

" Look here," said Roger, standing like the Faithful Centurion outlined against the darkening sky, " do you mean we can't get at that cave till the tide ebbs ? "

" That's right. Still, we may not need to get at the cave.

We may find what we're looking for in the car." Gingerly he began to make the descent. On one side of him was the face of the cliff, smooth, hard and pitiless as a wall of glass ; on the other a sheer drop to the toothed rocks below. Crook, like a good many other people, suffered agonies on heights, particularly when there was no rail to clutch in an emergency. He wished he had the moral courage to let the young man go down alone—he might be a human chamois from the way he was tackling the descent—but it was a point of honour with him to be in at the death, even if it was his own death, and so, inch by perilous inch, he descended, feeling every moment might be his last and telling himself that fly-bombs were child's play by comparison with this sort of frightful experience. Roger Trentham got down first, and had no chivalrous impulses to stay and help an older man. It is probable that he did not even think of Crook as being this.

He was bending above the car and flashing a torch on her when Crook, feeling as though his top skin had been scraped off, joined him.

" She didn't half come a crash," he said. " Glass smashed to blazes, of course, body a pretty good wreck, one door splintered, the other. . . ."

" Unless you want to commit suicide and sell your paper up the river you won't practise gymnastics here," said Crook sharply. " The main thing is there's nobody inside the car. Question is, was there when she landed here ? "

" I don't see how . . ." began Trentham, but Crook was flashing his natty little torch around him.

" Didn't you notice that ? " he said. He indicated the splintered glass of one of the windows. " That's a bit of a rug or a scarf or something. Now why should that be caught on the window unless—oh my Lord, I'd forgotten. One of the windows was broken by the girl, wasn't it ? "

" Would it be this one ? "

. " No," said Crook, more calmly. " It wouldn't. Because when she smashed the window she'd be in the passenger's seat, and I should say that when the car took her melodramatic dive to death, she was in the driver's."

" If she stayed there."

" She wouldn't have much choice. She was drugged, remember "

" So she was. Then your idea is that after she came down someone did a bit of rescue work ? "

" Tell you more in a minute. Look at this door. You say it's splintered and so it is, but look at that. What do you make of it ? "

" Blob of mud. Not so strange."

" Blob of *fresh* mud," said Crook impressively. " Curiouser and curiouser."

" Meaning that was made since morning."

" Don't it seem like that to you. Besides, look at that path." Both men shone their light on it. " You and me didn't make all those footprints. And they're fresh footprints because of the mud. No, someone came down here to fetch the girl. I daresay he hoped to get her up to the top and away in the car, but he found he couldn't make it. And if you ask me," said Crook with some violence, " Tarzan couldn't have made it either."

" Then where . . . ? "

" I suppose in the cave."

" Then hadn't we better go down and join the pair ? "

" We can't—not till the tide drops."

" How long'll that be ? "

" Matter of a couple of hours. But there's one thing. If we can't get in he can't get out. And presently we shall have the law with us. Hullo, what's that ? "

" Sounds uncommonly like the law," agreed Trentham. " Unless you think some enterprising agency's started a fleet of motor charabancs to the scene of the tragedy."

Crook moved gingerly. He wondered what the pair of them looked like to anyone on the face of the waters, supposing anyone to be on the face of waters and to be sufficiently keen-sighted to discover their presence in the fading light. Like two mysterious birds, he thought, and the unpleasant analogy returned to him—two birds of prey hunting on the rock for carrion in the shape of a body, alive or dead.

With what seemed to him the most intrepid courage the young man was still busying himself with the corpse of the car.

" All this stuff about the girl being dotty is all my eye and Betty Martin," he remarked. " My aunt said she was remarkably intelligent, and my aunt's standard is extremely high. I say, look over there, beyond the car. I can't swear to it because the light's so damned bad, but wouldn't you say there was a bit more of this rug or whatever it is on that thorn-branch on the further side ? "

" That fits in with your theory. Besides, if they didn't go that way there's only one alternative."

" Down there." Trentham leaned casually over. " Nasty drop. One thing, you probably wouldn't know much about it by the time you hit the rocks." He flashed his torch round on the ground. " I say, look at this." He stooped and picked up a grey suède glove. " My Auntie May might recognise that."

" She's be dead sure to," said Crook grimly. " I've met your Auntie May. If you took her somebody's chopped-off finger she'd identify it if it suited her book. And if you found an embryo elephant in the car she'd remember seeing the girl take it out for a walk on the end of a lead. You'd better save something for the police, though. They have tender consciences and they like to earn the bread and skilly we provide for 'em. Besides, I think I hear them coming."

" If they aren't grateful to us . . ." began Roger, but Crook said scornfully, " They ain't paid to be grateful. You should know that."

" They've taken their time anyway. The car might have been swept overboard in a gale before they arrived."

" If it had we should have been swept with it. You can be darn sure of that."

The next instant the police could not only be heard but seen clambering down the path towards the car. There were two of them, an inspector and his assistant, and as Crook had prophesied, they weren't a bit grateful, merely enquiring suspiciously how it was that he and his companion had found the car in the first place.

" Mainly because I was looking for it," said Crook.

The inspector wanted to know why, and Crook said because he was being paid to, and added his famous bit about the labourer being worthy of his hire but having to earn his hire just the same.

The inspector asked a number of questions and called to his assistant to come and help to examine the car. He stared balefully at Crook and the young *Daily Post* representative, who said afterwards that if there hadn't been witnesses present he was damned sure the chap would have driven 'em into the sea and pretended they'd done a suicide pact. The bull's-eyes of the police flashed, and Roger Trentham, under the impression he was being helpful, turned on his torch too until requested to put it away, and Crook nudged him with his elbow, and said, " May as well get any fun that's going out of this, seeing we have ring seats," and had the satisfaction of being questioned by the inspector as to the possible owner-ship of the car and the reason for its being found where it was. Crook didn't do as much talking as usual. He said he'd been called in by Sammy, who was probably going to bring an action against the *Post* for giving false impressions to the public, whereupon Roger said that it wasn't libellous to say that a more or less anonymous person called Sammy had tele-phoned, and that very likely he was telling the truth when he said he was looking after the girl.

The inspector, who didn't much care about the independent attitude adopted by the laity, said shortly that if the young lady had gone over the side there was very little likelihood of finding her. Except in very mild weather the rocks were unapproachable from above—except, of course, by suicides, murderees and sea birds. Every year during the season the authorities reported boating fatalities. In spite of all the warnings uttered by boat-owners and fishermen, gay young sparks staying in the Lestingham neighbourhood took unjusti-fiable risks, got caught by the current, found the boat out of control and were finally swept on to the rocks. It was a solitary place, but even if you were seen it didn't help you much. Even if a skilled climber could get down the face of the cliff he'd never get back. More than once the police had put notices up forbidding holiday-makers to go within a certain radius of the rocks but this regulation was evaded by bold spirits made eager by the very danger of the enterprise, and presently yet another owner would declare indignantly he'd not let his boat out to young town fellows that didn't know how to treat them.

" H'm," said the sergeant, " this wouldn't be the first accident we've had here."

" The local authorities did put up a fence round the edge of the cliff just before the war," added the inspector, " but then the War Office decided it would be a likely place to train the Home Guard—no one to watch manœuvres, see—and they tore the fence up."

His voice said you couldn't expect anything else from so irregular an arm of defence.

" I daresay they wanted the palings to drill with," suggested Crook in a brisk voice. " They were a bit short at the beginning."

The inspector looked as if he disliked him even more than he had done before.

" And anyway," Crook continued, " we don't think it was an accident."

" No ? "

" No. We think most likely it was murder—or attempted murder. It isn't likely if it was an accident that both the bodies would have fallen out of the car."

The inspector said time would tell.

" Well, consider the facts," Crook offered. " We've got plenty of time before we can go any further. That chap at the Boar says the driver only bought two gallons of petrol. What does that suggest to you ? That he knew he wouldn't be taking the car so very much further. If he'd wanted it to look like an accident he'd have filled up the tank."

" It might be suicide," said the sergeant meditatively. " This place used to be called Suicides' Leap, though why folk wanted to climb all this way when they could put their heads in a gas oven just as easy and no energy beats me."

Crook said kindly he didn't think they'd find this was suicide. In view of the facts. . . . The inspector interrupted to say that they hadn't yet identified the car as the one that had topped at the Boar. He flashed on his lantern again and they saw the number. XYZ.29.

" It's the car that was waiting at Holt Cross for the girl," Crook pointed out. " And there's no history of a second car coming this way. Besides, if he wanted to get rid of the car—say it's been stolen—he couldn't choose a better place. In the dark and not perhaps knowing the coast too well he couldn't be expected to know it would land on the platform. I daresay if he'd tried to put it there he'd have gone grey before he managed it."

" If he did want to get rid of it," agreed the inspector, grudgingly.

" Cars ain't like bodies," Crook urged with relish, " and we all know how difficult it is to get rid of them. They can't be shoved into ditches or under brushwood. They don't decompose beyond recognition. Moth and rust may corrupt but they can't finally disguise them. Whatever you do to a car, someone who once had it for a friend is going to know it again."

" You could put it in a car park," said the inspector drily. " And forget to come back for it."

" Too risky," opined Mr. Cautious Crook. " Someone else may back his car into yours ; then the police take the numbers and ask awkward questions about licences. Someone may want to borrow a match off you and remember your face when he sees it in a police court. You might even get one of these intelligent car attendants who remember the numbers of wanted cars and identify them. I don't say it's likely, I only say it's possible. After all, the history of murder is full of unlikely coincidences. And in saying that," added Crook earnestly, " I speak as a pro. One way and another, I'd say I know more about murder than any man living."

Roger Trentham broke in, " Look here, I don't understand about this cave. If the water comes up above the entrance anyone in it is bound to be drowned."

" The smugglers had thought of that," Crook told him. " The path goes down below sea-level—present sea-level that is—then it climbs again. The mouth of the cave is above that level, but it's impossible for anyone who isn't a monkey to get there, except when the tide's fallen below a certain point."

" You seem to have thought of a lot," said the inspector.

" Arthur Crook, the Human Ferret. Well, I'm like the lady in Victorian melodrama. My honour is at stake. I have to think of things."

" I suppose you're certain there's no other exit," enquired Trentham. He's as jumpy as a cat on hot bricks, thought Crook.

" Dead sure," said the inspector in a grim voice. There was one a long time ago, but it was closed when the authorities got wind of a big coup. coming off. They felled a great tree that stood near the exit, so that it blocked the passage. In the old days the fellows came up from the sands by a path that doesn't exist any longer, got into the cave with their stuff, and then oiled out the other end, where they had men waiting to cart the stuff away."

" Tickling authority's palm the while ? " suggested Crook.

" They say it was a long time before anyone could tell them where the other entrance was," continued the inspector, waxing expansive. " They tried following the chaps, but that didn't work, because they were up to all the moves, and one body more or less didn't make much difference to them. The authorities got it in the end by collaring one of the smugglers and burning the truth out of him. Then they blocked the

138

cave at the other end and waited. The fellows came that
night, found the entrance blocked and when they went back
to try and get word through to their mates they found themselves in an ambush. There was quite a lot of blood spilt at
the time. Fought like wild-cats, but they were overpowered
in the end. All who lived were hanged. Then the coastguards
sat down and waited, the same as we're doing now."

"Watch for the next instalment of this gripping romance,"
intoned Crook rapidly. "The smugglers came, reached the
beach, toiled up the path into the cave and found they
couldn't get out. When they came back to the cliff entrance
it was to discover . . ." He turned to Roger Trentham.
"Your shot," he said.

"To find a force of H.M. coastguards, supplemented by the
military, I daresay, equipped with pikes and halberds, waiting
for them. More blood."

"There's a headline for you," said Arthur Crook. "In a
remote and little-known corner of the English coast, where
once the sands ran red with blood of smuggler and coastguard
alike, duelling desperately beneath the unheeding moon, the
final act of a murder mystery that has baffled the police. . . ."

"That'll do," said the inspector, but he grinned in spite of
himself.

"Sure you haven't missed your vocation?" murmured
Trentham. "Well, what the hell do we now?"

"Ask the inspector," said Crook softly.

"We wait," said the inspector in laconic tones.

"Same like the coastguards," encouraged Crook.

"How long do we wait?"

"We-ell. What would you say, Inspector?"

"We ought to be able to get down in about an hour—always
providing there's something there when we do arrive."

"Well, you've only to use your common sense," said Crook
rather rudely. "Goliath himself couldn't have lugged a girl
up that cliff. I know you writing chaps spout a lot of hot air
about a girl being as fragile as a flower, but a flower who
weighed as much as Miss Deane would be put in the British
Museum—or the Chambers of Horrors."

"An hour," repeated Roger Trentham. "It's going to be
damned dark by then. And the inspector's right, whatever
you may say, Crook. The whole thing may be a plant. For
all we know the girl's a hundred miles away by this time."

"Don't forget she was doped before she was driven here,"

and the car's over the cliff. I doubt if the girl was in a state to walk a hundred miles."

" I suppose the chap who may be in the cave now . . ."

" The chap who drove that car here," amplified Crook.

" I suppose he's remembered it'll be damned dark in an hour, and is banking on no one being fool enough to risk his neck on the side of a cliff as slippery as glass on a hundred-to-one chance."

" He's going to have his work cut out explaining how he got there and why," the sergeant said.

" If you ask me," said Crook, undaunted by the unforth-coming manner of the inspector, " he'll say that he left the girl in the car for a minute and she grabbed the wheel and went off hell-for-leather."

. " That won't hold water. Why didn't he inform the police at once ? "

" If it was a stolen car he might have felt a bit delicate about it."

" He should have immobilised the car before leaving it," said the inspector, coldly.

" He'll say he had no idea she could drive—or he thought she was asleep—or she was shamming. . . ."

" If this is the right girl she couldn't," put in Roger suddenly. " Drive, I mean. My Auntie May asked her and she said she'd always wanted to learn."

" I could almost feel sorry for this chap if I wasn't on the side of the angels," said Arthur Crook. " Ninety-nine girls out of a hundred can drive. It must have looked a pretty safe bet." '

" He's in a worse jam now than ever," Roger muttered. But Crook said No, not really, because he was bound to get him in the end, whether the chap realised it or no.

" I'd like to be more certain about the girl," said Roger. He hauled something out of his pocket. " It's damned cold here," he said. " How about it, Inspector ? "

Crook, however, said grimly that they might need it for some more urgent reason, and Roger put it back.

It was the strangest vigil. Four men, on a bitterly cold autumn evening, perched on the side of a cliff like some new sort of bird, one brown, one blue, two nondescript, waiting for the floor of the sea to sink. They didn't talk very much. Roger wondered at the feelings of the trapped man when he came to the mouth of the cave, and saw he couldn't get away.

He might ruin everything, from a newspaperman's point of view, by diving overboard and taking his story with him. He looked thoughtfully at the inspector, and hoped he knew his onions well enough to prevent anything of that kind. He must, of course, have dumped the girl where it was unlikely she would be found for weeks, possibly months, and then come back, intending to re-ascend the cliff and make off in the car. But he'd left it too late. It had taken him longer than he had anticipated, or else the tide had come in more quickly. Now he must be waiting, just out of sight, waiting as tensely as the quartette on the cliff-side. Hope for his own sake he's warmer than we are, thought Roger. But he didn't really care about the cold. In his mind's eye he was planning headlines, deciding precisely where he'd start the story, how he'd phrase it. He'd have liked a photograph of the cliff, but he'd have to make word-painting do. Crook also thought of the man in the cave, of his tearing anxiety or furious despair ; the inspector and the sergeant were more tranquil so far as he was concerned. The Inspector did wonder if he was armed and if so, if it wouldn't be good economy to let Crook go in first. But he dismissed the idea with a sigh. It was part of British etiquette that the police took the first risk, like keeping a straight bat or a stiff upper lip. The sergeant eyed Crook balefully. If it hadn't been for his interference they'd all have got something warm inside them by now. Only a mug, he thought disgustedly, would ever have entered the Force. In ordinary occupations a man doesn't hang about, looking nearly as much of a fool as he feels, on a cold dark night, with three other people as crazy as himself—two of them crazier, in short, because they didn't have to be there at all. It was art for art's sake with them. He looked at Crook, who had seated himself on a bit of rock, that seemed no more immobile than himself, and who seemed to have no fears of the consequences said to accrue to middle-aged men sitting about on cold stone ; he looked at Roger Trentham, happy and excited and as wakeful as though this were morning instead of drawing on to one of the darkest and most miserable nights on record. Roger, in fact, was busily embroidering his theme. A chap who carried a girl from the platform to the cave must have got some nerve, he reflected. But of course he'd be keyed up by the immediacy of the situation, the danger, the dread. Men in a similar mood stopped runaway horses, braved flame and flood, yes, even men who were ordinarily alarmed by a woman's sharp tongue or the reprimand of an employer.

"What 'ud I do if I came out and found four men barring my path to freedom?" wondered the romantic young man. "Pitch myself down?" He looked into the now practically invisible depths and shivered. No, he'd sooner chance the scaffold. Then he began to think of the girl. Would she be dead? Impossible to say. If she'd been dead in the car, then surely X. would have left her there, instead of running this additional tremendous risk. Would he murder her in the cave? Again impossible to say, but not likely, because in that case he might still have left her in the car. But in such weather and in such surroundings she could be relied upon to freeze to death pretty soon. As for regaining consciousness and escaping, that wasn't very likely. To begin with it was improbable she'd be able to attract any attention, and it wouldn't be possible to prove she hadn't got herself down into the cave. Dead women can't talk—about the only kind that can't, he reflected. He wondered if there was an equivalent to the Trappist order for monks. He didn't suppose so. Human nature could be tried thus far and no farther, and there are some miracles even the most religious don't anticipate.

The wind blew colder; the moon, very wintry and aloof, looked out disapprovingly from behind a cloud. Disapprovingly is the word, he thought. I must remember that when I make my report. "The sea was almost black now under the icy sky. Nobody talked any more. Instinctively they husbanded their strength."

At last it was time to make a move. Crook got stiffly to his feet, thinking he was really getting too old for this kind of entertainment. He knew that even when they reached the cave, they'd still be a long way from the end of the case. He wondered if any of the other three appreciated that. Most probably not—but then they didn't know as much about it as he did. Why, there was even a chance they'd be singing "Now the labourer's task is o'er" for his benefit before they were through. This was true of all his cases, but it seldom occurred to him at this stage of the proceedings.

The sergeant thought, "That sea's taking a bloody long time to do its stuff." At home Elsie would be sitting by the fire, making tea and eating hot buttered toast. She always did that last thing. The kids would be in bed. Young Jim would give his eye-teeth to be here. He was glad it was too dark to see the young man's face. That chap would never tire of life till you got the millennium, when people stopped murdering one another, and there wasn't anything more for him to write about. All this, overturned cars, secret caves, ice-cold vigils, possible murder in the dark, it was all meat and drink to him.

Crook said, " Over the top, Inspector ? " and the inspector said, " Not long now."

Crook nodded. " Three fishers lay out on the shining sand. What bloody fools we should look to the rest of England now."

Roger Trentham grinned. " Not to my Auntie May. She'll most likely cut me out of her will for not somehow manoeuvring her into this."

And now at last they could continue the descent. The inspector didn't particularly want Mr. Crook there. Too spheroidal. The young chap was all right. He took his life in his hands, like war correspondents, and if he did break his blooming neck it wasn't the affair of the police. But Mr. Crook was notorious. If anything went wrong there'd probably be an enquiry ; he was quite capable of sending his ghost back from the dead to haunt the sergeant or accuse the inspector of deliberately shoving him overboard in order to retain all the kudos himself.

The odd-looking little procession reached the bend in the path, and began carefully to negotiate the ascent. This was easier than they had expected. The summer visitors made this trip under the most ideal conditions possible in the circumstances, and they had at all events worn a clear path that these night-hawks could follow.

" Better be careful," warned the inspector, " he may be armed."

" Not likely," said Crook in his confident way. " Not with all the precautions Uncle Herbert's been taking over a number of years."

The inspector didn't answer that one. Probably he thought it beneath contempt. They reached the entrance, and now Crook foiled the intention of officialdom to be the first to confront danger by pushing himself forward in quite an ostentatious manner and bounding towards the unknown like Dick Whittington's pantomime cat. The passage in which the four found themselves ran straight for a time, then turned abruptly to the left. Having been made for smugglers it was wide enough and high enough to be traversed in comparative comfort. Crook turned his head to say in a hoarse whisper, " It's to be hoped my creaking joints don't give him the tip, like the crocodile that swallowed the alarm-clock and warned its victim when it was coming."

He turned again and found himself in a large dark cave, with a second exit leading to blackness. Lying near this exit was a bundle in a green and grey rug. Bending above it and half-concealing it was a man in a loose grey jacket, with his back to the new-comers. He seemed absorbed in what he was doing and didn't at first hear their arrival. Only when Crook exclaimed " Eureka ! " did he turn and they saw who he was.

" Well, well, if it isn't Sammy Parker," exclaimed Mr. Crook, rubbing his hands because it was so damned cold upstairs, he told Roger afterwards. He gambolled into the centre of the cave, unscrupulously stealing all authority's thunder. " You didn't expect quite so many of us quite so soon, did you, Sammy ? Or—did you ? "

CHAPTER SEVENTEEN

Ef you wanter see sho' nuff trouble you des oughter go longer me : I'm de man wat kin show yer trouble.—UNCLE REMUS.

SAMMY, who had clearly been too much absorbed in what he was doing to hear their approach, leaped up and turned to face them. He was taller than Crook had remembered him, or of course, he reminded himself, it might be that the cave was low. He was on the short side himself and it had accommodated him comfortably enough, and perhaps the smugglers in that part of the coast had been small men, too. He looked, thought Roger Trentham, whose profession inclined him to think in terms more fantastic than those of his companions, like some avenging fate in a morality play. The inspector, a sensible man, crossed to the side of the bundle on the ground ; his sergeant took up a more or less—perhaps rather more— unostentatious stand by the man he supposed a bit dazedly they were going to arrest, Roger Trentham walked over to the inspector's side, and looked down at the unconscious girl. He stooped.

" She's alive ? " he asked quickly.

144

The inspector looked at him with unconcealed dislike. Then he said to the sergeant, ignoring the question, " Look out ! "

" If you mean Mr. Parker," said Crook, " that's all right. He's a client of mine."

As he had anticipated, the inspector was so staggered by this remark that he was momentarily silenced, and Sammy spoke for the first time.

." I must say you've taken a hell of a time to get here," he observed ungraciously. " How do you propose to get that girl up to the cliff surface ? "

" Who brought her here ? " demanded the inspector, before Mr. Crook could speak.

" I did. Well, she'd have frozen to death in that car. No thanks to the authorities she didn't."

" Be reasonable, Sammy," Crook urged. " This has only just become a police case."

" When they heard there was a car over the cliffs, I suppose ? Or are they going to run me in for leaving my car unattended ? "

" You say you brought her here ? " said the inspector sternly.

" I've already said so. It's no thanks to anyone if she is still alive. Haven't any of you got a drop of brandy or anything ? She's had all I had on me, which, thanks to our beneficient authorities, wasn't much."

" I told you you'd find good use for that before the night was over," said Crook to Roger Trentham. The young man produced his flask, and Sammy took it from him with a bare word of thanks and went over to the girl's side. The inspector would have forestalled him but Sammy pushed him aside. The girl was sheet-white and breathing. You couldn't say much more.

" What we want now," Sammy continued, " is a doctor and then a charge of dynamite to reopen the other entrance. Don't tell me you're going to try and get her up the face of the cliff. Why, even I couldn't do that."

The inspector's attitude was rather, " You got her here ; you can jolly well get her out again," but he couldn't precisely say that, so for the moment he said nothing. It was Crook who observed, " Any doctor who comes down here at this hour of night is going to win a medal."

" If that girl dies," said Sammy savagely, " I'll sue the

police for murder. And don't tell me you can't sue a branch of the Civil Service, because Mr. Crook and I know better."

Mr. Crook wisely kept his mouth shut, since he didn't know anything of the sort, and while he could make allowances for the distraught young man he couldn't really see that the police were to blame.

"It's damned cold here," said Roger Trentham, who had his own troubles. This was a magnificent story, and while there was no reason to suppose that any other press representative could steal it, it was undeniably true that the sooner he could contact his paper the better.

"You might at least give the girl your coat," said Sammy, bitterly.

Roger hesitated, then took it off. He might get pneumonia, but it added another picturesque detail to the picture, and so long as he got the story in before the symptoms manifested themselves, he was prepared to chance pneumonia. He was going to put the coat over the recumbent figure himself, but Sammy snatched it out of his hands and shoving the inspector aside did the job himself.

"I have an idea," observed Crook, in the voice of one who has the utmost confidence in his ideas. "No one's got anything on me or Mr. Trentham, and no doctor's goin' to materialise like a genie out of a bottle—or anything else out of a bottle, come to that," he added regretfully.

"I wondered when anyone was going to suggest getting a doctor," observed Sammy in the same injured voice.

"Too bad the cave isn't on the telephone," said the inspector.

"If that's meant for me," said Sammy, "you wouldn't have been a whit better off on the side of the cliff. Unless maybe you prefer a hearse to an ambulance."

"Mr. Trentham and me'll go back up the cliff," Crook hoped he didn't wince as he spoke ; the notion of that horrible climb galled his withers, as he'd have said, not quite sure what the phrase meant. "He can get in touch with his paper—all right, Sammy, all right, it is his job, you know, and half England's waiting for news of you and your young lady ; the other half," he added in soothing tones, "can't read. How about your police surgeon ? " he looked expectantly at the inspector.

The inspector clearly wasn't at all happy. He couldn't, of course, prevent Crook or the journalist leaving them, though he didn't much care for the sort of story the latter was clearly going to tell. But he felt that authority should contact the police doctor. He could, of course, suggest the sergeant going back up the cliff, but, not knowing the story from the inside as Crook appeared to, he wasn't anxious to be left alone with Sammy and the girl.

Crook appreciated his difficulties and kindly tried to dispose of them. "Show the gentleman you don't carry a gun," he invited the tall angry young man. "The armour of righteousness is all very fine but it don't stand much of a chance against two husky policemen."

"Of course I don't carry a gun," said Sammy impatiently. "Who'd give me a licence for it?"

"Never heard of breaking the law, I suppose?" said Crook, with a huge wink at the discomfited inspector. "You see," he continued, "he still don't know what you're doing here and how you knew where to look for the girl."

"That chap's stuff in his paper put me on to that," said Sammy. "He said the fellow made the rendezvous at Holt Cross. Well, I happen to know this part of the country and there are only two roads out that a car can take. The one runs back to Green Valley and the other comes to the cliffs. Oh, I know there's a branch road to Lestingham, but if you're going to commit a murder you don't choose a place like that. Too many Nosey Parkers about. Besides, if you tried to stage an accident there the local branch of St. John's Ambulance would bless you for a chance of showing what it can do. No, I remembered the simple arithmetic I learned at school and put two and two together, and decided that a car coming this way would head for the cliffs."

"Meaning to leave the girl in the cave?"

"Unless this chap who took her off was a gorilla he couldn't have done it," snapped Sammy. "I'm not exactly an invalid myself, but I wouldn't have cared to chance it."

"You brought her down from the ledge," the inspector reminded him.

"And wouldn't take the chance again for anything a grateful Government's going to give me by the way of gratuity and post-war credits in their own good time. Besides, I hadn't any choice. It was that or letting her freeze to death on the cliff. But I came by and stopped off at a pub. . . ."

"So you're the chap who got there before I did and began asking questions," said Roger.

147

Sammy looked at him offensively. " You only want a story for your paper," he said.

Roger didn't bear malice. It was too good a story 'for that. A lot more headlines began to whizz through his mind like rocket shells. He could polish them up as he went along.

" When I got here I saw the car," Sammy continued, " and guessing that it wasn't empty when it went over the side I crawled down. I had the devil of a job getting her out ; I thought the whole outfit was going over the side of the cliff more than once, which I daresay would have suited X's book very well, and by the time I got her down the tide had caught me. I couldn't get up to the top—and besides, once I did it meant the devil of a wait before we could get back and suppose she came round and found herself here—alone. She might have died of fright."

" We see your point perfectly, Sammy. And all things work together for good—you know the rest. Well, Inspector, how about it ? "

The inspector had no intention of being given his orders by a layman. He told the sergeant he'd better go back to the top and take the car and bring back the doctor. The sergeant listened unmoved.

" There'll be a moon later," he said.

" And there'll be arrangements for getting the young lady up to the top," the inspector continued.

" If she comes round . . ." began Roger Trentham, and Sammy interrupted him to say, " She's not going to find you sitting beside her ready to take down her story in shorthand, so you can put that idea out of your head."

" He means she might be able to give a bit of help on the upward road," interrupted Crook.

" Or she might suffer from vertigo," said the sergeant unexpectedly.

The inspector looked as if this were a nightmare, and he hoped he'd soon wake up. Crook thought it was an interesting situation. He wondered if the two men would have unbent by the time the police doctor arrived. Roger thought, " It's going to be damned cold going back without a coat, and Crook, reading that thought, said maliciously, " There's a nice rug in my car. You can play you're Baby Bunting from here to Lestingham."

And all the time the girl, Nora Deane, hadn't spoken or

stirred. Only her faint breathing showed that she was still alive.

The return journey was easier than Crook had anticipated. In the cave lighting had been by torches, but already the moon of which the sergeant had spoken was beginning to emerge. When his eyes got accustomed to the uncertain light Crook made commendable progress up the path. Roger went first and the sergeant came last, so he felt that if he did slip an official hand might prevent his crashing on to the Teeth. Up at the top they got into their separate cars.

" You coming back later ? " Crook asked his companion conversationally.

" You bet I'm coming back," returned Roger, who might have been Crook's Human Chamois, so nimbly did he tackle these nerve-shaking ascents and descents. " Haven't had a break like this for ages. I suppose," he went on, producing a cigarette case and passing it to Crook, who said No, thanks, he never did but a kind thought just the same, " you knew you were going to find that chap there."

" I had a hunch," said Crook, modestly. " Besides, who else could it have been ? "

" I expected the murderer," said Roger candidly.

Crook's eyes widened. " How come ? " he asked. " He'd have pushed the girl into the sea and taken his Flying Carpet back to Timbuktu. Only a chap who was silly with love would have chanced that road down to the cave."

" I hope she's going to pull through," murmured Roger.

" It'll be damned ungrateful of her if she don't, seein' the risks you and me and Sammy have taken," returned Crook in his vigorous way. " Anyway, the police 'ull see to it that she does They can't afford to have it said that she was getting along nicely until they appeared on the scenes, and then pegged out. Ah ! " he took a corner very prettily, " how wonderful is love."

" Love ? " Roger felt a little dazed by the swift procession of events and his companion's mercurial driving.

" Well, you didn't imagine Sammy was conductin' a social experiment, did you ? If he hadn't been demented about her she'd be either frozen to death at the wheel or at the bottom of the sea, most likely the first, though either would have suited the murderer's book."

" Think he knew the car had stuck half-way down ? "

" That's one of the things he'll have to tell us," said Crook,

pleasantly. " He wouldn't expect anyone to find her anyhow,
not in time, though naturally he'd rather there wasn't what
the novelists call a trace of the accident. Still, he might have
chanced his luck if he had known. Gents of fifty or there-
abouts don't take too kindly to crawlin' up and down cliffs at
twilight."

" Nice from you," said Roger.

" I said gents. You know, you ought to be grateful to us,
too. We're givin' you a grand run for your money. Murder,
abduction, vigil on the cliffs, staggering rescue, the corpse in
the cave, love triumphant—our Crime Reporter contacts
Arthur Crook—the Invincible Alliance—you know, I'm
practically writin' your article for you."

" In short, all that's left is to lay hands on the murderer."

" You've said it, boy."

" And I daresay you're getting all set to do that."

" Not my pigeon," said Mr. Crook tranquilly. " That s for
the police."

" Know who he is ? "

" Sure. Don't you ? "

" Know where he is ? "

" Mustn't steal all the policeman's little apples."

" I'd like to be in at the death," offered Roger.

" Stick around," said Crook, amiably.

" I suppose you wouldn't like to do an interview for the
paper ? " murmured Roger.

" Why waste time ? " asked Crook affably. " You could do
it better than me."

" How did you know Sammy 'ud be in the cave ? "

" Because Sammy was in love and chaps in love ain't sane.
No sane man would have taken those risks. Besides, he knew
about trains. I'd say he hired that car on the cliff. It's a
local number. Notice ? "

" You ought to be on the *Post*," said Roger admiringly.

" And then—I ain't the police. The police don't care if
there's motive for murder or not. Now, me, I think motive's
important and I couldn't think of a single reason why that
girl could be dangerous to Sammy Parker. She might be
dangerous to the murderer—the Lone Pit murderer, I mean
—or he might get the idea she was. But that man wasn't
Sammy. And I knew he wasn't on last night's job, because
before I left my office I rang his rooms. He has what they
call a service flat. That means you pay extra to listen to some

old crone explainin' why she didn't make your bed or dust your floor. Me, I don't have service, I have a char. It works out less expensive and I only keep the kind of beer I don't drink myself in an unlocked cupboard. Well, I rang the flat and presently the aforesaid crone answered, but not in too much of a hurry in case I should get ideas above my station. She said Mr. Parker was out. Well, I said, when did he go out ? She said, This morning. I said, I thought he wasn't there last night—being cagey, see ?—and she said Yes, he was, and his friends, from six o'clock onwards and kept going out for more bottles. Gave her a headache, she said. Y'know," Mr. Crook negotiated another curve, " there's somethin' rather nice about a woman that can get a headache just hearin' the bottles go up the stairs, without even wantin' to open them. Still, it told me what I wanted to know, that he spent last night at the flat. If he was at the flat he couldn't have been pushin' that girl over the cliff. He couldn't have done it in the time. Whoever did that made a night of it. He had to walk back afterwards, and I daresay he wouldn't put up at a local hotel, even if he could get in, in case uncomfortable questions were asked later. Q.E.D." he wound up triumphantly.

" Besides, he called you in, didn't he ? " said Roger. " Though that might have been a trick."

" More honoured in the breach than the performance," Crook assured him. " Meanin' it's done more often on the films than anywhere else. Mean to say, it's asking for trouble, when the chap happens to be me. And if you want to commit suicide, there's lots of cheaper ways. There's tanks, jeeps, despatch-riders, all positively urgin' you to choose your shroud, so why pay a chap to put you out of the way ? "

They reached Lestingham and commandeered telephones. Roger had a grand time. Mr. Crook rang up Bill. He hardly mentioned the girl ; that case was practically finished, and one of his mottoes was : All the past things are past and over.

Bill said, " That Jeffreys case is coming along. Could do with you in town."

" Shan't pass out this trip," Crook assured, and rang off after a little more technical conversation. When he rejoined Roger—or rather, was rejoined by him, since that young man's call was considerably longer—he said with a grin, " Well, which did you plump for in the end ? Abducted Girl Mystery. Lurking on the side of an impenetrable cliff, watching the light dissolve into mist, while inch by slow inch the sea dropped into the abyss, I spent one of the tensest hours of my life waiting for an opportunity to descend to the erstwhile smugglers' cave where, I had reason to believe, lay hidden the young girl, Nora Deane, who was so foully betrayed. . . ."

" Not betrayed," said Roger seriously. " To our readers that means something quite different. I think I'll be getting back now. I've got to collect my overcoat."

Crook said he was going to town, but he'd give his companion a lift to the Boar where he could collect his own car. Which he did and they parted on excellent terms. But Crook really got the better of the bargain, because he stayed in the bar of the Boar, drinking their incomparable beer and playing he was a deaf mute. You don't need words, if you're a civilised person, to buy yourself a drink.

CHAPTER EIGHTEEN

I wish my deadly foes no worse
Than lack of friends and empty purse.
                              —NICHOLAS BRETON

MRS. TRENTHAM sat at home talking endlessly to her new nurse. She made it perfectly clear that the post was only a temporary one, " because as soon as Miss Deane is able to return to her duties I shall have her back," she announced uncompromisingly.

The nurse, who wasn't interested in the murder and had a young man in Burma, said, " She hasn't come round yet, has she ? "

" Not yet. I believe the police and that extraordinary Mr. Crook are sitting by her bed night and day."

The new nurse sniffed. " Funny sort of hospital if they allow those goings-on," she said.

" He reminds me rather of Bulldog Drummond—Mr. Crook I mean," mused Mrs. Trentham.

" I wouldn't know," said the nurse, proceeding on an assumption common to her kind that all people over seventy are senile and should be treated as such. " Before my time."

" I can't imagine why you young women are so proud of

getting born so late," said Mrs. Trentham sharply. "You missed a great deal."

"Going to a better world than yours was," said the nurse.

"And you have us to thank for that. If we'd arranged to have you born into a perfect world—and I daresay we shall have to get a licence from the Ministry of Health before we're allowed to have children quite soon—what would there have been for you to do ? You're very able with your tongues," continued Mrs. Trentham, "but that's as far as it goes with a great many of you. Now Nurse Deane, though she *was* younger than you," her voice had all the stabbing malice of a darning-needle, "she was an old-fashioned sort of girl."

"If she'd been more wide awake she mightn't have got herself into this jam," said the new nurse.

"I think she has shown great enterprise," Mrs. Trentham defended her indignantly, "abducted and thrown over a cliff and she still has the sense to stay unconscious until she can get legal advice."

"Something to talk about afterwards, though," suggested the new nurse carelessly. Bert was having a lot worse in Burma than being abducted and thrown over a cliff, she shouldn't wonder. "Anyway, isn't she going to marry this young man ? "

"I thought you were a nurse, not a matrimonial agency," said Mrs. Trentham. "Isn't it time for my massage ? "

"Nor yet," said the nurse.

"Well, my watch says eleven o'clock."

"Your watch is fast."

"I've been setting my life by this clock for twenty-five years and I'll continue to do so with your kind permission. I'll have my massage now."

The nurse shrugged. It didn't matter really, and massage gave you a chance to let them know who was master.

Even massage couldn't keep Mrs. Trentham's tongue still. "I see they've found the owner of the car," she said, "the car the murderer stole and threw over the cliff. It belonged to some foolish young woman visiting in South Kensington. She parked it two doors away from the house and then was surprised when it disappeared."

"You don't have to immobilise them any longer," said the new nurse.

"She is making a ridiculous fuss," continued the dauntless old lady. "Do you mean to say it is really seriously injured ?

she said. I call it infamous. What do we have a police force
for if not to prevent the public from joy-riding. Joy-riding ! "
The old woman cackled. " That's what she said to my nephew.
He did an interview with her for his paper. Not much joy-
riding about it, he told her. You try being pushed over a cliff.
And what do you think she said ? The gentlemen I go about
with don't behave so rough. Can you beat it ? "

" Well, really," said Nurse languidly, " it seems a pity to
go to the trouble of riding in a stolen car if you're not going
to get any fun out of it. Anyway, I don't like the sound of
this young man, the one they call Sammy. And she doesn't
really seem to have known very much about him."

" She knew enough to know that he'd save her life if
necessary. What more do you need to know about any man ? "

" My Bert's fighting to save other women's lives," said
Nurse turning the old lady over.

" A very unpromising outlook for marriage," said Mrs.
Trentham, scoring the last point as usual.

Mrs. Trentham had not been guilty of much exaggeration
when she said that the three men most closely involved in the
affair were awaiting Miss Deane's return to consciousness with
an almost agonising eagerness. But when she said three she
meant Crook, Sammy and her nephew, Roger. Had she known
Crook better she would have realised that he never did anything he could get anyone else to do equally well for him. So
long as the two young men practically lived on the hospital
telephone and went tearing down at the first suggestion that
a change was imminent, he could devote himself to other and
more lucrative work. There was, however, a third person who
was watching with greater anxiety than any of them, and that
was the murderer himself.

Sammy, in one of his morose moods, had said to Crook, " I
suppose you don't give a damn if the chap has another shot.
He may, you know. The police—fools that they are—have
told everyone she's in Queen Anne's Hospital."

" Well, young Sir Galahad, what are you here for ? " asked
Crook pertinently. " My strength is as the strength of ten . . .
I'm only a poor yellow dog of a lawyer, not passion personified,
as one of the lower order of papers put it."

" But, good Heavens, we've got to stop him at any cost."

" No, we haven't," Crook contradicted him. " We've got
to hope he does. It's our one chance of getting him. Till he
comes out of his hole we're like cats at wainscots. In fact,

we're worse off than cats, because we don't know which particular part of the wainscot to watch."

" And you're going back to your other jobs ? Washing your hands of this, eh ? "

" I've done what you asked me to do," Crook pointed out mildly, " and that was get the girl back. What's more, I've got her back alive. It's the right time for me to drop out." His voice changed. " Be your age, Sammy. If this fellow knows I'm on the war-path he'll stay put. If I fade out of the picture he might come forward. I bet you that's the way his mind works."

As usual, Crook was right. The murderer was more frightened of what this unconventional and unscrupulous so-called lawyer could do than of the whole of Scotland Yard. Scotland Yard at least works according to a formula. It has certain standards. You can't always tell which way the official cat will jump, but Crook's cat was quite likely to come down the chimney or push up the lid of a drain. He didn't have a formula and would have been the despair of the Civil Service.

The murderer, therefore, was more afraid now than he had been from the outset. He considered that the luck had treated him abominably. At every turn some cog had slipped. He thought of those accursed small boys who had found the body in the pit, the damnably astute Sammy who had got the girl out of the car, the pertinacious police who hadn't contrived to drop her overboard while they got her up the face of the cliff, the serene and immovable Mr. Crook, that human toad, he thought viciously, who didn't care how many men hanged so long as he kept his laurels untarnished.

Ever since he heard the incredible news—and to him it had really been incredible—of the discovery of the girl, not only uninjured, so far as physical injuries went, but alive—he had lived in what poets call a burning hell. In vain he told himself that this self-torture was absurd. No girl could live through such an ordeal ; if she did live she couldn't be sane, and insane people can't give evidence. Surely, surely, she would die without regaining consciousness. He bought every edition of the paper, hung about wherever crowds congregated, forgetting, as murderers do, that one girl and the man who has tried to destroy her are of midget importance to the country at large ; he dropped into pubs and listened there, he even got into conversation with strangers, and casually intro-duced the question of the attempt on Nora Deane's life to find out if there were any developments. Most of the people in pubs were men who naturally weren't much interested. Once he ran up against a young detective novelist, who dis-missed the affair with a shrug and an angry, " If I put a thing like that into one of my books my publisher would think I'd got a screw loose. Any ordinary girl would have died of exposure before that chap, Sammy, found her. She must have been lying out since some time after tea till early the following afternoon."

" Why should she ? You were there perhaps ? Saw the car go over ? "

The young man stared. " Good Lord ! I never thought of that. Of course, this chap probably hung about on the cliff till the last possible minute. He'd got to get back to wherever he came from but I don't suppose it mattered much when he got back, and there's a rotten local train service from Lestingham. Probably he wouldn't get a train that night, and anyway he wouldn't want to take a chance of being recognised by trying to get a bed in Lestingham. P'haps he kept her in the car—she was doped, wasn't she ? —till the last minute, then sent it over and walked back to Lestingham at a time when there wouldn't be anyone about, and caught a workman's train. That makes things a bit clearer."

The murderer was regarding him with mingled fury and panic. " You said that, not me," he said sharply.

" Oh well," said the novelist, calling for Same again, " I daresay the girl will be able to tell us. Not that it matters much in the end."

" They haven't got the fellow yet," the murderer reminded him tensely.

The other laughed in a maddeningly confident way. " They will, though, now Crook's on the scene. Crook 'ud cut his throat if he missed his man, and Crook's one of those chaps who intends to die in bed." He dismissed the subject as though it were of no consequence at all and went on to talk about writers and the reading public. The murderer wished they were all at the bottom of the lake of fire and brimstone. He didn't stay much longer. There wasn't any sense. Besides, when chaps like this came so near to the truth he could feel his nerve breaking under the strain.

As the days went by and Nora was still reported unconscious

his hopes timidly rose. All the same, he dared not sleep, he found himself rehearsing sentences before he uttered them in case they betrayed him, he would watch his face in the mirror, leave his rooms full of apprehension lest somehow he be recognised, identified, taken, hanged. He had never supposed life could degenerate into this desperate mouse-trap existence. Sitting by the little popping fire in the room he now rented— for how could he return to his own house knowing that the authorities were after him ?—he wondered bitterly how any murderer could ensure final success. Of course, few did, but he hadn't imagined that this wretched fate would overtake him. How could he have guessed that the car would crash, not on the rocks as he had intended, but on the rocky ledge, and that the shock and the exposure would not combined be sufficient to kill the girl who constituted such a peril to him ? How, again, could he know that not only Sammy but also Crook would be leagued against him ? He had meant her to drown and, drowning, take her secret with her, the secret he couldn't afford to let anyone guess. He had anticipated that everyone would assume he had lost his life also. The fact that no second body was forthcoming meant nothing in such a place. It hadn't occurred to him to reflect that difficult questions would be asked about the imprisonment of one body in the shattered car and the disappearance of the second. Anyway, he hadn't meant the car to be found until the furious seas had battered it to pieces and, with any luck at all—only he'd had none—rendered the passenger unrecognisable. He had planned, if necessary, to say that the girl had got control of the car when he was momentarily out of it, and he hadn't been able to stop her mad plunge, but if he said that he'd have to report the accident to the police, and he couldn't afford to do that. He had thought that, once he was assumed dead, he could go to and fro over the face of the earth, unchallenged, free, seeking like Satan whom he might devour. And the sooner the authorities could be persuaded of his death the better. He leaned forward and turned up the fire. The room seemed unconscionably cold. The flame refused to respond and he realised that the greedy stove had devoured another shillingsworth of gas. He felt in his pocket but he had only half-crowns or coppers. He couldn't go down and ask his landlady for change; he was reaching the pitch where he thought everyone regarded him curiously. He didn't know from one hour to the next whether the girl

157

had come round and told all she knew. Of course, the police still didn't know where he was, but it was a terrible feeling that an army of nameless men were on his trail. It made you afraid to go out in the dark in case someone put a hand on your shoulder ; it suddenly woke you in the night, so that you lay rigid, scarcely daring to breathe, convinced that you heard feet on the stairs, and the slow noiseless opening of your door. Sometimes he almost screamed when bus-conductors said sharply for the second time, " Now then, fare please." So long as his money lasted he could, presumably continue to hide. It was fortunate that his brother-in-law had also visited his bank on that last day of his life. It had prolonged his period of freedom, but sooner or later he'd be down to his last pound note. What did men do when they were entirely without money ? The obvious answer was that they got work. Sociologists told you that a determined man with qualifications like his could always find a berth. But if you hadn't references, if you didn't dare come out into the open—what then ? You took an assumed name, presumably, perhaps you forged references—you lived on a trigger-wire of terror, knowing yourself liable to arrest the first slip you made. Besides, some time someone might say your own name aloud, and before you remembered, you might give yourself away. He used to practise saying that name aloud and watching his own reactions. He must look as though it didn't mean a thing to him, or perhaps say, " Oh, isn't that the chap who was mixed up in the Lone Pit affair."

He knew something about Crook—most people did. Crook used to say, " The successful criminal does his stuff and lies low. Stay out of the limelight, go on staying out. While you do that you're safe." He didn't mind broadcasting the advice, because he knew practically no one can take it. It's too hard. Will may be strong, but nerves have their breaking-point, and the wise hunter waits until the tension is too great, and then he leaps. If he hadn't sent that telegram, if he'd taken the minor risk, then he might still be safe. As it was he had virtually signed his death warrant. Here the dying fire gave a last sigh and the faint gold spark vanished. It was as if the room was suddenly filled with a cold rushing wind.

" It's easy to be wise after the event," he thought, " but what was so wrong in wanting a little of the money that was in the family, to which really I had a right ? If Adela had listened to me, taken my advice—but Adela was always an exasperating woman "—but what a triumph she must be enjoying now if she knew anything at all. What a revenge she was getting. He thought he could hear her flat well-bred voice speaking.

" But I can't do that without thinking about it more. You see, Herbert . . ." He thrust the thought aside.

But he could not blot out the memory of that last fatal interview. What had inspired that crazy visit to Askew Avenue ? The answer was simple enough—money again. It had spelt death for two men, for the one who had lain in Lone Pit, and for the other who shivered by the cold gas-fire—for what was this existence but a living death, a knowledge that sooner or later he must be trapped, if not before his store of money was exhausted, then afterwards. It was ironic to think of all that money lying intact, and he, its rightful heir, unable to claim a penny of it.

He thought of that sordid conversation in the dining-room at Askew Avenue, each man bluffing to the height of his powers, Herbert out for money to buy his partnership and holding the girl's story over Alfred's head, Alfred laughing roughly and telling him he'd no proof, and he'd only ruin himself if he went into the courts to accuse his brother-in-law of murder, when it came out that he himself was next on the list to inherit his sister's fortune. It had been bluffing all right. Herbert couldn't prove that Alfred had murdered his wife ; Alfred couldn't afford to let the matter be raised in the courts. At what precise moment, he wondered, unable to turn his thoughts into some more pleasant channel, had he known that murder was the only solution ? There was surely some fraction of time when the fatal decision had been taken. Was it, perhaps, as they walked out to Herbert Webster's car —Alfred had insisted on accompanying him. And once the decision was made it seemed irrevocable, was irrevocable, in fact, because the act followed almost instantly upon it.

" I had to do it," he writhed. " Oh God, what choice was there ? He meant to ruin me. I'd said too much by then. I had to shut his mouth. And it wasn't that I was such a fool. It was the luck—the luck that was against me." It was the cry of the weak man, doomed to failure.

He stood up. " I'm not beaten yet," he said defiantly, " not yet. I've not given myself away completely. I can still stop this—somehow. If this girl doesn't live to tell the story, I'll escape."

" Escape to what ? " his mind taunted him. " Escape to take some menial job in an office, to walk humbly because a middle-aged man's lucky to have work at all, escape to wear another name and another personality, escape to walk warily for the rest of your days and live as poor men live. . . . If you'd known how expensive murder is you wouldn't have risked it, even for that money, would you ? "

Suddenly he began to laugh, cramming his hands over his mouth because the people in the next room complained if there was any noise, and if they heard him laughing like that they'd think he was mad. In a sense he supposed he was. It would save a lot of trouble to throw up the sponge. Because there was nothing to look forward to. Even if he did manage to get a good position, that only made him ripe for blackmail if anyone discovered his secret. It was a case of heads they win, tails you lose, and why not lose once and for all instead of over a period of years ? He beat his hands against the sofa cushion in a sort of ecstasy of madness.

Outside an organ began to grind out revivalist hymns, and a draggled-looking old man began to sing.

" Peace, perfect peace, in this dark world of sin," he quavered.

The murderer flung up the window. " Quoth the raven, nevermore," he shouted back. The next instant he'd slammed down the sash. He'd have the police on him double-quick if he wasn't careful. " I'm going daft," he thought. The singer was warbling on in a dispirited manner. Someone in the street had stopped and was looking up, and a minute later he heard feet on the stairs. They paused at his door and his heart began its furious rat-tat once again.

" They've got me." He looked round. There was no way out from this second-floor room except by the window, and he hadn't the courage for that. Someone rapped authoritatively, and he heard his landlady's voice.

" Mr. Winter." That was what he'd called himself.

" Oh come in."

She opened the door. There was a man behind her in plain clothes. " What is it ? " he said, sharply. Even the window was better than this.

" I want to show this gentleman the room."

He scowled. " As a matter of fact. . . ."

" I've told him it's free at the end of the week." She pointed out its amenities—that didn't take long—and went away, leaving him a prey to every fear on earth. Presently he heard the front door close and she came back.

" The gentleman's taking the room from Monday," she said.

" I like that," he exploded. " It's mine. . . ."

" By the week. That was the agreement."

" It doesn't suit me," he told her sulkily.

" It doesn't suit me for you to stay." She had the whip-hand and she knew it. " I like a permanent let and besides. . . ."

" Well ? " He was sulky, apprehensive. He was beginning to understand how easily murder may become a habit, once you'd had a little experience. He could see himself with his hands round that skinny neck, choking the hard complacence out of that odious face. Sympathy, tenderness—why she couldn't spell the words. He wondered how she'd feel if he told her he was the man the police were after.

" He's a quiet gentleman," said the landlady.

" What about me ? Any complaints ? " His fingers curved. He had big hands, powerful and ruthless. They'd dealt out death before now, and if she had surprised his secret and meant to betray him—well, a man can't be hanged more than once.

" The couple next door have to go to work of a morning," she said coldly. " They need their sleep."

" Do I stop them ? "

" They don't like the radio going at midnight."

" That's only the news." His voice was breathless. He had to have that, there might be a police message. A man in his defenceless state couldn't afford to neglect any precaution.

" And then, the way you talk to yourself. . . ."

" That's nonsense," he cried, and then in the same breath, " What do I say ? "

" How should I know ? But it disturbs them. And they're permanents. They need their rest."

. He thought, " She's right. I must go. They're getting suspicious of me. I can't risk that. Does she guess anything ? " But her closed face told him nothing at all.

He pulled himself together. " As a matter of fact," he said and wondered if his voice sounded the same as usual, " I shouldn't have been able to stay much longer in any case. I heard from my Manchester representative this morning—I have to go up there."

" Yes ? " She didn't seem interested, and he remembered too late that she probably went through all the post and she

161

must have seen he hadn't had a letter with a Manchester postmark. He hadn't had any letters at all, except a few he'd
sent himself in a disguised hand, and none of them had the
Manchester postmark. " If you could make it convenient to
leave before the end of the week," she said, " that would suit
me. I want to get the place cleaned out."

He sighed with relief as she shut the door. She didn't
suspect anything, she just found him an unsatisfactory
lodger and would like him to get out. He began to count
his money.

" Perhaps I'd better go to Manchester," he reflected. " If
they do get on my track and find I've been here, would she
remember ? And if she did, would she tell them ? And would
they believe I was telling the truth ? Wouldn't they rather
suspect that I was trying to throw dust in their eyes ? " If
he could be sure of that, then Manchester would clearly be
the safest place for him to go to.

He got up and began to fling his clothes into a suit-case.
Then he stopped. He couldn't get out, not yet, not till he
knew about the girl. Any minute now she might speak—or
die. He must stay here till he knew which way the dice would
fall. All the same, he might send himself a telegram summoning him north, for the sake of appearances. He couldn't, he
thought, telephone from the house ; you never knew who
would be listening. There was a box not far off, he might go
there. On the way another thought struck him. This suspense
was more than he could endure. The enormity of his own
peril seemed to strike at him more powerfully than before.
He was a fool to stand waiting so patiently. A man worth
his salt would do something before it was too late.

" But what ? " he demanded.

The obvious answer was, " Stop the girl talking," and as he
thought that a new idea flashed into his mind and he was
resolved on his next step as irrevocably as when, on that fatal
walk to the car, he decided on murder for good or ill. There
was someone in the telephone box. He hadn't expected that.
It was a girl and she went on and on gabbling away about
nothing, he was certain. He chattered with rage, swung his
clenched fists, then realised she was looking at him oddly,
and hurried off, pulling his black-brimmed hat over his eyes.

At the post office he found a vacant instrument and rang
up the hospital where Nora Deane lay, closely guarded.

The hospital porter answered him. He had prepared his

story while he went along. He asked to speak to the Matron.
"Who is it ? " said the porter.

" In connection with Miss Deane."

" We aren't answering enquiries about Miss Deane over the
telephone," snapped the porter.

He thought, Damn your impudence, but refrained from
comment. He couldn't afford a row. Everything was too
tense. A lady with a cream-coloured pekinese on a lead pulled
open the door of the booth and said, " Oh, I'm sorry, I didn't
know there was—that is, I left a little diary somewhere. I
wondered if . . . Oh then I expect it was the place where I
had coffee." He shoved the door to and found he'd got cut
off, and had to dial all over again. Once more the porter
answered him. He assumed a chill authoritative voice.

" I am speaking for Miss Deane's only living relative," he
said. " My name is Winter and I am a lawyer. Would you
kindly put me on to the matron ? "

The fellow said, " Hold on, sir," and he was connected. It
was as easy as that. However, all the difficult part lay ahead.

" Is that the matron ? My name is Winter. I am Miss
Fenton's lawyer. Miss Fenton is Miss Deane's aunt, living in
Scotland. She has been very much distressed by the news,
and as I was coming south she asked me to get into touch
with you and find out the latest developments."

" I'm afraid there's nothing to tell you," said the matron
doubtfully. " That is . . ." There was a pause and he
exclaimed, " Are you there ? " because this sort of thing was
driving him crazy. She apologised, " I'm so sorry. Can you
hold on a minute ? There's an urgent call on the other
telephone—a doctor."

He hung on with what patience he could muster. This was
a dangerous game he was playing. He might be walking
straight into the little covered shed, but a man in his position
had to take a chance. If he could win the last round, prevent
the girl from speaking, diddle that young scribbling fool of his
triumph, black Mr. Crook's eye for him, destroy Sammy
Parker's hopes—even that wouldn't level the score. But it
would be something.

The matron came back to the line. " I'm so sorry to keep
you waiting, Mr. Winter. I wish I could tell you something
helpful about Miss Deane. But the fact is there's practically
no change."

" She's not spoken yet ? " He had been a pretty good

amateur actor as a young man, and he could put on a convincing Scottish accent.

" Not yet. Of course, Dr. Dacre hopes. . . ."

" Dacre ? Could I see him ? Miss Fenton's naturally very anxious. . . ."

, " We're very anxious, too. If we had known the name and address of Miss Deane's aunt we would have written, but she was unable to tell us anything and there was no record anywhere. . . ."

He allowed his voice to assume a severer note. " Miss Deane has no one but herself to thank if she does appear to be alone in the world. She's like all the young gerr-rls nowadays, want to stand on their own feet and won't take advice. She cut adrift from her auntie some while back. The foolish lassie didn't think it worth while writing to an auld body. . . ."

" If you'll give me Miss Fenton's address, Mr. Winter, we will certainly keep her posted."

He gave an address in Edinburgh. Before they could find out it was a fake, his job would be accomplished.

" And—what hope is there ? " he continued.

" Well, you know what they say. While there's life there's hope. Dr. Dacre will be along in an hour or so. If you'd care to see him. . . ."

" I would like that fine," he said firmly. " I promised Miss Fenton to see the lassie if I could. Miss Fenton is crippled herself," he added, " arthritis, the puir soul, and sore she suffers." It occurred to him that he might be overdoing the bluff Scotch lawyer and he became more restrained. " Miss Fenton would like her niece to come to her when the doctors let her travel, and it's where she should have been this long while. There's work in Edinburgh as much as in London or elsewhere."

" That would be very satisfactory," Matron commented. " We were wondering where to send her for her convalescence. For Dr. Dacre is afraid the effects of shock may be rather far-reaching." Then she said, " And may I have your address, Mr. Winter ? "

" I'm at the Station Hotel for two nights," he told her hurriedly. " But I was wishful to see Miss Deane, if only to tell Miss Fenton how she was."

" I'd have to get Dr. Dacre's permission. He won't be round for an hour or so, but if you'd care to come in then, you could see him at all events. So far he hasn't allowed anyone to see Miss Deane. It's very uncomfortable this being a police case. . . ."

" Oh ay," he agreed. " I'll be along in an hour, then. If the lassie's not conscious then I'll not give her a further shock by appearing, and if she is, then she'll be glad to know her auntie's waiting for her." He rang off before she could ask him again for his address. When he came out of the telephone booth the lady with the pekinese was still waiting. He wondered if she had been there all the time, if she was following him, if, after all, Crook was playing with him, like a cat with a mouse, if the secret he thought he'd so jealously guarded wasn't a secret after all.

" But, of course she's just what she seems," he told himself sensibly. " A silly woman who leaves her diary in a telephone booth. I ought to know the type, I've met enough of them. And as for the matron, why should she suppose I'm anything but what I appear to be ? An old aunt crippled with arthritis in Edinburgh is safe enough."

It was a dangerous plan he had in mind, many would have thought a hopeless one. His one chance now was to prevent the girl from speaking, and there was only one way to prevent this. It was impossible to plan every detail, he must take the first step and watch his opportunity. The matron had told him that the doctor wouldn't be round for an hour. He himself intended to arrive before then, though it was improbable that he would be allowed to be alone with the girl. Still, there was a chance. He went back to his rooms and completed his packing. He didn't intend to return here. Too late he wished he hadn't given the name of Winter. Still, they were bound to find out soon enough that he was an impostor. He slipped nervously down the stairs, carrying the suit-case. He had left some notes on the table in his room, more than sufficient, he calculated, to cover the landlady's account. He shook with nervousness lest she should suddenly appear, but this hour of the day was one she usually devoted to shopping. He himself took a roundabout path away from the shops. At the station he deposited the bag and bought a ticket for London. This was to put spies on the wrong track. Then he bought a ticket for Lestingham and waited impatiently for what seemed to him hours and hours for the next train. He thought people looked at him suspiciously as he alighted on the platform, but told himself he was a fool and the victim of his imagination. He walked a short way, but when he was near

165

the hospital he got a cab and drove up as Miss Fenton's lawyer would certainly be expected to do, knowing that he could charge the fare to his client's account. He explained his identity to the porter and was allowed to come in. The door swung behind him and he began walking up a long passage. Every step he took, he reflected, took him nearer his fate. A crazy tune began to swing in his head.

> Will you walk into my parlour ? said the
> spider to the fly.

And then from somewhere another line he'd read :

> Perseverance is a virtue, said the spider to
> the fly.

" Will you wait in here, sir ? " said the porter, opening the door of a small room. He went in and sat down and the porter shut the door behind him. He heard the footsteps going away and terror smote him again.

" I'm past the first mile-stone," he reminded himself. " I'm inside the place."

Now he had to move on to the second stage, which was altogether more difficult, more dangerous, and from which there might well be no going back.

CHAPTER NINETEEN

We never are but by ourselves betrayed.—WM. CONGREVE.

THEY left him in the little room for a long time. Outside he heard footsteps going up and down ; sometimes they seemed to slow up as they approached his door, and he prepared for a fresh encounter. But eventually they all went past. There was a little mirror hanging in a corner and he went over and looked at himself. It seemed impossible that he shouldn't instantly be recognised as the man whose photograph had been in all the papers. For all he knew, the porter had recognised him already. He hadn't dared do much in the way of a disguise. Wigs and moustaches were untrustworthy, they were too easily detected and might later be traced. He had a plate in his upper jaw which, removed, displayed a gap in his front teeth ; he felt that with this taken out he presented quite a different appearance. That and a pair of horn-rimmed glasses to replace the usual pair with invisible rims wrought a considerable change, and he was actor enough to know that an extravagant disguise is worse than no disguise at all. Besides, it's by mannerisms, a particular walk, a tone of voice, that men are recognised.

He got up and walked over to the window. The hospital was on the high road. Just below him two women were talking eagerly. The air was so quiet that when he raised the window a little he could hear what they said.

"Bensons—shredded suet," one was observing earnestly. It was hard to believe in a world where shredded suet assumed such importance.

Over the road a number of women waited in a fish queue, and more were standing at the bus stop. The whole world seemed normal except himself. A little boy went past dragging his blunt-toed boots through the pile of gold leaves in the gutter ; a dog chased a red cat. . . . The door opened suddenly and he turned.

It was the matron, a pleasant sensible woman of about fifty, wearing pince-nez.

She said, " Mr. Winter ? I hope we may have better news for you soon. Dr. Dacre has just arrived."

"Is he with Miss Deane ? "

" He has an operation case first, and then he's going along."

" I'd like to see the young lady . . ." he said nervously.

" I daresay she'll seem very changed," Matron warned him.

" I've never set eyes on her myself. And Miss Fenton hasn't seen her since the war."

" Of course, it was a terrible experience. . . ."

He shook his head. " These young girls ! " he said. " And this mysterious young man. In my young days they introduced their young men to the home circle."

" But Miss Deane hadn't a home circle." Matron's tone was brisk.

" Will the doctor be a long time ? " he asked, fighting to keep apprehension out of his voice.

" Oh, not very long, I think."

Suddenly he was convinced that she was playing with him, that she knew who he was, that it was all a trap. Yet why should it be ? You don't look for a hamadryad in a sideboard, said G. K. Chesterton, because hamadryads don't live in sideboards, and you don't look for a murderer in the person of a not very spruce Scotch lawyer.

" I have an appointment," he mumbled. " How would it be if I were to come back in half an hour ? "

" Oh, Dr. Dacre won't be as long as that. Besides, Mr. Crook's coming at any minute."

" Crook ? " Now terror had him fairly by the throat.

" Yes. He's the lawyer acting for Mr. Parker. In fact, he was with the police when they found Miss Deane," a version of the case that would have turned Crook green with rage.

The murderer said nothing, and Matron enquired, " Have you ever met Mr. Crook ? He's quite a personality."

" We haven't heard of him in Edinburgh."

Matron smiled. " Really ? I should have expected the whole legal profession to know Mr. Crook by reputation at all events."

He thought, " That was another trap and I've fallen into it. Damn it, they have rumbled me. I've got to get out double-quick."

He said he'd wait till the doctor was ready, and Matron agreed placidly that it wouldn't be long. He stood up, expecting her to go ; as soon as he was alone he'd oil out and they could think what they pleased. Putting one over on Matron was one thing, but getting past Crook was something quite different. Because in spite of what he'd just said he knew a lot about Crook, and he'd sooner be cornered by a rat. You can kick a rat off sometimes, but Crook would be as difficult to escape as an octopus. Matron went on standing there, damn her, making polite conversation to which he could barely find replies. And all the time he expected the door to open and Crook to come in. She went away at last, and the instant he could no longer hear her footsteps he tiptoed across to the door and opened it. The passage was empty ; there wasn't even a probationer in sight. He thought he could make a bolt for it now, and then speculated if there might still be a chance to put his original plan into practice. There were some patients on this floor in private rooms, with the doctor's name on a slip in a slot by the door. Of course, if the girl wasn't alone it was hopeless. He found the door and stood staring at it. He couldn't believe he'd got so far. There was no one in the corridor and he put his hand out to turn the knob. He'd made the necessary preparations before he left his rooms. Now he needed no more than half a minute. Just in time he heard a movement in the room and shrank back. This room was almost on a corner, and he could hide himself and watch developments. The door opened and a nurse came out. She walked in the opposite direction, round another corner. He was nearly choked by the beating of his heart and the drumming of the blood in his ears. Stealthily he emerged. Now or never. Are there not, dear Michael, two points in the adventure of the diver ? One when, a beggar, he prepares to plunge, two, when, a prince, he rises with his pearl ? Festus, I plunge. . . .

" Hullo, hullo, hullo," sang out a cheerful voice. " Little Bo-Peep has lost her sheep. . . ."

He swung round. A large short common-looking man wearing a common-looking brown suit had appeared apparently out of the floor and was regarding him with a cheerful grin.

" Devil of a place a hospital to lose one's way in," the newcomer continued. " What were you making for actually ? "

" I was—er—trying to find my way out," he said. " I have to put through an important telephone call, and . . ."

" You're on the first floor. You'll have to go down. But there's a telephone here that's used by friends and relatives of the victims. I've used it myself more than once. I'll show you."

The wretched man did not need to be told that this was the ubiquitous Mr. Crook ; not could he hope that his ridiculous story had been accepted. As they walked along the corridor he pulled himself together.

" As a matter of fact," he said, sounding the Scottish accent which had escaped him in the moment of crisis, " my name is Winter. I'm Miss Fenton's lawyer. Miss Fenton is Miss Deane's only living relative." He decided that by the date of their next meeting Miss Fenton should have had a stroke which would make it impossible for her to answer letters or to see visitors. This thrusting pugnacious fellow looked perfectly capable of chartering an aeroplane to take him to Edinburgh to check up on his companion's statement.

" Nice to meet you," said Crook, heartily. " I'm a lawyer myself though you don't have to believe that if you don't want to. So Miss Fenton sent you down to look after the young lady's affairs. Bit late in the day, wasn't it ? "

" I came as soon as my other engagements permitted," said

ANTHONY GILBERT

the·spurious Winter stiffly. " In any case, I understand that
Miss Deane is hardly in a fit condition to receive visitors."
" Oh, but we're changing all that," said Crook, heartily.
" Dacre thinks there's definite improvement. That's why
I'm here." He pushed open the door of the identical room
the murderer had been occupying a few minutes before and
shouldered his companion in.
" We'd better wait here," he said.
" I—the telephone," said the other, whose one desire now
was to make good his escape.
" Someone 'ull be along in a minute, I daresay, and they'll
show you. Naturally we're all hangin' on Miss Deane's words."
" It might be happier for the puir creature if she didn't
remember what had occurred," said Winter primly.
" Happier for the murderer," Crook agreed. " I'll bet you,
wherever he is, he's shaking in his shoes this minute." He
wagged his big red head and chuckled.
" Ye know who he is," ventured Winter.
" I could lay my finger on him any minute practically,"
said Crook.
The poor wretch started. What did that mean ? Was he
being hyper-sensitive and reading meanings into casual
phrases that they were never intended to bear ? or was Crook
playing with him, a fat red cat playing with a mouse ?
" I suppose," he managed, " it's just a matter of time."
" So's the Last Judgment. You know, Mr. Winter, I'm not
a soft-hearted chap in the ordinary way, you can't afford to
be in my line of business, as you know as well as me, but I
give you my word, I'm sorry for the fellow when Sammy
Parker gets wind of him. Tearing him limb from limb will be
child's play to that young man. Boiling him in oil, roasting
him over a slow fire, leaving him out for the vultures, those
are some of Sammy's ideas."
" The police will prevent that, fortunately."
" If they're on the spot. They don't seem to have been
specially up to time so far. But there's a space for repentance,
no doubt. Hullo, who's this ? "
The door opened like a whirlwind and Roger Trentham
came in.
" Give you three guesses," offered Crook hospitably to his
brother practitioner.
" I'm afraid I've no idea."
Before Crook could effect introductions the door opened

170

again and Sammy came in. The pseudo-Mr. Winter rose unsteadily to his feet. Now was the time to press his demand for the use of the telephone. They could hardly offer to accompany him, and once he was out of their sight he'd run like the notorious rabbit. He half-smiled, forgetting the gap in his teeth.

"I'm afraid I must just put through that message," he said. He looked at Sammy. "Mr. Crook's been telling me about you. I'm afraid you have had a shocking time, anxiety and so forth, but they seem to think Miss Deane will pull round, after all."

"Bad luck for them if she doesn't," said Sammy.

Crook intervened. "This is Mr. Winter, Miss Deane's aunt's lawyer, from Edinburgh where the rock comes from."

Before Sammy could speak, young Mr. Trentham, who had been the first young man to put in an appearance, broke out, "I say, can't that call of yours stand over for a minute? Can't you give me a line on the aunt? I mean, my readers are beginning to get impatient. You know what they are. Always wanting something fresh. A chap I know in the theatre says that in a play you have to bring on a new character or start a new subject every three minutes, if you're to stop the audience coughing and dropping their programmes. Miss Deane's been like this for forty-eight hours, and when you've told them that you've told them all there is to tell. You're a godsend to me. Now then, about the old lady. Does she breed parrots or go in for spiritualism or anything like that? My readers like their old ladies to be a bit original. What does she look like? How old is she? And maybe you can open up a bit about Miss Deane. My readers are nuts on mystery, but they don't want too much of it."

"That'll do," said Sammy. "Miss Deane's going to marry me. Get that into your thick head if you can."

"Well, is the old lady going to leave her any priceless pearls or anything of that kind? My readers want a bit of romance."

"I've told you, I'll supply all that."

"I—really I couldn't say," protested the hapless Mr. Winter, feeling like a besieged Christian with lions all round him. "Miss Deane had not kept up with her aunt as she should. . . ."

"Well, look here," interrupted Roger, "will you go along and have a talk with Mrs. Trentham, my Auntie May, before you go back ? She had Miss Deane for a nurse at the time it all happened—in a way she really dragged the girl into it."

" I'm really at a loss," almost shouted Mr. Winter.

" It's quite easy," said Crook. " The girl knew too much about the death of a lady called Adela Newstead. That was the beginning."

" But—how very strange ! I understood from the papers it was Mr. Newstead who was killed."

" That was later, and there are lots of chaps going round saying it served him jolly well right. I wouldn't know about that, of course. He may have killed his wife—but I never did approve of all this interference in a chap's private affairs. If the girl had had any sense she wouldn't have touched the thing with a barge-pole."

" She couldn't help it," exclaimed Sammy, indignantly.

" She didn't have to go and see this chap, Webster, did she ? " Crook was watching Winter carefully as he spoke. " That's when the trouble began. But for her Mrs. Newstead would have been quietly disposed of ; and the dogs could have gone on snoozin' as before, instead of which she set 'em barking up every tree in sight."

Mr. Winter looked shocked. " But if she had reason to suspect foul play. . . ."

" Now then, you and me play in the same yard," Crook admonished him. " We know how often citizens come tooling up to the Police Station with their tongues hangin' out to give information, unless they think there's somethin' in it for them."

" And—dear me ! —do you suggest that there was anything in it for Miss Deane ? "

" Oh, she's the exception that proves the rule—ain't she, Sammy ? The woman with a conscience. If you ask me, a conscience is like a Rolls-Royce. It's ostentatious unless you're sure you can afford it."

" I, of course, only know the story as it has appeared in the press," said Mr. Winter. " I confess to being a leetle confused. It appears that Miss Deane had information that made her dangerous to someone. . . ."

" And that someone was the Lone Pit murderer," amplified Crook. " But the pieces are all beginnin' to fit together."

" If Miss Deane should not recover or should not altogether recall the details . . ." hazarded Mr. Winter.

" I'd have a shot at fitting the thing up myself," Crook offered. " It's just a sum in simple addition. And you'd think the same if you knew all the facts." He looked round the circle. "Why, boys, here's a golden opportunity while we're waiting for the sawbones. Suppose we tell Mr. Winter the story as far as we know it and see what conclusions he comes to. Sammy, you start. You were in on Chapter One and the rest of us can carry on when it's our turn."

CHAPTER TWENTY

My way is to begin with the beginning.—LORD BYRON.

"CHAPTER ONE," announced Sammy, "begins in a fog. In that fog I met Miss Deane on her way to Askew Avenue to take up the job of nursing Newstead's wife. It was a very bad night, shocking, in fact, one of those fogs when anything may happen." He looked meaningly at Crook.

"Don't mind me," said Mr. Crook. "Fogs help me to pay my income tax."

Mr. Winter looked perplexed, but Sammy gave him no opportunity to ask questions.

"I'd overshot my station and was waiting at the entrance wondering what I'd better do—it was about eleven o'clock and as much hope of the fog lifting before morning as of the Japs winning the Far Eastern War—when a girl came up the steps and walked past me. She stopped just in front of me, as if she wasn't quite sure of her bearings either. I'm not precisely a clever chap," explained Sammy modestly, "what was good enough for my father is good enough for me, and I don't like to see a young girl—and Miss Deane's no amazon—hanging about alone at that hour of the night and in that sort of weather. All sorts of nasty things happen in fogs and some of them happen to young girls."

"Sometimes the young girls want 'em to," contributed Crook, unsympathetically.

"I could see she wasn't that sort of girl. For one thing, she carried a case, and in the glimpse I got of her as she came up from the station I could see she was wearing a uniform coat. So naturally I asked if I could help. I didn't know the neighbourhood, but you remember what they say about two heads being better than one, so we started off together to look for Askew Avenue. We talked a bit on the way—she told me she hadn't got a relative living (well, I daresay she didn't count her Edinburgh auntie, seeing they hadn't had much to do with one another for some years) and I got the idea that this was a girl I'd like to see some more of. So when we reached Askew Avenue I said I'd look in the next day during her time off. She didn't know a soul in the place, and nursing a serious case isn't much fun, and anyway I thought if we staged a meeting by daylight we might know if we wanted to call it a day or pass on into Chapter Two. I managed to get a lift back to London after I'd landed her at the house she wanted—one of these night lorries taking chaps to and from factories—and next day I went down as I'd promised to collect Miss Deane. When I reached the house the blinds were down in the upper room and nobody answered the bell. I waited some time and presently Mr. Newstead turned up and asked me my business. When I explained he told me the girl had gone back to town, and he couldn't give me the address. I thought that was a bit thin, seeing he must have got her from somewhere, but he said it was the doctor. I found out at the local which doctor had been attending the house and went along to see him, but my luck was dead out, he wouldn't tell me anything either. I suppose Mr. Crook would have discovered her whereabouts somehow, but I seemed to be in a blind alley, and when I got back to London there was an official letter telling me to move on that night, and—well, that was the end of it for the time being. Only I felt pretty sure we should meet again some time and I kept my eyes skinned."

"Trentham's turn," said Crook, judicially, "unless Mr. Winter's got any questions he'd like to ask."

"Not yet," said Mr. Winter, looking painfully at the young journalist.

"My paper features crime," explained Roger, "and we keep a sort of register. For instance, if anybody finds a baby's body in a well, we turn up the register and see how many other babies' bodies have been found in wells, and so on. We didn't hear anything about Mrs. Newstead's death, but then we wouldn't expect to. There didn't seem to be any mystery about that—but when the body of a man was found in Lone Pit we began to get cracking. We didn't know any more than any other paper, not at first, and though we went down and interviewed the local people we didn't learn any more than the police did."

" I understood," observed Mr. Winter, moistening his dry lips, " there was very little doubt as to the identity of the murderer."

" Once we knew who the dead man was there was no doubt at all," agreed Crook.

" You mustn't think we by-passed the whole thing," Roger was earnestly assuring Mr. Winter, " but from our point of view there wasn't much of a story to handle. One middle-aged man has a row with another middle-aged man and biffs him over the head and puts the body in a quarry—very regrettable, of course, but not uncommon. And definitely not romantic. What we want is a lovely girl—and until Miss Deane flashed into the picture we couldn't find one. Of course we made enquiries about Mrs. Newstead, in case there had been any funny business about her death, but the result was we got pushed off doorsteps and got earache listening at key-holes without getting any forrader. It was a pity, because we were short on murders just then, and they don't like you to take to the good on the *Post*, but just when I was beginning to think the whole case was folding up, I got my stroke of good fortune. My Auntie May rang me up from Green Valley that she had a girl there who'd been in the house when Mrs. Newstead died, and had carried a very fishy story to the brother-in-law some hours later."

" You didn't—er—think it rather surprising that she had not mentioned the matter before ? "

" She was a girl with a living to get," cut in Crook. " Also she seems to have had some sense, though not enough. She knew that gettin' mixed up with the police wouldn't do her any good."

" Anyway," continued Roger enthusiastically, " it seemed a dead snip for the *Post*. And at that time no one else had the story at all. I put in that original para. to establish the fact that we were head of the queue. . . ."

" And practically signed the girl's death warrant," cut in Crook drily.

" I didn't say where she was," protested the young man.

" No. But you warned X. that she had evidence to give that might lead to the discovery of the truth. When he read that para.," he added, turning politely to Mr. Winter, " X. decided to nip in first. He phoned the matron of the nursing home with a cooked-up story and managed to find out from her where Miss Deane was employed. Then he dashed out

175

and sent both telegrams—oh yes, I think he sent both tele-grams. If she'd only got the one signed Sammy she might, bein' a girl of spirit, have shoved it into her pocket and done nothing. But he put the wind up her a bit with the first wire, and then followed it up with another."

" And she thought it had been sent by the real Sammy," explained Roger. " Well, so did my Auntie May. So did we all."

" No reason why she shouldn't," Crook agreed politely, " unless, of course, she'd wondered how he got the address. Still, no one thinks of everything, not even murderers."

" And it's hard to blame the young lady," put in Mr. Winter. " Why should she not suppose Mr.—er—Sammy had sent it ? "

" Well, since Sammy tells us he didn't, it's obvious there's only one person who could, and that's X. himself."

" I couldn't have sent it," said Sammy. " I didn't know her address. Admittedly someone telephoned the matron, but it wasn't me. I didn't know the matron's address."

" Precisely," said Crook. " Remember what Sherlock Holmes used to say ? Eliminate the impossible and what remains, however improbable, must be the truth. It's a pity," he added thoughtfully, " we haven't got Miss Deane here to tell us the rest of the story, but in her absence we must reconstruct it as well as we can. She supposed the wire to be the real article and she went off to meet her death, as they used to say when I was young and education wasn't so fussy as it is now."

Roger Trentham, like one of the famous oysters, hurried up all eager for the treat. " When I got down to Green Valley my Auntie May was hopping with excitement. First time in her life she'd ever been connected with a murder at first-hand, so to speak."

" You mean she had already assumed that there was a plot against the girl ? " Mr. Winter sounded puzzled.

" You don't know my Auntie May," said Roger kindly. " She could beat any thriller-writer at his own game. When she heard that we'd found her in the car over the cliff, she just folded her hands and said, " Exactly what I expected. But what's the good of talking to the police ? "

" They'd have to be issued with an extra pair of ears apiece if they did," said Crook rudely.

" And when," enquired Mr. Winter, " did you first realise that Miss Deane was not coming back ? "

" Oh, I left that bit out. A chap rang about six-thirty or
so and said he was Sammy. . . ."

" Did he say it ? " asked Crook, " or did you put the idea
into his mind ? "

" Now you come to mention it, I believe I put it into his
mind. Of course, we'd no idea there was anything wrong at
that juncture."

" Nice present to him," suggested Crook. " Still, I daresay
it don't make much difference in the long run."

" My Auntie May and I thought she'd gone off with this
fellow to prevent being dragged into any unpleasantness,"
explained Roger. " And I can't say I blamed her, though
Auntie May thought different. Auntie May would like nothing
better than getting mixed up good and proper in a criminal
case."

" And I suppose she'd give the girl beans if she hung back
like a modest violet."

" If you ask me," said the young man, " it was as much to
avoid Auntie May as the police that she cut and run. And
I'm with her there, too. I'd as soon face a young tank—and
I'm a man who fought with the Eighth Army—as my Auntie
May on the war-path."

Mr. Winter leaned forward. The conversation had a painful fascination for him. He felt like a man walking on a tight-
rope, knowing that any second he may crash. And yet he
couldn't stand still. He had to go on walking. " And may I
ask when you had any reason to suppose all was not well ? "
he enquired.

" When Mr. Parker here came bounding into my office
asking what the hell I meant by it ? "

" And lucky I was in too much of a hurry to do more than
bound," put in Sammy indignantly.

" Hold your horses," said Crook. " There was nothing you
could do—in law."

" And that's justice ? " exploded Sammy.

" You ain't the only chap in this world called Sammy,"
Crook explained mildly. " And Mr. Trentham was only giving
his public the news it wanted. A fellow called Sammy rang
up and said he had taken Miss Deane away—and Mr.
Trentham printed the story. That's fair comment."

Mr. Winter spoke again. " And it didna occur to ye," he
stressed the Scotch note in his voice, " Mr. Parker will forgive
me maybe, but I'm an auld man and a lawyer at that—it

didna occur to ye that Mr. Parker might be wishful to put
you off the scent ? "

" You don't miss much, do you ? " said Crook in appre-
ciative tones.

Mr. Winter smiled, though the missing front tooth made
the effect a rather ghastly one.

" I am a man over whose head many many years have
passed, Mr. Crook, and the one thing I have learned, sad
though it may sound, is that the human heart is deceitful and
desperately wicked."

Crook reflected that it seemed to have taken the chap a
long time to find that out, but forebore from comment.

" Of course I thought of it." Roger Trentham was indignantly answering Mr. Winter's remark. " It's what any chap
would think of. But I'm not a lawyer. I'm just a journalist,
and I tell things the way they happen."

Crook's admiration for him knew no bounds. A young
fellow who could make that sort of statement and get away
with it should go far.

" However, as I've already told Sammy here, I rang his
landlady and discovered he'd been at home all the previous
night, which simply couldn't be the fact with the fellow who
pushed our little girl over the cliff, and that only left X. It
was quite simple really," he added modestly.

" I must, as they say, hand it to you," commented Mr.
Winter, with another of his ghastly grins. " You didn't forget
much."

Crook looked at him thoughtfully. " That ain't good
enough. When you're plannin' a murder, Mr. Winter, you
can't afford to forget anything. A chain's only as strong as
its weakest link. Miss one detail and you're dished. One of
my aunts," he added expansively, " used to give me hand-
painted texts—painted by herself—to hang over my bed.
One of them was ' He that is faithful in little is faithful in
much ' and it's as good a motto for a murderer as he's likely
to find."

Sammy said, " How did you know I should be down in
Southshire ? because you did, didn't you ? "

" You had Young Lochinvar stamped all over you
when you came into my office. And you knew that part
of the country, which I didn't, so I didn't see why you
shouldn't blaze the trail. You remember tellin' me," he
turned to Roger, " that some other chap had beaten us to it,

called at the Boar before we did? Well, that chap was Sammy."

" And you knew it ? "

" No one else was likely to get there before you and me."

" And you let him get away with it ? "

" I had something else to think of," acknowledged Crook, and now he was as serious as a judge pronouncing the death sentence. " It was a thing that worried me and Bill quite a lot and that was," he leaned back, stretching out his pudgy legs and folding his big freckled hands, while he eyed his audience who hung on his words with an absorption that would have been a compliment to Mr. Churchill, " why did Webster wait three days before taking any action ? "

" But he didn't," said Roger, " he went down to Charlbury directly he'd seen the girl. Or don't you agree ? "

" I do agree," said Crook. " But he didn't kill Alfred Newstead that day, because Alfred Newstead was at his wife's funeral. Alfred Newstead didn't disappear till the Friday. Mrs. Newstead died on the Tuesday. Now, Webster was a lawyer." He turned to Mr. Winter. " You'll appreciate this point, I know. He wasn't a fool, so I argued he must have some point in waiting, but to a common or garden chap like me that don't make sense. If he'd gone to the police while Mrs. Newstead was still above ground he'd have a case. They could rout out the doctor and make him give evidence, they could pull in Miss Deane, and our Mr. Newstead would be in a very nasty spot. But instead of that he holds his hand, he telephones to Miss Deane that he's decided to take no action, and then, three days too late, he pushes brother-in-law Alfred into a hole in the ground. No, that was my problem. Lawyers act logical on the whole, and there was some answer if I could find it. And till I found it I reckoned I was just wastin' time. When I'd got it I knew I'd be on the home stretch. So while our two young men were runnin' a neck-and-neck in South-shire, I stayed in London and figured things out."

" And—you found the answer ? " Mr. Winter eyed him carefully.

" I think so. Yes, Mr. Winter, I really and truly do think so. I got a line on Mr. Webster's movements. We know he was at his office on the Tuesday morning at eleven o'clock, because Miss Deane left him there. After she'd gone he put a call through to Mr. Cradock to say he could start drawin' up the documents for the partnership. Everything was O.K., he said, and he'd be writing. That gave me my cue."

" I haven't got there yet," said Roger, blankly.

" Well, look at it straight. Cradock was the chap he was going into partnership with. The thing had been hangin' fire for a while, and not because Webster couldn't make up his mind. But when you enter into that sort of agreement there's generally a clause sayin' you'll put up so much cash, and if the agreement hadn't got through it was because Webster was findin' difficulties in layin' hands on the ready. Now, mark you," he leaned forward impressively, " the minute after Miss Deane tells him that his sister's dead, he rings up Mr. Cradock and says, Go right ahead. See where that gets you ? "

" You mean, he knew he'd have the money ? But I thought it was all left to the husband ? "

" It was,' said Crook.

" You mean, he'd already made up his mind to commit murder ? "

" No. He was a lawyer. Lawyers know better than most people that murder don't pay. But there's another line. . . ."

" Blackmail ! " exclaimed Roger Trentham.

" Don't the facts suggest that to you ? He knew his brother-in-law couldn't afford to have an enquiry, and it wouldn't help him to have the chap swung, even if he could have worked it, which I doubt. What he did want was a sum of money and here was a chance to get it. It wouldn't have been ready cash, but he held most of his sister's securities. There wouldn't have been any trouble about raising the needful."

" Gosh, what a story ! " exclaimed Trentham. " But, look here, where did it go wrong ? "

" I fancy it went wrong because Alfred Newstead, having had all the trouble and all the risk, didn't propose to be milked of half his profits by a chap who hadn't even had to take a walk in the rain to get them. Don't you think so, Mr. Winter ? "

" It was a very indiscreet attitude to adopt, in view of the consequences," said Mr. Winter glassily. " It appears to have cost Mr. Newstead his life."

" That's the way it appears to me, too," said Crook.

Sammy frowned.

" And after the funeral ? What happened then ? I take it Newstead stalled for a bit. I can't go into all this while my wife's still above ground, he must have said, or words to that effect, but afterwards we'll come to terms."

" I'm like Mr. Crook," said Roger, " that's the bit I don't understand, either. If Webster wasn't a complete fool he must have seen he was weakening his case by waiting. Suppose Newstead did play crooked—and it wouldn't be the first time, if he had—what steps could Webster take ? The police would look at him pretty old-fashioned and want to know why he'd waited such a hell of a time, and he couldn't afford to have it known that he'd been prepared to sell his silence."

" That's a nice phrase," said Crook generously. " No, I agree with you. There was something damned fishy going on, and I had to find out what it was. It held me up quite a while. Anno domini, I suppose. I asked myself not only why did he wait three days but where the hell did he spend those three days ? He didn't go to his hotel in Wolverhampton, he didn't go to his own house, no one's come forward who remembers seeing him. His car was taken from the garage on the Tuesday and reappeared in the Midlands on the Friday afternoon. No one seems to have seen it in the interim, any more than anyone seems to have seen Mr. Webster. So, after a bit, it struck me there was only one place where it could have been."

" And that was ? " No holder of a shilling ticket in the gods could have listened more spell-bound to the drama being played out before him than Mr. Lawyer Winter.

" In Mr. Newstead's garage. No one would look for it there."

" And—Webster ? "

" In Mr. Newstead's house. Oh no, I think having arrived he stayed there till the Friday."

" How about luggage ? " enquired the practical Roger.

" I don't think he'd worry about that."

" And rations ? "

" He don't seem to have worried about that either."

There was a moment's silence. Then both young men spoke together.

" You mean. . . . ? "

Mr. Winter's voice drowned both. " If he could persuade his brother-in-law to yield him a large sum of money the provision of a change of underwear and a little food would present no great difficulties."

" But it did," objected Roger. " At least, they don't seem to have hit it off for long. I suppose Webster got violent. . . ."

" Why suppose that ? " asked Crook.

" Why, otherwise, was the body of Alfred Newstead found in the Lone Pit dump ? "

" It wasn't," said Crook.

His audience stared.

" But, my dear sir," Mr. Winter sounded agitated beyond belief.

" Wasn't ! " Sammy was scowling. " Aw, nuts, Crook."

" Give the man a chance," urged Roger, as pleased as a young hound scenting its first fox.

" You asked me just now if I knew where Herbert Webster was," said Crook to the spurious Mr. Winter. " I said I thought I could guess. I bet anyone present five pounds that he's lying at this moment in a grave in the Middlesex County Cemetery, alongside his sister."

The storm burst. " Golly ! " exclaimed Trentham. " That would explain the disfigured face all right. I always wondered . . ."

" And the fact that he didn't take so much as a toothbrush with him. . . ."

" And that no one ever seems to have seen him at Charlbury. It's damn difficult to hide a dead body, but it's nothing compared with tryin' to hide a live one. You ask any girl who'd had a little mistake. . . ."

" And the wrist-watch ! " Roger Trentham was hard on the scent. " We thought it was damned careless to smash up the face and then leave the watch on the wrist. But, of course, that was to serve for identity purposes."

" And the chap we're really looking for isn't Webster but Alfred Newstead."

" I thought you'd get there presently," observed Crook kindly.

" Well, now we can go ahead filling in the gaps," said Roger.

Mr. Crook turned to his contemporary, who had risen to his feet and looked as though he discovered himself in a circle of fire.

" Well, that's where you can help us, Mr. Newstead," he said. " What precisely did happen after you took the girl away from the Blue Boar ? "

CHAPTER TWENTY-ONE

No question is ever settled
Until it is settled right.

—E. W. Wilcox.

Pandemonium broke out.

The shouting, bellowing, questions, cries, disclaimers, would have done credit to a cattle market in full swing.

Sammy spoke first. " So that's him ? All right. No need to trouble the police this trip."

Roger and Crook caught him by an arm either side.

" Don't be a bloody fool," said Roger.

" Let me go," said Sammy, and his voice was enough to freeze your blood, though the fury seemed to have been choked out of it.

" Now be your age ! " Crook pleaded. " He can't get away. And you pay your rates for police protection, don't you ? Besides, Mr. Trentham likes his stories to have a happy ending, and it won't help him for you to swing for murder."

" I think," said the man Crook said was Alfred Newstead, " you've taken leave of your senses. Webster, so far as I know, is still at large, and the man they buried, again so far as I know, is Alfred Newstead."

" We'll see what your dentist says about that," suggested Crook. " He'll have a map of your jaw, I take it. And I daresay when you put your plate back quite a lot of people will recognise you—including Mrs. Forbes."

" Why not bring in the whole of Charlbury while you're about it ? Anyway, no sane man would take Hattie Forbes' word for anything."

" Hullo," said Crook, " how come you've heard of the lady's reputation ? You hail from Edinburgh, you said."

" Quit fooling, Crook," exclaimed Sammy, wrenching at Roger's arm. " We know the fellow's Newstead."

" Because I say so ? That's handsome of you."

" You've forgotten—I've met him before."

" Didn't recognise him when you came in though, did you ? "

" That's true. He has changed himself, you know. And I only saw him for a moment in the rain. . . ."

183

" What the soldier said ain't evidence. No, we'll want more than that, but, believe me, we'll get it. As a matter of fact . . ." he stopped as feet sounded outside and a bevy of people came sweeping into the room. They included the matron, two plain-clothes men, a police officer in uniform, and Nora Deane dressed in nursing clothes.

" What's all this ? " demanded one of the plain-clothes men.

" Murder, if you don't hurry," Crook told him.

The girl, Nora Deane, let out a low cry and stepped back a pace. Sammy freed himself with a great lunge and came to stand beside her. Crook closed up on the other side.

" You needn't look at me like that," said Mr. Winter.

" It's Mr. Newstead," said the girl, " I didn't know him at first. But—you've knocked out one of his teeth."

" His dentist did that. Rough chaps, these dentists. But I daresay he'll soon be able to put it back again. All right, we needn't keep you. You've done fine."

" I'm not frightened," said she. " Not while Mr. Crook's here."

" You're a honey," said the grateful Crook, shooting a malicious glance in Sammy's direction. " Now, if the authorities want to ask the young lady any questions . . ."

" Do you identify this man as the driver of the car that was crashed over Dead Man's Point ? " asked one of the plain-clothes men.

" It's Mr. Newstead—yes, I do."

" You've still got to prove that," said Newstead.

" I wonder exactly why you came here to-day," drawled Crook. " I daresay I could guess, though. You thought you'd take a last shot at putting Miss Deane where she couldn't do you any harm. I wonder what you intended to do. Another sleeping-draught ? "

" I—I don't know what you mean."

" Murderers, the police tell me, generally stick to the same method in their crimes. You've tried poison—that was your wife. . . ."

The plain-clothes man pulled him up sharply. " You can't say that, Mr. Crook."

" It's what all England's going to be saying in twenty-four hours," he pointed out. " All right, what you mean is the police are allowed to say it first. But I suppose, Mr. Newstead, you won't deny that you put Herbert Webster into the pit,

that you killed him in your house and hid his body till after
the funeral and then . . ."

" No need to answer any of those," said the plain-clothes
man.

" Ain't you even going to search him ? " asked Mr. Crook
plaintively.

The wretched creature's hand was fumbling near his pocket.
The inspector saw it, gave an order. The next minute
his pockets were being turned out. In one of them was a
syringe, loaded, as was subsequently learned, with a charge of
morphia.

" Enough to put us all under the daisies," said Crook. " So
that was the idea. He meant to get into Miss Deane's room
when it was unguarded and then to do his dirty job. Funny
thing is," he looked at the lost man with less pity than he'd
have looked at a rabbit he'd accidentally run over, " it occurred
to me that that might be his idea. I told the matron to put
me wise the minute she got a message that anyone, not the
press or the police, wanted to see Miss Deane. We happened
to know she had no relations, she told Sammy so, and when
this gentleman rang up to say he represented her old Scotch
auntie, Matron rang me. Afraid I kept you waiting, Mr.
Newstead, but it couldn't be helped. I was being paid by
Sammy here to find Miss Deane and when I'd found her finish
up the story. I sort of guessed you might get restless and go
looking for the room, so I suggested that the young lady in
charge—the nurse, that is—should just oil out for a minute or
two and—see what happened. Sort of experiment, see ? And
it all worked like a time machine. You came huntin' for the
room, and the nurse, who could see through the glass panel,
saw you and walked out, and that was my cue. I was around
the other corner."

" It was damned risky," said Sammy.

" Not with me on the job," Crook assured him. " You've
forgotten my motto—Crook always gets his man."

The authorities had finished emptying Newstead's pockets.
In one of those belonging to the waistcoat they found something they didn't expect—a little trinket of moonstone on a
broken silver chain. When she saw that the girl, Nora Deane,
moved forward.

" My locket ! " she said. " It broke that afternoon while
we were waiting for the petrol, and he accused me of doing it
on purpose. Ask the woman who was there," she implored,

turning to Crook. " She'll remember. That proves it was him, that proves it."

Roger Trentham slipped past them and made a dash for a telephone. The story had been a whizzer from start to finish. Even when it seemed as though it was going to fold up there had been some new development. He told his paper to hold the front page and he'd be right down. He was, in his own way, as inhuman as Bill Parsons. To him the people were nothing and the story was all.

Back in the room Crook was saying, " You know, my father never gave me much, he wasn't that kind of a man, but he did hand me some good advice every now and again and one of the things he told me was, Always go through your pockets every night, before your wife gets a chance. It'll save a lot of trouble in the long run. And I'll say," he wound up, his brown eyes bright with conquest and hard as stones fixed on the stricken face of the man he'd so successfully cornered, " I'll say my old dad was a hundred per cent right."

Nora Deane, slim, trim, the colour back in her delicate cheeks, violet eyes shining, sat incongruously enough in Mr. Crook's big shabby office and said, " I haven't come to waste your time, which I know is valuable—why, at this very minute someone may be threatened with death and I'm stopping you saving her—but I must say Thank You."

Crook waved a huge paw. " Matter of business," he said.

Nora smiled. " You like to give out you're hard-boiled," she said.

Crook, looking at her, thought he hadn't any use for janes himself, they were so incalculable, but when you met one like this you began to understand why impetuous fellows like Sammy Parker took their one and only life in their hand to get the girl out of a jam. It didn't make him feel that way, he'd have told you, but he didn't precisely blame chaps like Sammy.

" Sammy," continued Miss Deane serenely, " says you're a charmer. He says you could have a harem if you chose, without any trouble."

" If your precious Sammy had any experience of harems he'd know he was talking through his hat. And if I were your father I shouldn't allow you to marry a fool."

" Marry ? " Nora Deane looked at him wisely. " Well, I don't know. . . ."

"Sammy does. That's half women's trouble; they never think the man knows anything. Sammy knew from the beginning he was goin' to hitch up with you, and if you think you can teach an obstinate chap like that any different, well, you've got your work cut out for the rest of your days."

Nora let that pass. "I still don't understand how you knew it was Herbert Webster in the Lone Pit and not Mr. Newstead," she said.

"I daresay I'd never have known if Newstead had laid low. But when that telegram came signed Sammy, and when Sammy told me he hadn't sent it, then I was sure. You see, Herbert Webster had never heard of Sammy. You told Mrs. Trentham you'd never mentioned him to anyone, and Webster had never had a chance of meeting him. But Newstead had, because Sammy went round to Askew Avenue the day Mrs. Newstead handed in her checks. And then, though you might have given your London address to Webster, I didn't think you'd have given him the address of the matron, where as we know Alfred Newstead had it. Then, of course, there was the point I made at the time, the fact that he recognised Sammy directly he came in, though there was no reason why he shouldn't have thought Trentham was the fellow. No, he didn't treat you well, but I'll say you got your own back, and a bit over, when we found we had you safely tucked up in bed."

"You knew he'd try and kill me again?"

"He hadn't much choice," said Crook, tolerantly. "If he'd stopped to think, he might have known that he hadn't a hope with me on his tail, but that's the trouble with all these murderers. They don't think long enough. If ever you go in for murder, take my tip—and you can have this for a wedding present—remember it's not enough to look at the road ahead and avoid all the obstacles in sight, you need what another Sammy—Weller this time—called a pair of patent double million magnifyin' gass microscopes of hextra power to see all the dangers just round the corner."

He grinned in his turn; he went on grinning till he looked like the wolf after it had eaten Red Riding-Hood's grandmother and heard Red Riding-Hood at the door.

Nora stood up and held out her hand. "Thank you very much," she said, "for everything." Then she laughed. "I always wondered if it was true."

"If what was true?"

" That most of the wedding presents people give you aren't any use afterwards."

And before Crook could think of an answer to that one she was gone.

THE END

›› If you've enjoyed this book and would like to discover more great vintage crime and thriller titles, as well as the most exciting crime and thriller authors writing today, visit: ››

The Murder Room
Where Criminal Minds Meet

themurderroom.com

www.ingramcontent.com/pod-product-compliance
Ingram Content Group UK Ltd.
Pitfield, Milton Keynes, MK11 3LW, UK
UKHW040435280225
455666UK00003B/95